THE SORROW AND THE TERROR

THE HAUNTING LEGACY OF THE AIR INDIA TRAGEDY

Clark Blaise & Bharati Mukherjee

VIKING

VIKING

Penguin Books Canada Ltd., 2801 John Street, Markham,
Ontario, Canada L3R 1B4
Penguin Books, Harmondsworth, Middlesex, England
Viking Penguin Inc., 40 West 23rd Street, New York,
New York 10010 U.S.A.
Penguin Books Australia Ltd., Ringwood, Victoria, Australia
Penguin Books (N.Z.) Ltd., 182 - 190 Wairau Road,
Auckland 10, New Zealand

First published by Penguin Books Canada Limited, 1987

Copyright © Clark Blaise and Bharati Mukherjee, 1987

Printed in Canada

Canadian Cataloguing in Publication Data
Blaise, Clark, 1940 -
The sorrow and the terror: the haunting legacy
of the Air India tragedy

ISBN 0-670-81204-8

1. Air-India Flight 182 Incident, 1985.
I. Mukherjee, Bharati.   II. Title.

TL553.5.B58 1987   909′.096337   C86-094677-0

THE SORROW
AND THE TERROR

THE FACTS

On June 23, 1985, at 2:19 A.M. (EDT), a suitcase belonging to a certain Mr L. Singh exploded during baggage transfer at Narita Airport in Tokyo, Japan. CP Air Flight 003 had arrived at Narita fifteen minutes ahead of schedule.

Two baggage handlers were killed, four injured. Mr L. Singh did not board the flight.

Fifty-five minutes later (3:14 A.M. EDT), 110 miles off the south-west coast of Ireland, a bomb exploded in the forward baggage hold of Air India Flight 182, bound for New Delhi and Bombay, from Toronto and Montreal. The flight was approximately an hour and a half behind schedule at the moment of its destruction. A certain Mr M. Singh had persuaded officials to put his bag on board the flight in Vancouver, for transfer to the Air India flight leaving Toronto. He did not board the flight.

Three hundred and seven passengers and twenty-two crew members were killed. Over ninety percent of the passengers, most of them holiday-bound women and children, were Canadian citizens. The death toll of 329 stands as the worst at-sea air crash of all time. As a terrorist act, it is the bloodiest of the modern era.

He seeks at least
Upon the last and sharpest height,
Before the spirits fade away,
Some landing place, to clasp and say,
"Farewell! We lose ourselves in light."

In Memoriam, Poem 47
Alfred, Lord Tennyson

This verse was cited by two men left widowed and childless in the Air India disaster of June 23, 1985. They said, "Our children were lost in light."

INTRODUCTION

As Canadian immigrants ourselves, with twenty years' involvement in the Indian-immigrant life of North America, we were driven to write this book as citizens bearing witness. We saw it then, and see it now, as fundamentally an immigration tragedy with terrorist overtones. What we have read and whom we have talked to and what we have learned are for the most part available to any private citizen with the time and passion to devote to seeking them out.

When we began our research in January 1986, it seemed as though the Air India disaster (as it has come to be called) was in the process of disappearing from the larger Canadian consciousness. Politically, the tragedy was "unhoused," in that Canada wished to see it as an Indian event sadly visited on these shores by uncontrollable fanatics, and India was happy to treat it as an "overseas incident" with containable financial implications.

India does not want its communal violence — the Sikh-Hindu conflict — to gain the international spotlight. It does not want the weaknesses of Air India security exposed. It does not want the shortcomings of its democracy discussed overseas. It does not want the spokesmen for Sikh independence to gain the romantic legitimacy of "freedom fighters" by the use of dramatic film clips and the commentary of instant experts. Within India itself, the government has shown understandable reluctance to "fan the fires of communal discord" by publicizing the presumed role of members of one minority community (Sikhs) in causing the deaths of so many innocent tourists (mainly Hindu). The wiser course is to see it as a Canadian problem.

The Canadian government has its own political agenda. The Air India crash and the revelation of terrorist cells operating freely on Canadian soil are uncomfortable reminders of policy failures. Untrained, indifferent and complacent airport security, an unresponsive and unprepared ministry of transport (Transport Canada) and even an insensitive prime minister were exposed within hours of the crash.

Beyond the immediate deficiencies, however, lies the problematic policy of multiculturalism itself, the nation's desire to preserve and even foster ethnic diversity. Multiculturalism has become a cornerstone of Canada's eternally agonized self-definition. (Any Canadian school child can tell you that "we" favour multiculturalism and the ethnic mosaic; "they" — meaning the United States — stuffs everyone into its melting pot.) When the Air India disaster is looked at from the perspective of Canadian immigration and racial policies reaching back over eighty years, it can be seen as a long time in the making, with many precautions ignored.

Like India, Canada does not welcome scrutiny of its communal difficulties. Both Canada ("the peaceable kingdom") and India ("the world's largest democracy") pride themselves on their images in the world. Canadian racism, though now at least acknowledged, conveniently pales beside the historical models of Britain and the United States. Indian democracy, whatever its faults, avoids the blatant abuses of Pakistan. Self-serving comparisons with one's immediate neighbours often inhibit serious self-examination. Conversations in both countries often begin, "With all our faults, at least we're not like them..." The Air India disaster temporarily removed those comforting blinders.

There is one other assertion — this coming from the Sikh extremists — that requires the most serious examination of all. They would like to distract the world from their alleged role in the Air India disaster, and to do so they have exaggerated the motive of vengeance.

Vengeance is a powerful emotion. Vengeance is universally understood, even when deplored. It is the great, simplifying tool, the Rambo inside Hamlet, the unstable, subversive element in justice. Like scapegoating, it's a recurring battle cry in the rhetoric of tyrants and demagogues. Vengeance, however, neither explains nor justifies a complicated event. At best, it recruits adherents, provides ready-made justification and numbs any moral doubt. It plays well to the very fringe of the uneducated, unemployed, unstable and violence-prone young men to which it is directed. It appeals particularly to the Punjabi code of *izzat*, embracing honour, self-respect and blood-for-blood revenge, which is the unofficial law of Sikh-dominated Punjab.

And what of ourselves? We have a political point of view. We have been moved to tears and to fury. We know there are larger stories, wheels within wheels (the main one turning on CIA involvement in the Afghan conflict, the role of Pakistan, and the ups and downs of Indo-U.S. relations) that only an investigator with off-the-record contacts can track down.

The world of terrorism involves as much shadow as act, and in the bureaucracy of terror (or terror prevention), one set of interests can be served even as others are being destroyed. One thinks of Winston Churchill's wartime decision to permit the destruction of Coventry, which could have been avoided, but at the cost of alerting the Germans that their codes had been cracked. Thousands died in order to keep a secret.

Many terrorist acts are planned for the direct damage they cause, but many more for the *response* they wish to provoke, which they hope will be bloody, repressive and politically embarrassing. When a terrorist act succeeds in its mission, credit will be claimed. If it fails — as surely the Air India attack failed — *provocateurs* can still be blamed. (The phoned-in claims of responsibility on behalf of extremist organizations, received in New York, Washington and Toronto the day after the crash, are dismissed as further provocation.) India lost an insured plane and a few lives, say the extremists, but gained a propaganda victory. If they benefited, isn't it logical to assume they planned it?

The terrorist cells in this account are a combination of criminal underworld and religious cult. Many of their activities are inexplicable to outsiders or nonbelievers. Grandiose schemes are planned for self-promotion or as "messages" sent to rivals or for morale building within the group. Sophisticated political analysis is often beside the point.

We have spoken with the extremists, with Indian government representatives, with moderate Sikhs, with Canadian officials, with journalists, doctors, engineers, administrators, lawyers and scholars. We have visited Vancouver, Toronto, Montreal, Detroit, Ottawa and Ireland, and we have received information from contacts in India, Japan, Europe and California. We have read backfiles of newspapers and of government documents. We have attended trials and studied transcripts. Mainly, however, we have visited the bereaved families and tried to see the disaster through their eyes.

The Air India disaster was a truly national tragedy. Of the 307 passengers, 21 began that terrible day in western Canada, 181 in Toronto (some originating from Buffalo and Detroit) and 105 in Montreal. Although there were 11 victims with Caucasian names, almost all were immigrants or the children of immigrants who had come to Canada in the sixties and seventies. Eighty-four were children; two were infants; many were women.

One thing we've come to appreciate during the course of our research is the meticulousness of police work, and the genius — and limitation — of the law. We have also been appalled at the abuse of justice, both from the accused and from the law that permits Canada's super-secret police force, the Canadian Security Intelligence Service (CSIS) to intervene in a criminal trial and declare a judge impotent in his own courtroom. Such a legal environment satisfies most normal definitions of a police state, yet the Canadian public remains ignorant, or quietly supportive, of the threat that this law poses to every citizen's civil liberties.

It is further evidence, we fear, that Canada still has a long way to go in absorbing the lesson of the Air India disaster as an intimate tragedy with implications for everyone.

The police have been close to "solving" the case — naming names and booking the suspects — for over a year. One early account of the disaster had the police nearly closing in just as the book went to press. As late as August 1986, the normally tight-lipped Commissioner of the Royal Canadian Mounted

Police, Robert Simmonds, reported that three individuals in Canada were likely to be brought into court "soon" in connection with the disaster and the Narita explosion. Delays, after such expectancy, foster skepticism and enormous frustration. Among the bereaved families the call for justice today is louder, the bitterness and cynicism sharper, than at any time since the crash.

At the moment of this writing, eighteen months after the event itself, it can be said that the circumstantial case against a Vancouver-based Sikh extremist cell is very strong. Authorities know who made *a* bomb — but did he also make *the* bomb that exploded in Japan? They know who bought the precise stereo tuner that housed the Narita bomb — but did he also place the bomb inside it? And what, precisely, are the links between the Narita bomb that killed two baggage handlers and the Air India bomb that killed the 329? Until the couriers are also arrested (and many of them are in India), the police cannot bring charges. The judgement of Britain's respected *Flight International* magazine remains valid:

> However strong the circumstantial evidence might be, it still looks as though any "Singh" who appeared in court, charged with causing the Air India disaster, might walk away free.

To lose the most expensive case ever investigated in Canada (total costs by now in excess of $60 million; over $500 million in civil damages) on a technicality would mean to lose it forever.

Our commitment in writing this book, however, has not been merely to probe for motives or to reconstruct events. Our purpose is not just to retell the story and clarify the issues in our own minds, but to honour the 329 lives, each of them a lawsuit without limits, something unpayable except in the currency of shared remorse.

Clark Blaise and Bharati Mukherjee
New York City

BACKGROUND

Sikhism: It is pretentious to attempt a definition of a religion in anything less than several volumes. For the purposes of this book, it is more important to say what Sikhism is *not*, before venturing upon any kind of theological description.

Sikhs are not terrorists. Sikhs object to the headlines that link them with terrorist acts ("Sikh Bomb Suspected") and court appearances ("Five Sikhs to go on trial") of suspected terrorists. In this book we will reserve the term "Khalistani" to describe the people engaged in or supporting activities directed towards the creation of a separate Sikh state in India (the so-called "Khalistan"), or engaged in violence outside of India directed towards Indian targets. All Khalistanis are Sikhs, but not all Sikhs are Khalistanis.

As a religious community, Sikh males are generally recognizable by their distinctive beards and turbans. Males must not cut their hair. They will bear the name "Singh" as either a middle or a family name. The distinguishing characteristics of a Sikh male include the wearing of a ceremonial dagger, a comb in the hair, a steel bracelet and short outer pants, along with the hair and the turban, which are known, collectively, as the "five K's," for the first letter of the Punjabi word for each sign. Obviously, not all of the five K's can be worn in contemporary Western society.

Sikhism is a visionary religion, the creation of one inspired leader, Guru Nanak (1469-1539), who was born a Hindu in the Punjab village now known as Nankana Sahib. It is a religion intimately connected with the region of the Punjab, a flat, fertile area drained by five rivers ("punjab" means, literally, "land of the five rivers"), and with the devotional hymns and

prayers composed by Nanak and the next nine gurus in the
Punjabi language. To the west of the Punjab, Muslim empires
stretch in an unbroken arc through the Middle East and North
Africa all the way to the Atlantic. Immediately to the east
begins the Hindu heartland of India.

True to its geographical position, Sikhism is a fusion of
devotional strains in both Islam and Hinduism. Both *bhakti*
Hinduism and *sufi* Islam stressed the openness of the faith,
castelessness and the one unknowable god without attribute,
whose presence was felt through prayer. For Nanak, the vision
of god was so powerful that it embodied certain secular truths
as well. Honesty, truthfulness, sexual faithfulness were regarded
as self-evident virtues, flowing from the union with god. A
Sikh cannot harm his fellow man, cannot bring hurt to anyone.
Nanak's great contribution to the faith, beyond his poems, was
the installation of a guru as guide and leader, but not as a god.

Inevitably, the success of the teachings led to conflict with
the Mogul (Muslim) emperors of the region. The peaceful
religion was gradually transformed into an army of the faithful
by the attempts of Emperors Jehangir and Aurengzeb to destroy
it, root and branch. The fifth guru, Arjun (1563-1606), the
most distinguished and saintly leader after the founder, was
tortured to death by Jehangir.

Thus began the final phase of early Sikh history, an almost
constant series of battles, murders and intrigue, ending two
hundred years after its founding with Guru Gobind's announced
birth of the *khalsa* (the "pure") — the militant army of the
faithful.

Sikhism's major contemporary scholar, Khushwant Singh,
recounts the transformation in Sikh thought from the time of
the peaceful Nanak to that of the militant Gobind:

> Whereas Nanak had propagated goodness, Gobind Singh
> condemned evil. One preached the love of one's neighbor,
> the other the punishment of transgressors. Nanak's God
> loved His saints; Gobind's God destroyed His enemies. *

After Gobind Singh, the institution of the single guru was

*Reprinted with permission from Princeton University Press (Khushwant Singh, *History of the Sikhs 1469-1839*, vol. 1. Copyright © 1963 by Princeton University Press)

ended. Thereafter, the faithful were to look to the scriptures —
the collected writings of the earlier gurus — for their guidance.

We mention these historical events only because of their
bearing on contemporary events. *Khalsa* is a word with many
connotations: a community of the pure in faith has come to
mean those dedicated to the political agenda of Khalistan. Yet
at the same time, a great many Khalistanis have no particular
attachment to the fundamental articles of the Sikh faith. A
Sikh who is baptized into the faith today is almost assuredly
following the priestly leadership of a militant Khalistani.

Perhaps no great injustice is committed if the Western reader
simply thinks of Sikhism as a religion like Christianity or Islam,
with a noble theology, a saintly founder and a confusing set of
mutually exclusive teachings. Humble and arrogant, persecuted
and aggressive, militant and pacifist.

Khushwant Singh continues his thoughts on the transformation of the faith with two more paragraphs as appropriate to
events in today's Punjab as they were nearly three hundred
years ago:

> The complexion of the Sikh community also underwent
> a radical change. Up until that time the leadership had
> remained in the hands of the non-militant urban Khatris
> [a caste of warriors and artisans]. They had been quite
> willing to pay lip service to the ideal of a casteless society
> preached by Nanak, but they were not willing to soil their
> lips by drinking *amrit* ["nectar"] out of the same bowl, as
> Gobind wanted them to do. Few of them accepted con-
> version to the new faith. They remained just Sikhs, better
> known as *Sahajdharis* ("those who take time to adopt"),
> and separated from the *kesadhari* ("hirsute") Khalsa. The
> bulk of the converts were Jat peasants of the central dis-
> tricts of the Punjab who were technically low in the caste
> hierarchy. They took over the leadership from the Khatris.
> The rise of militant Sikhism became the rise of Jat power
> in the Punjab.

The same words are used by Khalistanis to condemn shaved,

unturbaned Sikhs even today, and the same arguments about assimilation and purity can be heard in Vancouver or Amritsar.

Khalistan: An unborn "land of the pure" for Sikhs and Sikhs alone, to be carved from existing Indian territories, including the present-day states of Punjab, Haryana, Himachal Pradesh, and sizeable chunks of Jammu and Kashmir, Uttar Pradesh, Rajasthan and Gujarat, along with the federal territory of Delhi. Present-day Indian Punjab is roughly the size of Costa Rica; expensively produced maps of Khalistan, as distributed in Vancouver, envisage a Sikh empire stretching from the Himalayas to the Arabian Sea, an area the size of France.

A separate Sikh state has been discussed for centuries. In the early nineteenth century, under Ranjit Singh, there was even a Sikh Empire centred in the original Punjab (the current Pakistani West Punjab, and the Indian states of Punjab, Haryana and Himachal Pradesh, as well as much of Jammu and Kashmir). It collapsed shortly after the emperor's death in 1839. Most historians agree that the time for a "Sikhistan," as it was then called, was the 1930s, when Britain turned a responsive ear to India's Muslims and eventually granted them a Pakistan. After that time, given the immediate hostilities between India and Pakistan, further partition of the Indian nation was unthinkable.

Khalistan was given modern utterance in 1971, by a former Punjab cabinet minister, Dr Jagjit Singh Chauhan, who first fled to Pakistan, and then to England, where he has operated a "Khalistan House" and a "Council of Khalistan" since that time. Wherever Sikhs have settled in the world, especially in England, British Columbia and California, Khalistan is likely to be represented with an "embassy," maps, currency and passports. As the only apparent shadow government of a non-existent state, Chauhan's Khalistan has suffered or profited with the fortunes of the cause. Until the rise of the late fundamentalist priest, Jarnail Singh Bhindranwale, and especially since the invasion of the Golden Temple in Amritsar, which politicized Sikhs around the world, the cause was open to ridicule from all sides. Since then, it has struggled to control the forces it so enthusiastically released. Events, in the form of more violent organizations and less respectable leadership, have passed it by.

Punjab, the heart of any "Khalistan," is India's frontier state along the northwest border with Pakistan. Culturally, religiously and linguistically, Punjabi-speaking Indian Sikhs are wedged between Muslim Punjabi Pakistanis, who speak Urdu, and Hindu Punjabi Indians, who speak Hindi. The language distinction is quite arbitrary. Many Sikhs prefer to use Urdu, and Hindu Punjabis are likely to favour Punjabi over Hindi or Urdu. Though the scripts of the three languages are different, the spoken languages are very close.

Historically, relations between Sikhs and Hindus have been far closer than relations between Sikhs and Muslims. In the 1947 partition of the subcontinent, when Britain carved up "the jewel in its crown" and made one sovereign country for the Hindus and another for the Muslims, Sikhs in the new, constitutionally Muslim Pakistan pulled up stakes and fled to secular India. (By doing so, they became the greatest losers in blood and land.)

Relations between Sikhs and Hindus in the Punjab were traditionally so close that many Hindu families "gave" a son to Sikhism. Worship at the Sikh *gurdwara* (temple) is a common practice among Hindus of the Punjab. Most Hindus, without thinking too deeply about it, consider Sikhism one of the many variant forms of Hinduism. The Constitution of India even considers a shaven, unturbaned Sikh a Hindu.

In this, perversely, Khalistanis, would agree. They, too, would call a shaven, unturbaned Sikh a Hindu — or something worse. The new Sikh fundamentalism, inspired by the preachings of Jarnail Singh Bhindranwale, places absolute emphasis on the maintenance of the "five K's." To have been "born in a Sikh family," but not to maintain the external forms of the religion is to show contempt for the *khalsa*.

The birth and death dates of Bhindranwale (1947-84) encapsulate much of the drama of contemporary Sikh history. He was born with independent India, and killed in "Operation Blue Star," the Indian Army "invasion" of the Sikh's holiest shrine, the Golden Temple. In revenge for having ordered the invasion, Sikh bodyguards of Mrs Gandhi assassinated her on October 31, 1984. In revenge for her assassination, nearly three thousand innocent Sikhs were killed by rioting Hindus — or by paid criminals masquerading as rioters. In presumed revenge for those riots, Khalistanis and criminal, nonpolitical elements within Sikh society have killed hundreds of innocent Hindus and moderate Sikhs in the past two years.

The 329 victims of the Air India crash are part of that ongoing, self-generating, self-justifying vengeance.

The fear and hatred between Sikhs and Hindus currently sweeping Punjab is felt by many to be artificial and unthinkable. Sikhs raised with the notion that all of India is their home, and that secular education, travel, and self-improvement are their birthrights, feel that Khalistan is a mediæval farce, an invitation to join the seventeenth century ("and become the Palestinians of India," as one successful Toronto Sikh businessman put it) at a time when Punjab is the wealthiest and most progressive state in India.

Many of us remember an easier time in India, in riding the trains at night and seeing the hooks above each seat hung with the confectionary colours of the prewrapped turbans of the sleeping *sardarjis* (as Sikhs are known in India). It was a stirring sight, like a rainbow of muted lights. And in the morning, the men would rise at dawn and begin the combing of their hip-length hair, its oiling and elaborate swirling back on top to be set by the comb and tucked beneath the turban. Not without its vanity and macho; and certainly not without its beauty. Watching it was to behold one of India's many minor miracles.

It is important to retain that sense of basic warmth and trust, and to stress the difference between "Khalistanis" — the supporters of Sikh independence, of the exacting of "blood for blood" revenge against India or against Hindus or even against dissenters within their own community — and the 15 million Sikhs in India and now around the world who constitute the community of believers.

Singh (which means "lion") is part of the name, or the full name, of every male member of the Sikh religion. All females take the name "Kaur" which means "princess." The original ideal of Sikhism was to eliminate all references to one's former (Hindu) caste, and merge identity in the new brotherhood of the faith. In practice, however, the last name has stayed, and "Singh" often appears as a middle name.

To complicate matters, "Singh" is also a common Hindu name throughout north India. All Sikhs are Singhs, but not all Singhs are Sikh. The pilot of the doomed Air India flight was Commander Hanse Singh Narendra, a Hindu. His closest friend, in New Jersey, is another Hindu, Saravjit Singh. The co-pilot of Flight 182 was a Sikh, Captain Satwinder Singh Bhinder.

Apart from certain victims, all Singhs mentioned in this book are of the Sikh religion.

PART ONE

New York City, October 31, 1984

It's not unusual for bearded men to dance in the streets of New York, so the ecstatic, turbaned men in yellow "Dash Mesh (Tenth Guru) Regiment" T-shirts dancing and distributing sweets outside the Indian Consulate on East 64th Street in Manhattan on Hallowe'en Day 1984 seem only slightly bizarre to passersby, only mildly curious to the assembled reporters.

They're Sikhs, and they hate Mrs Gandhi. They're happy she's dead and that her Sikh bodyguards pulled the trigger. This is the first eruption of Khalistani fervour in the mainstream press.

The leader of the demonstration is an exceptional individual. His name, which he gives in a brief interview with a Reuters reporter, is Gurpartap Singh Birk. He's thirty-four, married, with a wife and two children still in England, where he did his graduate study. This moment is the high point of his life.

In England, he was vice-president of Data Application International (a Belgian company with branches in fifteen countries); in New York, he is a six-figure, six-day-a-week, twelve-hour-a-day executive associated with one of DAI's clients, Automatic Toll System of White Plains. He holds a Ph.D. in computer science. He designed the Belgian Parliament's computer system, and now he is working on a system to automate toll-road collections in the United States.

He has one other obligation, squeezed in between his corporate duties. In 1982, while he was still in England, he became a member of the Dash Mesh Regiment of the Sikh Students Federation. Inevitably, given his skills, he became its president and one of the editors of the *Khalistan Times*. He is one of the brightest lights in the Khalistan movement, the New York head, the man in charge of organizing protests and publicity for that unborn nation of the pure called Khalistan.

Dancing with him that day are several of his recruits, among them Lal Singh Lally and Ammand Singh Dhaliwal. They often drop their final name, as good Sikhs are enjoined to do by Sikhism, to designate their brotherhood in the faith. Birk also has a *nom de guerre*. In some of his dealings, which are soon to become complicated indeed, he is known as John Singh.

The death of Indira Gandhi, he tells the reporter, partially avenges the insult to the Sikh religion sustained in the desecration of the Golden Temple and the killing of the Khalistan leadership there. She has paid in blood for the murder of the Sikh priest Jarnail Singh Bhindranwale; the leader of the All-India Sikh Students Federation, Amrik Singh; and the military strategist, Major-General Shahbeg Singh.

The assassination, Birk goes on to say, indicates the depth of passion, and the outrage. It shows that the enemies of the Sikh people cannot hide. Everyone involved in the planning of the Golden Temple operation is known, and will be dealt with.

In the meantime, Birk and his comrades stage their celebration with dancing and sweets on East 64th Street. In the Sikh religion, sweets are traditionally offered when God has answered prayers.

Delhi, India, November 1, 1984

Birk could not have known it that day in New York, but even as he danced, horrors were going on in Delhi. The riots, as they have been called, a pogrom against the Sikhs, which is what, in fact, it was, had already begun.

The violence got under way quietly enough in the Delhi twilight of October 31, the day of Indira Gandhi's assassination, and continued for the next two nights. The focus was on the Delhi slums. First, individual male Sikhs were pulled from their taxicabs and trucks (traditional Sikh employment in India) and beaten on the streets. Sikh shops were looted and burned as police and soldiers looked on. In middle-class districts, Sikh schools and *gurdwaras* were attacked, again with no intervention from the police.

Then, later at night, the full horror descended. In the slum districts entire blocks of Sikh settlements were sealed off, then systematically attacked and burned. Looters seem to have known in advance precisely which houses to attack, and to have known how many males or unprotected females were living inside.

Independent investigators feel the rioters had been armed with information from ration-card or voters' lists. Under the guise of an uncontrollable surge of popular reaction, a goon-squad of thugs and petty criminals was allowed three nights to murder, loot, rape and burn. Intimidation of Sikhs seems to be the reason, a demonstration of what *could* happen on a larger scale if the dogs of communal violence were finally let slip.

Lists of the sixteen guilty of this second operation against the Sikhs (lists that include much of the Congress (I) party high command in New Delhi, fervent Gandhi loyalists, whom Rajiv inherited as a brain-trust) circulate all over India, and in *gurdwaras* in the West. Already, two men named in the lists, a New Delhi politician and labour leader named Lalit Makan, and General A. S. Vaidya, planner of the Golden Temple operation, have been assassinated. The chief suspect in the Makan killing is Lal Singh.

It is estimated that 2,700 Sikhs were killed in the three nights of the pogrom. The brutal tales of stonings, rapes and torture deaths are as graphic as any in this century's repertory of horrors. Madhu Kishwar (a Hindu, incidentally) writes in an impassioned thirty-seven-page article entitled "Gangster Rule — The Massacre of the Sikhs" in the feminist monthly *Manushi*:

Unfortunately, an overwhelming majority of people in Delhi seem to feel that all the killings and arson were, in some way, justifiable. They believe this not just because they are possessed by the desire for revenge for the murder of Indira Gandhi, but because they have been convinced by years of vicious chauvinist propaganda that a purging operation was necessary in order to "save the nation" and "keep the nation united." The ruling party has made itself the arch-symbol of a so-called united nation. Its opponents are invariably accused of "weakening the nation" in the face of the dangers of the "foreign hand." Once such a chauvinist, nationalist fever infects the brains of people there is little hope that rationality or humanity or logic will prevail. The vision of the nation begins to act as a monster devouring its own people.

Dolomite, Alabama, November 8, 1984

Frank Camper is just the sort of redneck commie-bashing gun-nut from the G. Gordon Liddy school who inspires a rush of warm loathing in most parts of the world. He plays to the image every chance he gets ("Watch out for the snakes, boy!" being one of his favourites) during guided tours of his mercenary-training school, a booby-trapped little jungle in the piney woods outside of Birmingham.

Until the events of June 1985 caught up with him, bringing in the world press (Pritish Nandy, one-time Calcutta poet and now editor of *The Illustrated Weekly of India* came all the way over to write a properly incensed cover-exposé), plus the camera crews of *60 Minutes*, Frank Camper had been running a quiet little operation. His clients were the usual readers of *Soldier of Fortune*, the weekend Rambos howling on their Harleys. The training was tough and authentic, and graduates looking for employment in any of the world's hotspots could presumably use it to profitable effect.

On November 8, less than a week after the Delhi pogrom, Frank Camper received tuition — paid by VISA — from three prospective students. Lal Singh, Balraj Singh and Sukhvinder Singh. He remembers them as "average people except for the fact that they wore three-piece suits with their turbans and tennis shoes."

He immediately realized that in these three he'd lured an entirely different sort of fantasist out of hiding. "All they wanted was to kill Indians," he later wrote in *Penthouse*. They wanted to poison food as it came out of Punjab, they wanted to spread pestilence through the water supplies. And, most of all, once their training was complete, they wanted advanced instruction in assassination and major demolition — blowing up trains and bridges, even atomic reactors — and they wanted the hardware to do it. Rajiv Gandhi would be coming to New York in June 1985, and they wanted to be ready for him.

In Camper, they'd come to the wrong man. He looked right and sounded right, but he was, and always had been, an FBI undercover agent. The Mercenary School was an FBI sting operation. He was happy to provide them with everything they wanted, including their own private arms supplier — an even more convincing-looking agent from the FBI's Birmingham detachment — who offered the best prices this side of Crazy Eddie's.

In December 1984, Lal Singh invited Camper up to New York to show his hardware and to meet the Khalistani hierarchy at the Sheraton. First came Lal's superior, Gurpartap Singh Birk, who was using the alias John Singh, then Birk's superior, Major-General Jaswant Singh Bhullar, a white-turbaned, sixty-year-old with a white handlebar moustache and military bearing. The old military man had come up from his Washington headquarters to size up a possible ally and to assess the quality of the arsenal (Ingram machine guns, with silencers) that Camper had brought along for sale.

And that's how Camper — and the FBI — infiltrated the leadership of the Khalistan movement in the United States. Gurpartap Singh Birk, the weekend commando who'd been dancing in the streets just a month and a half before, and Major-General Bhullar, Indian Army (ret'd.), President of the World Sikh Organization (WSO) and Khalistani Washington-based lobbyist, would be working unwittingly for the FBI right up to the time of their (respective) arrest and deportation.

Major-General Bhullar had fled Punjab just before the invasion of the Golden Temple. The movement's other ranking general, Shahbeg Singh, was killed in the attack. A known associate of Bhindranwale, Bhullar had nevertheless been allowed into the United States in October 1984, on a B-2 visa (a tourist visa given for stays of up to six months and extendible for a maximum of two years at the discretion of the Immigration and Naturalization Service). Towards the end of his second six months, he applied for a change to an H-1 visa (temporary work visa for persons of exceptional ability), but the request was denied by the INS, which subsequently began deportation proceedings.

December 1984, when these meetings were being held at the Sheraton, was a traumatic time for all Sikhs. The twin shocks of the Golden Temple invasion and the Delhi riots had politicized the entire community. Khalistan, which had been little more than a joke to North American Sikhs up to that time, was suddenly seen as a sanctuary for a threatened people. And among the more aggressive fringe, vengeance was the only acceptable response.

Only two months after arriving in America, then, General Bhullar was meeting with Camper and Birk in New York. In that meeting, even more drastic terrorist measures were being discussed. "If only we could poison the water in Bombay," Camper recalls them saying, "they would die by the thousands. Is this possible?" Around the time of their meeting, Bhullar also addressed the international conference of the WSO. That conference — attended by many Sikhs who were anti-Congress (and not too keen on Hindus) but not pro-Khalistan (one might call them nonpolitical Sikh chauvinists) — was a sign of things to come.

We met a Sikh who had been an invited speaker to that conference, a bureaucrat with the Ontario government. "The first thing was placards of Khalistan, which I am totally against. A Khalistan that has no Hindus or Muslims in it is a Hitler Khalistan. Second thing was the speeches. The policy speech which was read by Bhullar himself was about downing — no, the word wasn't downing — it was about *disrupting* Air India flights, and killing — no, I'm sorry, not killing, the word used in Punjabi to *mean* killing — but the phrase was 'giving a ticket to heaven' to those people who advocate the case of the Indian government. I have no hesitation in saying that this is not Sikhism."

Another Canadian Sikh at the conference (who would later be questioned in the spring of 1986 in the assassination attempt against a Punjab Cabinet minister, Malkiat Singh Sidhu, in British Columbia on a family visit) was remembered as swearing, "We will bring back the heads of fifty thousand Hindus in return for the Golden Temple attack."

"And there were other speakers," this delegate went on. "A speaker for Azad Kashmiri [the Kashmir Liberation Front], and another from the Afghan rebels. What is their relevance to this meeting? The Azad Kashmiri and the Afghan Mujahadeen speakers were given standing ovations because they said we will bring together all movements against India because India allies itself with the Third World and the Soviet Union."

That conference was probably the high-water mark of the Khalistan movement in the United States. Already, however, the waters were receding, and not simply because of the infiltration of the FBI. At the time of this writing, Major-General Bhullar has found temporary refuge in Belgium. The WSO no longer exists in the United States, but operates as a splinter faction out of Canada.

New York City, January 6, 1985

Not long after the WSO conference, the passions of Gurpartap Singh Birk and his two close associates, Lal and Ammand, ripened into a plan of action. They had met Camper, they knew where to get weaponry and training. Birk is an organized, impatient, arrogant leader. In January 1985 his plans crystallized.

On January 6, he wrote his New Year's resolutions, and he drafted a six-point statement of intentions for the Sikh Students Federation of North America. It was a direct appeal to Sikh youth to join in the Khalistan effort.

Birk's activities were centred on the plan to assassinate Rajiv
Gandhi, and on causing major economic and social hardship in
India. His arrest and trial and the seizure of certain documents
offer the clearest glimpse we are likely to have of the Khalistani-
terrorist mind.

The ultimate aim was the liberation of Sikh lands and the
avenging of the murders of Sikhs in the Golden Temple. He
wished to reunite all Sikhs in India and abroad to fight for the
same cause on one front. He foresaw the closing down of all
Indian consulates and embassies around the world. By provok-
ing a brutal response from the Indian government against
Sikhs, he hoped to gain the sympathetic assistance of the
United States, Canada and Britain. He intended to avenge the
death of Jarnail Singh Bhindranwale and the "two thousand"
(perhaps as high as one thousand) other Sikhs in the Golden
Temple (later, he would state that there were more than 10,000
deaths in the Delhi riots; the figures cited for both are much
inflated) by the deaths of Rajiv Gandhi and the president of
India, the "Sikh traitor" Giani Zail Singh. His final intent was
to raise a Sikh Liberation Army from those same three foreign
countries, which have large Sikh populations.

His New Year's resolution went into slightly more detail,
naming some names and spelling out intentions more graphically:

> My New Year's resolution is to make Khalistan. In order
> to achieve it we have to unite all the Youth of Khalistan
> irrespective of their castes. In North America I have
> united the Youth. R. Shergill is possibly the next to me in
> every case. Other *jatha* [i.e., those who go out and court
> arrest] are very small in their gray matter. Perhaps Toronto
> is the worse example, because all the people from there
> are after the leadership, *chamcha giri* [sycophancy], etc.
> Blind faith doesn't get you anywhere.
>
> The youth has to think [in] constructive ways. I have an
> idea which I have only shared with two other people. One
> is Lal and the other is Thariwal [probably Ammand
> Singh "Dhaliwal"]. I don't think Thariwal, as ex-army,
> really understood my ideas; but Lal is all for it. In a

nutshell what we have to do is to defeat the Indian Economy. Many different ways are available. What I am propagating is to make India financially so poor that it falls on its knees. Stop each and every industry in each state of India. For example, leave Punjab aside, there are approx. 20 states. Select five commandoes for each state. One as the organiser and four [for] blowing the shit apart. Start with big industries by bombing the industry on same day same time. Four people farther divided into two groups. I have [found] that groups of two are most effective. Each state will fall to five people [who] are told which to select, and provide the back up. Select two targets and do to them what they did to my people in the Golden Temple.

One of the main targets is the Bhabha Atomic power station. I have the information that by simply contaminating the water they use we could blow the Atomic power station. How easy it can be done. Only one group will work on this. This should be the first, because after it the security is going to increase [and] it may happen that we may not be able to break the security.

The next target is chemical firms such as Union Carbide. [Note: The disastrous chemical spill that killed over 2,000 residents of Bhopal had already occurred. No suspicion of Sikh-extremist tampering is suggested.] Once the poisonous gas leaks take place, let the nature take its course. All I need is the 100 people and I could bring the Indian puppet government on its knees for good. I feel I have two or three already: R. Shergill, Lal, myself. Vicci and Sukhi [This is probably a reference to the two other New York Khalistanis in Birk's cell who were arrested with him in early May in New Orleans: Virinder Singh and Sukhvinder Singh.] can be only back up since they have no foresight and not enough intelligence to think for themselves. With appropriate organisation I can get one group of five people from N.Y. R. Shergill should be able to get the second group. This makes ten people. We must convince Dhillon [i.e., Ganga Singh Dhillon, founding

member and head of the U.S. chapter of the WSO] to get
five people committed to do all this. Balbir should also be
able to get five people from Montreal. Vancouver is
another five people. I myself probably have to go to
Toronto to raise five people. Bal and Randhawa are not
right people.

This makes six groups and 30 peoples. England has a
rich resource of people. We have to stop making conver-
sions and start acting. Can it be possible that we can get
70 people from there? When we have this then we have to
have three workshops. The first for the co-ordinates which
includes everything from making time bombs, contami-
nants, poison of food crops, biological warfare, to
organization.

The second group and third group is a team-member
for each group. Once we have done that we can reach the
ultimate aim.

We must be aware of all the people who are after the
leadership or any office. Baldev Singh or Khalon are not
useful for any office whatsoever [both are New York area
spokesmen]. Bhullar is army advisor and should only be
used as such. . . .

Person's background has to be clean. Has to be clean
Sikh. . . .

[One cannot help noting Birk's near-despair over the perceived *moral* lapses of the Khalistan leadership. He is talking,
analogously, of the Washington and Jefferson of the Khalistan
movement when he states of one: "He will cheat, lie, bribe and
kill to get his ultimate aims." He alludes to the man's drinking,
his sexual promiscuity, even his black marketeering. Of an even
more eminent leader, Birk writes, ". . . should not be trusted. He
will insinuate, may not lie, to make you believe he is the purest
person in the world." Always and most damagingly, Birk (and
others like him) return to obsessions with purity.]

On January 26, 1985, Birk — known as John Singh — Lal and
Ammand, and FBI undercover agent Thomas Norris — known

as Tom Nichols — met in a video-bugged room in the Hilton Hotel in New York City to discuss their need for fake passports, explosives, guns and training. Birk was being sucked deeper and deeper into a situation where he could be charged with conspiracy to wage war against India. He spoke freely of his large-scale schemes for destruction. He promised to arrange for a "camp" out in western New Jersey along the banks of the Delaware River, where commandos could train intensively under "Nichols's" direction.

On April 27, they drive out to Columbia, New Jersey, in a bugged truck — Birk, Lal and Ammand Singh, and Nichols — to scout the desolate terrain. They have directions, and the name of a truck stop where they are to park; they are to enter the fields behind. This is where the weekend commandos are to be trained, but they get lost on the property, and they can't find the house they've supposedly rented.

Nichols drives back to New York, dropping Birk, Lal and Ammand off at the house of a Sikh friend in New Jersey.

There probably never was a house or a farm. A year later, there is only a truck stop and no house. Across the highway, there is a gas station, owned by Sikhs, where a shaved Sikh works, recognizable only by his steel bracelet.

New Orleans, May 4, 1985

On this day, the terrorist career of Gurpartap Singh Birk, a.k.a. John Singh, comes to an end. The notoriety of Lal Singh and Ammand Singh, who will elude the pick-up, just begins. In a hotel lobby a few blocks from the LSU Medical Center, four Sikhs are arrested by the FBI. Their names: Gurpartap Singh Birk, Virinder Singh, Jasbir Singh and Sukhvinder Singh, of New York. On May 11th, they will be joined by Jatwinder Singh Ahlu- walia, of New Orleans. The charge: conspiracy to assassinate a protected foreign personage, Bhajan Lal, Chief Minister of the Indian state of Haryana, in the U.S. for private medical matters. The weapon: a revolver in Birk's car, purchased on the trip from Frank Camper's small private dealership in Birmingham.

To civil libertarians, like Birk's lawyer William Kunstler, and court-appointed attorney Ron Rakoski, they were picked up merely for being Sikhs in a hotel lobby. They were unarmed and politely behaved. To the FBI and the prosecution, they were conspiring to assassinate a foreign official.

For the first time in the United States, the word "Sikh" will be identified with the plotting of violent crime within the country's borders.

Toronto, May 12, 1985

In a private home in the Toronto suburb of Brampton, one of the last agreements between Sikh factions and law enforcement officers in Canada is about to be worked out. Present are Ron Prior of the Metropolitan Toronto Police (who is in charge of Minority Group Relations), John Piper, then Director of Public Relations for the United Way in Toronto, and representatives of moderate and militant Sikhs in Toronto. In total, nearly twenty people.

In the winter of 1983, Piper had proposed that the world's most popular female vocalist, Lata Mangeshkar (who has made over twenty-five thousand recordings in twenty different languages), give a charity concert at Maple Leaf Gardens in Toronto, to benefit the United Way. Announcements had been delayed, first in September 1984, and then in December, at the time of the Bhopal disaster. In India, she raised some $50,000 at a concert for Bhopal emergency relief.

Finally, an agreement is reached. This will be the first time in Canadian history, and perhaps in world history, that a "Third World" artist raises funds for a "Western" charity. The United Way estimates that $100,000 can be raised in a sold-out concert. Lata's American manager demands first-class treatment for the star — an official political greeting from the mayor of Toronto and premier of Ontario at the airport, first-class accommodations for the entourage and prominent press coverage. All of this is arranged.

Since the Indian Consulate in Toronto has been contacted for its aid in endorsing the project, and has in fact, provided important early support, the Sikh community has expressed its objections, and indicated it might be forced to disrupt the concert if the Indian government appears in any way to sponsor or to take credit for her appearance. They have already objected to the United Way's having sent blankets to India after the Bhopal disaster through the Indian government, and not through private charities. In return for their agreeing not to disrupt the concert, the Sikh community representatives extract the promise that the Indian Consul-General in Toronto, Surinder Malik, will not be allowed to speak at the event — and the name "India" will not appear in the official brochure.

In return for a promise of nonviolence from Sikh protesters or Khalistani demonstrators, Lata Mangeshkar, a devout Hindu and personal friend of the Nehru/Gandhi family, will be brought to Toronto under the auspices of the United Way of Greater Toronto and the South Asian Community.

Ottawa, May 13, 1985

On this day, the Indian High Commission requests that certain Indian government installations in Canada (notably Air India) be provided with extra security in light of threats levelled against them. The RCMP, assessing the threats, concur. Air India is assigned extraordinary protection, both on the tarmac and at its ticket booths.

June, it will be recalled, is the month of the one-year anniversary of Operation Blue Star, the Indian Army invasion of the Sikh's Golden Temple. Memorial month is treated very seriously in Sikh temples across North America. Boycotts of all Indian institutions, especially Air India, have been demanded in *gurdwaras* around the world.

Duncan, British Columbia, June 4, 1985

On the east coast of Vancouver Island, just an hour's drive
north of the provincial capital of Victoria (where the dowager
dames of the Empire still take their tea in the Empress Hotel),
three hours by ferry west of Vancouver (through the bungalow-
bedecked islands of the Strait of Georgia), a harsher version of
Canada still hangs on. It's found in the chain of old logging
towns pinched between the uplands and the shore, from
Duncan through Nanaimo, Ladysmith and Courtenay, all the
way up to Campbell River.

Duncan is a typical Island city, a one-time railway junction,
where logs from the north met logs from the interior, and were
cut into lumber to build the West. Timber and mining built
these towns and still sustain them, forming their character.
Sawmills and dockwork, shunting and repairing — steady
labour for men willing to suffer the low pay rather than endure
the loneliness of the lumber camps.

But the shopping-mall culture of the mainland has also
found its way to Vancouver Island. A plaza at the edge of
Duncan boasts a Woolworth's and the usual Shacks and Huts.
The town-centre has fought back with a pedestrian mall and
much wood-trimmed renovation: there's a small Eaton's, T. N.
Singh's law office, computer stores, boutiques along the mall,
some restaurants. One, called Khyber, serves a fair Punjabi-
style lunch. Public money has been invested in an impressive
cluster of civic buildings clumped in hexagons of stark concrete with more wood trim. The court house is there and the
civic services and the office of an RCMP detachment.

In his home on Kimberley Street, Inderjit Singh Reyat has
been awakened by a collect call at four o'clock in the morning.
He is accustomed to predawn messages; there have been four
calls, all from the same Vancouver number, and four calls he's
immediately returned, in the past ten days. Generally, he has
received the call, hung up and then dressed and driven down to
his place of work and phoned the same person back. The
anxious caller, according to Reyat's testimony many months

later, has been calling because he is *very* interested in getting his car converted to propane use.

The man has come to Duncan with a young straggly-bearded associate. They've been driven from the ferry to Reyat's house by another friend, Joginder Singh Gill, who has now left.

At six-thirty in the evening on Tuesday, June 4, 1985, Reyat, the man from Vancouver and his young associate exit Reyat's house on Kimberley Street, get into a dark brown Mercury bearing the vanity plates "I. Reyat," and drive into town, stopping in the parking lot of Auto-Electric Marine on Canada Avenue. The two older men are wearing the tall turbans and long, free-flowing beards of baptized Sikhs, not the tidier, more ornamental turbans and gathered beards one associates with urbanized Sikhs here and in India. The third man is much younger; his beard is still straggly.

Inderjit Singh Reyat is a skilled worker. He is considered the best auto electrician in Duncan, and he was considered the best player of *tabla* (Indian drums) in Vancouver before he moved to the Island. He is from a large family, most of whom still live in Vancouver, where he continues to be well regarded within the Sikh community. His older visitor is Talvinder Singh Parmar, a Sikh priest and political organizer. He is identified by the Indian government as a killer and is being actively sought by that government for the 1981 murder of two policemen in Deheru, a village in Punjab. However, Talvinder Singh Parmar, who has also sometimes used the name Hardev Singh Parmar, describes himself in Canada as an unemployed janitor. The home he built in 1982 in the Vancouver suburb of Burnaby is valued at $350,000.

Many in the Canadian Sikh community and among the Khalistani commandos consider Parmar rude and arrogant, remembering his way of entering the temple and appropriating the front row for himself. Many object to his political organizing and to the Khalistani group, Babar Khalsa ("Pure Tigers"), whose Vancouver cell he heads. Even within the Babar Khalsa, his "ego" is a problem for some. His disregard for the sacrifices made by others working in the cause — some of them with families, some of them in jail — has alienated even his hard-core supporters. As a priest, he claims to have baptized over 12,000 Sikhs worldwide. In his own words, the whole Sikh nation is his concern and is in his heart.

Nine times during interrogation in the months to come, Inderjit Singh Reyat will deny knowing, or having heard of, Talvinder Singh Parmar.

After twenty-five minutes inside the shop, the three men exit and speed back up Somenos Road to the Route 18 intersection, make a left, and proceed to the Hillcrest Road intersection. They back the car down the sloping gravel path to the concrete barrier. The young man stays with the car. Parmar and Reyat take something from the trunk of the car and disappear with it down the trail.

Reyat, the skilled technician, has been here before. A couple of weeks earlier, he tested a device composed of a twelve-volt battery, cardboard cylinder, gun powder, a light bulb and filament and some dynamite. It didn't work. This time he has made a device using priming powder from a .22-calibre cartridge. It works.

Fourteen minutes later, a woman sitting in a parked car behind a mound of dirt on Hillcrest Road a few hundred feet to the north is nearly knocked from her seat by the sound of an explosion. She is Margaret Lynne McAdams, a surveillance agent for the CSIS. She and her partner have followed Parmar and his young companion all the way from Vancouver. Her partner has taken position several hundred yards away, closer to the detonation. The three men leave Hillcrest Road immediately, heading back to Kimberley Street. The young man stays with Reyat for the week; Talvinder Parmar spends the night and then returns to Vancouver. The next day, Reyat and the young man go to the Woolworth's store in the mall and buy a very large, outmoded Sanyo AM-FM stereo tuner, model number FMT 611K for slightly more than a hundred dollars, charging it on Reyat's VISA card. He later tells police that it was a gift to the young man, whose name he says he never learned.

Maple Leaf Gardens, Toronto, June 9, 1985

Shortly before the sold-out Lata Mangeshkar concert at Maple Leaf Gardens, police receive a phoned-in bomb threat. A man with an Indian accent, calling from a restaurant in Montreal, claims to have overheard Sikh plotters discussing a bomb. A search of the facility reveals nothing, and the concert goes on to raise $123,000 for the United Way. Sikhs appear to have boycotted the concert, but do not interfere with its staging.

The *Globe and Mail* headline asserts that police are taking the threat seriously. Police later deny the gravity of their investigation and speak off the record of "some crazy" having phoned in a call. Sikhs are incensed and feel betrayed, denying the possibility of such a plot after having given their word. They immediately accuse the Indian Consulate of having originated the call as a bad-faith provocation. Consul-General Malik reacts angrily. Already denied the right to welcome the singer, he withdraws from the head table at the official banquet. His name plate will stare out from in front of his empty chair.

From this moment on, doubt will be cast on *everyone's* credibility: the media either for appearing gullible or for overcompensating out of hostile suspiciousness; the Indian Consulate for manipulation; the Sikhs for their limitless spleen and violence.

These suspicions only harden in the months to come.

Vancouver and Toronto, June 1985

The month: June. The "memorial month" for the Golden Temple invasion. Spectacular vengeance has been promised. Rajiv Gandhi is coming to Washington and New York in June, but the planned assassination has been prevented.

The only direct Air India flight out of Canada departs from Toronto and Montreal every Saturday evening. It is part of a continuous round trip between Canada and the Asian subcontinent, beginning as Air India 181 in India, going on to Frankfurt, and landing in Toronto, where the crew changes. Then, heading east with some passengers from India or Frankfurt still on board, the flight makes a final stop in Montreal, where it changes its number to Air India 182 before making the journey back to India.

The dates available for carrying out a major attack on an Air India plane during this memorial month are the 8th, the 15th, the 22nd, and the 29th. But the June 8th departure from Toronto has been cancelled due to engine failure. Perhaps the 15th is too soon — the remote timers for the explosive device are tricky, and parts are still missing. This leaves the flight on the 22nd, departing from Toronto at 6:00 P.M. (EDT) and Montreal at 8:10 P.M. (EDT) and making a stopover in London at 2:25 A.M. (EDT) on the 23rd. It is to land in New Delhi at 11:30 P.M. (local time) on the 23rd and will arrive in Bombay at 2:05 A.M. (local time) on the 24th. On the 23rd there is also a Canadian Pacific flight to Japan connecting with Air India 301 to Bangkok.

Though Air India makes a special request for — and receives — extra RCMP surveillance of their aircraft for this month of maximum threat, there is only one irregularity in the security arrangements. The Air India station manager at Toronto's Lester B. Pearson International Airport, who is in charge of the overall operation of unloading and loading of both passengers and cargo, will be away on vacation on June 22nd. It is not clear who has been assigned to replace the station manager and assume his duties.

Vancouver, June 16, 1985

June 22, 1985, was target day. Two Air India jets would be blown out of calm skies over two distant continents on June 22nd. It thrilled Singh to be part of the spectacular operation. He was one of the chosen.

Singh dialled the CP Air reservations number. An agent picked up the phone, suspecting no sinister designs.

Singh told the agent he wanted to take a Vancouver-Tokyo-Bangkok flight on June 22. He expressed his preferences, and the agent booked him confirmed seats on CP Air 003 to Tokyo on June 22, connecting with Air India Flight 301.

The ticket agent asked for a name.

Singh gave an initial instead of a name. (Why not confuse eventual police trails?) *A. Singh.* "A" for "Ammand"? *Ammand Singh* had made headline news all May. A mystery man named Ammand Singh was being sought by Interpol for conspiracy to assassinate Rajiv Gandhi. Gurpartap Singh Birk, alleged to be the leader of the assassination cell, had been caught by the FBI and was currently in jail. But Birk's two accomplices had fled the net. There were rumours of the fugitives surfacing in Brooklyn, in Vancouver, in Los Angeles.

Why not use "A. Singh" for the confirmed ticket?

The agent needed a phone number where the passenger could be reached.

Singh didn't hesitate. 324-7525. It was the number of the Ross Street *gurdwara* in Vancouver. No member of the congregation would dare question or betray.

The ticket was never picked up, never paid for, but the reservation was never cancelled. The name "A. Singh" therefore stayed on the flight-manifest throughout the coming scrutiny.

Vancouver, June 19, 1985

The phone rang at about 6:00 P.M. PDT in the CP Air reservations office, and Martine Donohue answered. The caller identified himself as Mr Singh. He didn't have a strong accent, but she could tell right away that he was foreign. He had to be an East Indian. But not the usual rough logger or labourer type, she decided. This one had a suave voice and a cultured accent, sort of like Rajiv Gandhi's, the new prime minister of India.

The caller with the suave East Indian voice wanted to make two separate reservations for two separate male passengers, both named Singh like himself, and both departing from Vancouver on June 22nd.

Donohue punched up the details on the screen. There were no complications for passenger Mohinderbell Singh, who wanted, the caller said, to travel from Vancouver to Bangkok through Tokyo. She booked this Singh onto CP Air 003 to

Tokyo, then on to Air India 301 from Tokyo to Bangkok. Mohinderbell was willing to pay a higher-than-economy fare (called Royal Canadian) on CP Air 003 in order to be certain to link up in Tokyo with Air India 301. Linking was the important thing. The caller rejected Donohue's suggestion of an economy booking on a later flight.

The second reservation was for a Jaswand Singh, who planned to fly from Vancouver to India through Montreal. This was a little harder. Donohue booked this Singh onto CP Air 086 to Montreal's Dorval Airport, and then onto Air India 182 out of Mirabel Airport in Montreal the same day, June 22nd.

She asked for a contact telephone number.

The caller was prepared. He gave Donohue a misleading number: 437-3216. Until a year before, it had been the home phone number of Hardial Singh Johal, a heating engineer for the Vancouver school system, a man known to be an ardent supporter of Harchand Singh Longowal, the leader of the non-Khalistani Akali Dal party in Punjab, and known equally for his outspoken criticism of the Khalistan movement. Johal had been physically beaten for his views.

Donohue entered Johal's number.

This Mr Singh's call lasted about half an hour.

Singh reported his success to other members of his cell. He had the two necessary confirmed seats on two Air India flights racing towards India from opposite directions, three days hence. Sparks would fly. It would be a spectacular display of strength.

He had expected to be congratulated. But he was not. The bag-bomb destined to blow up Air India 301 would be safe, the leader conceded, because it would be interlined (automatically transferred to a second carrier) in Tokyo. But how was the bag-bomb arriving on CP Air 086 at Dorval Airport to be safely checked in at the Air India counter at Mirabel Airport, which was an hour away from Dorval by bus? A cell-member would have to board the plane, accompany the "luggage" and risk arrest.

Singh left it to one of the others to correct the mistake.

The cell discussed the options. At least one of the members was accustomed to frequent transcontinental travel on business. A connecting flight to Montreal was out of the question, because of the baggage transfer between the two separate airports.

The solution was simple, and they should have thought of it in the first place. The imaginary Jaswand Singh would have to connect with Air India 181 in Toronto, not in Montreal, and get his deadly bag interlined all the way to India at the CP Air counter in Vancouver Airport itself.

It took the cell an hour and a bit to work out the transfer problem.

At 7:20 P.M. PDT another cell member called the CP Air reservations office. Donohue was off duty by then. Another ticket agent worked to accommodate Jaswand Singh's changed travel plans. The agent got Mr Singh a confirmed seat on CP Air 060 to Toronto easily enough. But Jaswand Singh, the agent informed the caller, would have to be wait-listed on Flight 181 out of Toronto. As the flight made the final leg of its incoming journey — from Toronto to Montreal — sixty-eight passengers from Frankfurt or India would still be on board. They would be disembarking at Montreal, making room for more India-bound passengers, but until then, the flight was fully booked.

This was a devastating blow to the cell. Without a confirmed ticket, Jaswand Singh's bag would not be interlined all the way when he checked it in, in Vancouver on the morning of June 22nd.

The cell didn't despair. They had advisers who were travel agents. Something could be worked out at the last minute.

Over the phone the caller made a quick decision. He abandoned the reservation on CP Air 086 to Dorval and the confirmed Montreal connection on Air India 182 for Jaswand Singh. Instead he took the CP Air 060 seat to Toronto and the wait-listing on Air India 181. It would work out.

Vancouver, June 20, 1985

Shortly after noon the next day (at 12:10 P.M. PDT), a tall, well-built Sikh gentleman estimated to be in his late thirties, walked into CP Air's downtown office to pay for the tickets reserved for Jaswand and Mohinderbell Singh. He wore a grey windbreaker and a saffron turban.

The ticket agent on duty, Gerry Duncan, told the man in the saffron turban how much he owed for the two round-trip reserved tickets. The man pulled out a fistful of cash, and discovered he didn't have quite enough for two round-trip tickets, especially not for the imaginary Mohinderbell's imaginary journey by Royal Canadian class. So, on the spot, the turbaned man changed the booking to one-way.

Gerry Duncan remembers the buyer's salt-and-pepper beard. It was gathered in a fine black mesh. He remembers a diamond ring. And he remembers that the man took cash out of his right pocket — hundreds and fifties. Duncan remembers the turbaned man as being very confident — he seemed to know airline procedures rather well. Duncan thought of him as a travel agent picking up tickets for his clients.

The man in the saffron turban peeled off a total of $3,005. Then he changed the names on the reservations. Jaswand Singh became M. Singh, and Mohinderbell Singh became L. Singh. So from then on the screen showed L. Singh, and the previously reserved "A. Singh" as passengers on CP Air 003 to Narita and on Air India 301 from Narita to Bangkok, and it showed M. Singh as a passenger on CP Air 060 to Toronto and wait-listed on Air India 181 to Montreal.

Perhaps it was a gesture meant to mislead and to show off. "L. Singh" would evoke memories of Lal Singh, the second fugitive who had eluded the FBI and Interpol nets.

Duncan counted the bills. He put away the cash and handed over two consecutively numbered tickets.

Vancouver, June 22, 1985

It is still very early on the second-longest day of the year. Dark clouds frame the snow-capped mountains north of the city. It will be a typically cool, cloudy morning in one of the world's most beautifully situated cities. Two young men are preparing to leave for the airport. Their names are Singh. We picture these Singhs in their late twenties or early thirties, unemployed, unskilled, but consumed with a mission.

Heavy bags — one grey, headed for Tokyo and transferring to Bangkok, and the other burgundy, going east to Toronto and transferring to New Delhi — are crammed with clothes and electronic gadgetry. In bags like these, on every flight to India, the good life of this continent is being exported piecemeal to the villages of India.

The stereo tuner is heavy and must be handled very carefully. The Sanyo factory packing — carton and foam plastic — has been preserved for maximum protection. Normally, in the good-natured game of smuggling (there's even an Indian party-game called "Contraband," a kind of jet-setters' Monopoly, where the winner smuggles the greatest amount, with the blandest lying, through customs), the "overseas Indian" would disguise his purchases, discard the factory wrappings and pretend the equipment was used personal property, not a gift. But this tuner will never reach Indian customs. No need for disguise, no need for warranty cards. The workings of the tuner have all been gutted anyway.

One of the Singhs calls himself "Manjit" for today. Manjit is more nervous than might be expected of a man packing for a vacation trip to his homeland. Much later today, he believes, the world will register his deed as a blow for the honour, dignity and self-respect of his religion and the restoration of Sikh pride everywhere. He burns with *izzat*.

He is worried about one critical detail. His seat on Air India
out of Toronto is still unconfirmed. He's not worried for
himself, since he has no intention of flying anywhere today, not
even to Toronto. But with a confirmed seat on Air India, there
would be no question about interlining his precious cargo. The
whole mission hangs on solving this one complication. He
keeps calling CP Air. He has been calling ever since the bad
news about his wait-listed status, and still no seats have opened
up. It is now just an hour before he has to leave for the airport.

At 6:30 A.M. he calls the downtown ticket office. "This is
Manjit Singh," he says in his laboured English. "What is my
status on Air India 181?"

Just as he fears, the clerk's news is still discouraging.
"Wait-listed only," comes the response, as it has for the past
two days. This time, however, Manjit detects a familiar accent
from the clerk. He continues the conversation in Hindi, itself a
foreign — even hated — language, but one that at least grants
him fluency, with the aid of some Punjabi additions.

The clerk is Aziz Premji, an African-born Muslim of Indian
origin. In multi-ethnic Vancouver, this is multiculturalism
working precisely as it was intended to work. It is almost
charming — this cross-cultural conversation — if one ignores
the motivation for the call.

"I must get my suitcase on board," he insists. "Even if I do
not fly today, what about my bag?" He inquires about giving his
baggage tags to friends with confirmed seats, just to make
certain that his bag is boarded.

Premji explains the impossibility of the request. He can only
suggest that Mr Singh fly to Toronto on the nine o'clock CP
flight, for which he is confirmed, and try again in Toronto.
Perhaps a seat will open up.

"You don't understand," Manjit pleads. That the plan should
stumble now over so simple a detail as a seat he doesn't even
intend to occupy is grotesque.

Obviously, Manjit Singh — though willing — is not able. His
role in the entire drama is little more than that of a bag carrier,
a porter of vengeance. Now that he has failed to coax baggage
tags out of the Hindi-speaking Premji, the bag will have to be

entrusted to a singh who can handle himself more persuasively, to a singh whose English is more fluent. In the movement, the minor players are all called "singhs," as in "we're sending you five singhs," meaning five young men willing to undertake any assignment without questions.

The second singh fills the bill. He is more "acceptable" to an anglo-saxon counter-clerk. He arrives at the airport shortly after eight o'clock, stands in a long line and finally finds himself in front of CP Air passenger clerk Jeannie Adams for seat-assignment and baggage check-in. She remembers this singh as "sparkly eyed and smiley faced," not gaunt and sinister. This singh, a man of medium height and medium build, is in his thirties. He wears a good grey suit. He doesn't wear a turban. To Jeannie Adams this man's deportment seems pleasantly Canadian.

She looks his ticket over and twists a Toronto baggage tag around the handle of his burgundy bag. He stops her. Desperation makes him peremptory. He demands that Adams check his bag all the way to New Delhi though he has only "RQ" (wait-listed), not "OK," status on the Air India flight out of Toronto. She looks at his ticket again and calls up the reservation list on her screen. His status still shows as "RQ." She explains that interlining his bag would be against the rules. He bullies and cajoles. Panic does not make him less fluent. He acts as if he is very knowledgeable about baggage tags and baggage transfers. Adams stands her ground as long as she can. The passenger check-in line gets longer and longer. "You jerk," she keeps thinking. It is time either to get firm and possibly alienate a passenger who has indeed paid a great deal of money — $1,697 — or give in and let Air India handle it in Toronto.

Desperate, the second singh tries one last manœuvre. "I called Air India," he claims. "They told my seat is confirmed now."

Adams looks at him, irritated and skeptical.

"I'll get my brother," he insists. "My brother will tell you." He leaves his burgundy bag on the scale, drops his ticket on the counter and turns to leave. This is an astute psychological gesture on the part of the well-spoken, well-dressed singh. A shout or threat might have alienated Jeannie Adams completely.

Adams watches him for a moment as he turns away from his ticket and his suitcase, unaware that the decision she makes next will affect the fates of 329 people.

"I don't want to talk to your brother," she snaps at him. "I don't have time. Look at the line behind you." Waiting is something a harassed check-in clerk cannot do. She thinks again of dumping the problem in Air India's lap. After all, they can deal with him better.

Finally she interlines the bag. Young Mr Singh walks out of the airport and disappears. There are one hundred thousand Sikhs in British Columbia, half of the Canadian total, and there is the Punjabi Pipeline from Vancouver to Los Angeles, paid for by Sikh doctors and entrepreneurs, that run illegal singhs up and down the Pacific coast and out through Mexico when their jobs are done. Manjit Singh, if that's what his name really was, is probably on his way to the border-crossing village of Abbotsford and into the state of Washington, or back in some safe-house awaiting transport into the interior, before the plane even takes off.

There is another singh leaving Vancouver today. "L. Singh" checks in a new grey vinyl bag packed with clothes and a bulky Sanyo FMT 611K stereo tuner, its factory packing intact, its works gutted. He is ticketed on CP Air 003 to Narita Airport, Tokyo, and he has a confirmed seat on Air India from Narita as far as Bangkok. Although he has no intention of boarding, his confirmed seat represents real security. There are no baggage hassles for "L. Singh." His bag will be interlined at Narita as a matter of routine.

Lester B. Pearson International Airport, Toronto, June 22, 1985
Mirabel International Airport, Montreal, June 22, 1985

Ethnic airlines at their weekly departure: how quickly the hidden essence of the homeland emerges, once the adopted country is left at curbside!

For the India-born travelling to India on Air India, India begins at the check-in counter. It may begin with a groan: Air India 181 is already late! Just like India, they think — we hurry to get here, afraid of the rainstorm (such a shower, a regular cloudburst! A bad omen, perhaps — or is it good? There's always someone around to contradict any interpretation), others build in extra time for the long trip in from Detroit or Buffalo in case (as they often do) they get lost in those superhighways outside Toronto, only this time they didn't get lost, and they arrived in plenty of time. Too much time. What to do for three or four hours? Chat, drink tea, talk to old friends.

Behind the glass, with their families around them (the women wearing their gold jewellery and brand-new saris, the girls in new pant suits, the boys in their T-shirts and blue jeans) the men find their confidence restored, the noise level rises, the little children are running about, the families cluster according to language. Many of the men are smoking, but not the Sikhs, of course, for whom it is expressly forbidden; and why are so many *sardarjis* at the airport tonight? At least if *they're* on the plane, it won't get blown up, someone jokes nervously. No, only hijacked, someone retorts.

These moments are the best of all, when the clothes are crisp, the children alert and playful, the families greeting each other and making plans to get together in India, even if they fail to see each other in Toronto. For these few hours it is possible to contemplate a perfected version of Canada and India. Seeing the children, you know why you emigrated. Anticipating the joy in India, you know why you cannot cut the ties.

It is the high point of several dozen lives today: going to India, showing off the material success, showing off the tall, strong, confident children (who still haven't lost the culture and the language of their parents). How many suitcases have been packed just with gifts, all those weeks of dedicated sari shopping and appliance buying down on Gerrard Street in the Indian stores? Toronto is one of the world centres of Indian settlement, just after London and New York. The X-ray machines will be working overtime, with all those stereos and televisions and Cuisinarts.

Whatever the children will do with their lives — and with their 90-plus grades and their parents' savings and frantic blessings, everything will be open to them — it will entail a commitment to social service or some sort of international development. These are the first generation, born in India but carried here as infants, precisely like the earlier generation of Jewish immigrants, only these parents did not suffer a generation of sweatshops and poverty or raise themselves from ghettos. For the most part, the families flying to India today arrived with the skills and the determination to do well wherever they would settle, and statistics show they are, in terms of income, the most successful immigrant group in Canada.

Statistics also show they are socially the least esteemed, the most discriminated against — in social distance tests, the only group to come in below blacks.

Passengers are still connecting in Toronto from various western flights. The plane itself, named the *Emperor Kanishka*, one of the few planes named for a Hindu, and not a Muslim, emperor of India, is still out on the tarmac near the Air Canada hangar. Work has been proceeding on the cargo doors ever since the plane's arrival from Frankfurt at 3:00 P.M., because this return trip to India is going to involve a rather complicated, but still routine, manœuvre. An entire engine — the one that failed and caused the cancellation of the June 8th flight — is being loaded onto the plane. Part of it is being put in one container in the forward cargo compartment; the rest of the engine is being stowed on four pallets in the rear cargo compartment. Flight 181 (182 after it leaves Montreal) will carry no cargo apart from the engine this week — only the baggage of its passengers, which even now is going through the X-ray prior to loading. The "pod" of the engine — its empty shell — is being fixed to the left wing of the aircraft. Again, a routine procedure for authorized personnel, who are swarming all over the plane at the moment while an RCMP officer, parked under the wing, checks everyone out for proper ID.

Meanwhile, the X-ray machine has broken down. M. Singh's bag has not yet passed through. The Air India security chief, John D'Souza, can't get it started, although for some reason it will be working perfectly again the next morning. Rather than opening the remaining bags, he issues a hand-held PD-4 Sniffer (the machine with the notorious Transport Canada history) to the Burns International Security agents on duty, James Post and Naseem Nanji, and instructs them on its use.

Over six months earlier, there were concerns about security. According to the Canadian Aviation Safety Board's report:

> ...Prior to the inaugural Air India flight out of Toronto on January 19, a meeting on security for Air India flights (Toronto) was held with representatives from Transport Canada, RCMP and Air India. At this meeting, a PD-4 Sniffer belonging to Air India was produced. It was explained that it would be used to screen checked baggage, as the X-ray machine had not yet arrived. At that time, an RCMP member tested its effectiveness. The test revealed that it could not detect a small container of gunpowder until the head of the sniffer was moved to less than an inch from the gunpowder. Also, the next day the sniffer was tried on a piece of C4 plastic explosives and it did not function even when it came directly in contact with the explosive substance. It is not known if this was the sniffer used on 22 June 1985.

Although it's against Transport Canada regulations, they've never had special instruction. D'Souza activates the sensor by holding a lighted match directly under it. The loud whistle caused by the open flame is not duplicated by any of the sealed suitcases passing before them. One burgundy suitcase (the same one that has been loaded without a passenger coupon) emits a few low beeps, but since it doesn't match up with D'Souza's dramatic demonstration, agent Post lets it pass.

After the plane finally takes off from Toronto, an hour and thirty-eight minutes late, on its way to Montreal, the various men, couples and women who've said goodbye to their husbands and children and wives will return to the home or apartment, or go to a quiet party.

An hour later, while the last bags are being X-rayed at Mirabel Airport in Montreal, the pilot of the flight, Commander Hanse Singh Narendra, steps into a booth and calls his good friend Saravjit Singh, in New Jersey. This is to be the last unofficial communication from Flight 182. The fifty-seven-year-old commander has spent the week in Toronto on a kind of mini-vacation with his girlfriend of nineteen years, London-based Air Canada ticket agent Valerie Evans. But their return trip to London has been frustrated — he couldn't get her on board his Air India flight. The chap who usually handles that sort of complimentary staff travel had stepped out of the office, and Narendra was reluctant to get someone else to take authority. So she'll just have to get back to London by Air Canada. They'll be getting in at about the same time anyway. But Narendra and Valerie, and the Saravjit Singhs of Spotswood, New Jersey, will all be getting together again, he promises, this time in Vancouver in the fall.

By now the Mirabel security agents have detected three "suspicious" bags, and pulled them from the belt. They notify Air India security — D'Souza again — but he can't come right away to open them. No one else is notified, and by the time D'Souza arrives half an hour later, the plane has already taken off. The suspicious bags turn out to be perfectly harmless.

Mr and Mrs John Laurence, parents of the celebrated young dancers Krithika and Shyamala, who are going to India for a summer of intensive study of Indian classical dance, take the short drive back from Pearson International Airport to their home in suburban Mississauga, and find that a niece has broken a glass in the interim. "Auntie, you're going to be so angry with me," the niece declares, and to the niece's great surprise, Sarojini Laurence *is* upset, far more than a glass is worth. She's suddenly remembered her daughters' reaction to the invasion of the Golden Temple slightly over a year before: "We'd better not take Air India!"

Saroj will be unable to sleep that night as the plane crosses the Atlantic. She'll still be awake at 4:00, when, unknown to her, her daughters lie at the bottom of the North Atlantic, 110 miles off the coast of Ireland.

Sikh Temple, Malton, June 23, 1985

While the plane was over the Atlantic, there were celebrations at the Sikh Temple in Malton, near the Pearson International Airport. A pizza deliverer remembers that a big party was going on there, at three in the morning. He later identified one of the suspects from a mug shot.

Narita Airport, Japan, June 23, 1985

CP Air Flight 003 with 374 passengers and a crew of 16 left Vancouver seventeen minutes late, at 1:37 P.M. (PDT) on June 22nd, and arrived at Tokyo's Narita Airport some nine hours (and one calendar-day) later, at 2:41 P.M. local time, fourteen minutes ahead of schedule.

Three hundred and sixty-five pieces of luggage, stowed in nine Duralumin containers, had been sent from Vancouver. Four of the containers had been unloaded by handlers, when, suddenly, at 3:19 P.M., the luggage-handling area erupted in flames, smoke and flying debris. A twenty-four-year-old cargo handler named Hideharu Koda had just checked the "Bangkok" ticket on a grey vinyl suitcase and passed it to his colleague, twenty-five-year-old Hideo Asano, for placement on the transfer-cart. Both young men were obliterated; four others were seriously injured.

The Punjab conflict had just claimed its first non-Indian lives.

51° N, 12° 50'W, 3:14 A.M. *EDT, June 23, 1985*

Breakfast had just been served, and people were moving about
in the cabin. One can imagine the commotion. The passengers
were mainly women and children. There were eighty-four children aboard, typical of summertime flights to India from North
America — particularly this flight, the first after school closing.
Little Suneal Dhunna, seated in the last row of the plane, was to
be brought forward in just a few minutes to visit the cockpit.
In the cockpit itself, the co-pilot, Captain Satwinder Singh
Bhinder and Flight Engineer Dara Dumasia were searching for
the customs seals that were routinely placed on liquor bottles
that had been brought on board to serve passengers, but had
remained unopened.

PART TWO

CHAPTER 1

On the morning of June 23, 1985, Thomas Lane was the radar controller at the Shannon Air Traffic Control Centre. At six minutes past eight Irish time, he received an identifying "Good Morning, Shannon" transmission from Air India 182. The speaker was the co-pilot, Satwinder Singh Bhinder. Lane assigned Air India 182 a special identification number, 2005, for the half-hour it would be in Irish airspace. As soon as Bhinder punched the number into his on-board transponder, sending it along an electronic information beam to Shannon, the position of Air India relative to Shannon radar was automatically locked in.

On the ground station's radar screen, all planes are rendered equally — each is a diamond shape accompanied by labels stating flight number, position and updated altitude. Actually, the ground radar is "blind" — it doesn't bounce an electronic signal off a plane, as we're used to seeing in movies. Instead, it merely responds to the data-flow provided by the plane's transponder beam. The result, in effect, is of two machines talking to each other through the medium of electronic signals.

Because ground radar responds to the signals, and not the plane's physical presence, it is not unusual for the diamond image to disappear entirely for a few seconds, or for several sweeps of the radar. Electrical interference, human error or some other disturbance can disrupt the signal beam. In that event, ground radar radios the pilot, alerting him to the difficulty. If a plane were going down, it might very well remain in contact with the ground station by transponder up to the moment of impact. But if the plane had exploded and the transponder was damaged in the process, nothing dramatic would be registered on radar — just a slow fade and eventual "deletion" from the screen.

Lane's last voice communication with Bhinder was at 8:09:58 A.M. local time, confirming Air India's routing into British airspace, which it was due to enter in another twenty-five minutes. But Bhinder was making minor errors in his transmissions to the Shannon tower. First, he began transmitting on the wrong frequency, which Shannon corrected:

Shannon: 182, your correct Shannon frequency is 131 15.

Second, Bhinder misestimated (or misreported) his arrival time over the checkpoint by a full minute — negligible over the course of an entire flight, but this error occurred only nineteen minutes after he had originally called it in. The third error is more difficult to understand. Bhinder misread the code number that Shannon radar gave him to "squawk," or punch into his transponder. All planes controlled by Shannon are given a baseline of 2000; his number was 2005, but he was squawking at 3005.

> *AI 182:*　　AI 182 Good morning.
>
> *Shannon:*　AI 182 Good morning. Squawk 2005 and go ahead please.
>
> *AI 182:*　　3005 squawking...

A minute and fifteen seconds later:

Shannon: AI 182 would you squawk 2005
I repeat 2005

This was the last instruction from Shannon to Air India 182.

Fifty-five minutes after the Tokyo blast, at 3:14 A.M. EDT (8:14 local time) at a point 110 miles off the southwest coast of Ireland, Air India 182, a Boeing 747 carrying 329 passengers and crew, disappeared from Shannon radar. There were two other planes — one a TWA at thirty-five thousand feet, the other a CP Air Empress at thirty-seven thousand feet — still on his screen. Three planes is a light load for Shannon. The first European landfall on the North Atlantic run, it is equipped to handle up to two dozen aircraft at a time.

Lane, alert to alarming causes for deletions, called Air India 182 right away. But, except for a less-than-six-second carrier wave at 8:14, Air India 182 remained silent, and invisible on the screen.

The officers in the Shannon control tower tensed. The situation with Air India 182 was no longer routine. Lane telephoned the Air Traffic Control Centre at Ballygreen, three miles from Shannon, to find out what sort of response they were getting from Air India 182. Ballygreen was not picking up any response either. The vanishing of the diamond image from the radar screen seemed to Lane curiously precipitous. There were no May Day calls, no switching on of the emergency beacon. What this meant to Officer Lane was that no crew member on board had had time or physical capacity to request help before disaster had wiped the plane's image off the Shannon screen.

Lane then called the TWA airliner and asked if its pilot could sight any aircraft ahead of him. Travelling at ten miles a minute, however, the TWA plane had already passed the crash site. The weather was clear enough for the TWA crew to scan the airspace in front of them, but they didn't see the *Emperor Kanishka*. The situation was obviously an emergency one. Lane and his co-workers called Aircraft International Emergency Section. They called the CP Air jet. They called their radio station at Selce. They went into an "Alert" phase.

Lane sensed he was dealing with a major disaster. "I felt that something was wrong," he said later, at the inquest. "It never happened before. I never saw anything like that before."

As Lane frantically attempted to raise a signal, Air India 182 was in its death roll. The crippled airplane, having lost its wing-support almost immediately, plunged nearly six miles in a mere forty-five seconds. The curve of descent was similar to an automobile's dive off a high cliff at full throttle. The plane had been travelling at nearly six hundred miles per hour, or ten miles per minute, yet it hit the water at a point only five miles — or thirty seconds — ahead of its last reported position. Engineers have estimated the velocity at water-impact to have been nearly nine hundred miles per hour.

CHAPTER 2

The words "black box" imply disaster with a hint of miraculous revelation. The black box is the soul, a link to the beyond. When the apocalypse comes, we'll probably tell it to the stars on a loop of tape in an indestructible box, flung into space.

Air India Flight 182's black box — comprised of two recorders, one containing the computer data on the aircraft's systems, the other containing all cockpit voice recording — was recovered from a depth of about 6,500 feet on July 10, seventeen days after the crash. The hoped-for answers all came as negative information: nothing was wrong; conditions were normal; the pilots had no warning. The death of Flight 182 was sudden and unpredicted, and that was the most important clue of all. It could only mean (barring Star Wars testing, space debris, Russian rockets and UFOs, all of which journalists and lawyers at the coroner's inquest in Ireland discussed as open possibilities) that a bomb had exploded near the electronics bay, severing the power line and the transponder feed at the same instant as it had knocked the airplane from the sky.

No suspicion attached itself to the plane's airworthiness. Its servicing was up to date — in fact, it had just received a complete overhaul. The *Emperor Kanishka* was Air India's fourth-youngest 747 in a fleet of ten. It had been commissioned in February 1978, and until that morning in June, had made well over seven thousand takeoffs and landings — an average of over three a day — and had been airborne over twenty-six thousand hours, or 43 percent of the eighty-eight months of its life. Extraordinary as that sounds, it is reasonably light service. The *Kanishka* was capable of handling much more, everything but the stress it was finally subjected to.

The interesting anomalies, small as they are, come from the Cockpit Voice Recorder (CVR). The CVR records in an endless half-hour loop; thus, in the event of disaster, investigators will always have the final thirty minutes of cockpit sound, but nothing earlier. Since Flight 182 vanished at 8:14 A.M. local time, we know everything that was said in the cockpit from 7:44 on.

The co-pilot, Captain Satwinder Singh Bhinder, and the pilot, Commander Hanse Singh Narendra, didn't see eye to eye on a number of issues; the cockpit of the *Emperor Kanishka* was a small parliament of political division. Bhinder was an observant Sikh with *"khalsa"* tendencies and some very hard-line Khalistani friends in Toronto. The two pilots had flown into Toronto on June 15th from Frankfurt, and laid over for the week, waiting for their departure on the 22nd. Many people saw them during the week, though they did not spend much time together. Their relationship was doubtless professional, but could hardly have been cordial. Indeed, given the realities of life in North India at the time, and what we know of their associates and personalities, it's a wonder they were able to tolerate each other's presence.

Narendra, who was fifty-seven and in his final year of active flying for Air India, considered his forty-three-year-old co-pilot an extremist. The context for that particular judgement is not really clear, but with Narendra's outspokenness, and Bhinder's friendship with Toronto Khalistanis, disagreements were inevitable.

According to his friends, Narendra could be counted on to say precisely what he felt. He was not diplomatic. Worldly and aristocratic, he'd been raised for the sporting and hunting life on a large estate in the Mathra District of Uttar Pradesh. The family was *thakur*, high-caste Hindu landowners, though, like many families in North India, it included Sikhs through intermarriage.

"He was a vocal man," his close friend, Saravjit Singh, recalls. "He was totally opposed to the Khalistan movement, and he voiced his opposition to the Sikhs, including the Sikhs within his family. He said that these terrorists belong in a 'lunatic asylum.'" He was mentally prepared for a hijacking attempt, but never spoke of other fears. It should be remembered that the Air India tragedy occurred while much of the world, and particularly the United States, was preoccupied with the prolonged TWA hijacking and hostage negotiations that were going on at the same time in Beirut.

By all accounts, politics aside, he seems to have been a delightful man — generous, gregarious and a bit of a rogue. In his early years on the New York—London run, he would call his friends from John F. Kennedy International and go straight out to their Queens Indian neighbourhood for dinner and a party, then end up sleeping on the livingroom rug. He'd wake up before dawn and sneak off to his suite in the Biltmore to get some rest. The friendships remained intact through the Indian-immigrant ladder-climb from bachelor pads in Queens to marriage and suburban split-levels in New Jersey.

Now, with retirement very much on his mind, he was pulled between the outdoor attractions of a small farm and the urban charms of a luxury apartment in a New Delhi "pilots' colony." These were significant choices, because he was making them for love, and the open life he could finally lead. His wife was living with their son in Air India's comfortable staff residence outside Bombay. They had not lived as husband and wife for the past seventeen years.

Narendra's life was complicated. There was his twenty-two-year-old son, excessively involved in the Bombay high-life. There was the admittedly failed marriage, not yet officially ended. There were the retirement options. But the major complication was Valerie Evans, his girlfriend of nineteen years. Now forty-three, she expected to settle down with him and live in India. Narendra, in fact, had chosen this particular Air India assignment for the extra week it would give the two of them in Toronto and the United States. Since she couldn't fly back to London with him on the same flight, she returned via Air Canada. When Valerie Evans arrived at the airport in London, Flight 182 was still listed as "late."

Co-pilot Satwinder Singh Bhinder, a forty-three-year-old ex-Indian Air Force jet pilot, was unmistakably Sikh. Turbaned and bearded, he'd spent some time over the week with an old friend from India, Jagdev Singh Nijjar. The Nijjar connection raises problems.

Nijjar, the editor and publisher of a Khalistani paper in Toronto, was considered no friend of India. He'd been watched, and his dinner with Bhinder was reported back to Air India. It's not known whether Bhinder himself was under surveillance. We know that he had carried at least two plain-wrapped packages aboard the flight on his private trolley as personal effects. There were reports that Nijjar had handed them to Bhinder at dinner the night before. Initially, some credence was given to the possibility that the packages might have contained explosives. Indian sources have subsequently discounted the rumour as the fabrication of a "fanatic Hindu."

When the RCMP compiled a series of depositions taken from interviews with all known contacts of the two pilots, they accepted Nijjar's description of the friendship at face value: it was nonpolitical, based on mutual acquaintances in India. He even asserted that Bhinder disagreed with him on Khalistan. We are in no position to challenge the specifics, except to note that the deposition flies in the face of logic and experience. Khalistani supporters hated pro-India Sikhs with a ferocity that has been proven several times to be murderous. And most disturbing of all: Khalistan supporters, when questioned by authorities about their actions and connections, have denied even the simplest, most obvious facts. Inderjit Reyat, out on Vancouver Island, initially denied knowing the Sikh priest and political organizer Talvinder Singh Parmar, or being able to recognize the name Rajiv Gandhi, or having heard of an Air India crash.

Rumours run rampant in Indian society, especially in times of communal strain. Nothing is ever forgotten or ever lost. Slivers of fact exist to support nearly any contention. Nijjar's brother is a well-known militant currently working for the Khalistani cause in Ecuador; therefore, the rumours went, Nijjar is also a fanatic — why wouldn't he blow up the plane? No, say others, these Vancouver and Toronto Punjabi papers aren't sincere enough to take *any* stand. They'll publish anything that pays. They'll publish libellous statements, then solicit money to retract them. Their motives aren't political — they're financial. All these newspaper chaps play a double game: one year for Congress (I) (Gandhi's party), another year for Khalistan. Whoever pays the most, that's the way they go.

What to trust? We have entered a war zone of half-truth, of charge and countercharge. No one seriously suggests that co-pilot Bhinder, whatever his politics, carried explosives aboard. No one suggests that Mr Nijjar gave him such a package to carry. What one *does* find remarkable is that a friendship could exist between a Khalistani sympathizer and a pro-India Sikh.

Even if one comes cold to the final cockpit recordings, one can't help noticing the disapproving tone in Bhinder's conversation with Flight Attendant Jamshed Dinshaw (a member of the Parsi community — probably India's most "liberal"), and later with In-flight Supervisor Sampath Lazar, a Christian, concerning the number of liquor customs seals requested by the crew. (Crew members on many international airlines often pilfer liquor intended for the passengers, and ask for extra seals for those bottles.) The very last words recorded, in fact, concern the extraordinary number of seals.

On the CVR Bhinder says in English, "Everybody is having that whiskey and beer...that is what I am saying. Without fail, all of them, whatever is allowed."

Lazar helpfully suggests (in Hindi) that it's a hard-core problem, what can one do?

But Bhinder isn't mollified. "All, I mean, all girls, all cabin crew, everybody!"

Narendra joins in. Maybe the women flight attendants are carrying liquor for their friends.

But Bhinder remains enraged. "Somebody ten beers!"

What these retrieved recordings of casual conversations do is support the personality sketches provided by friends after the accident. And more importantly, they portray that the flight, up to the last minute, was one of utter routine, one of devotion to bureaucratic details.

CHAPTER 3

At 8:30 A.M., within sixteen minutes of Air India 182's disappearance from the radar screen, Shannon Air Traffic Control called Marine Rescue Coordination Centre (MRCC) and notified them of an emergency.

MRCC combines the Naval Service and Air Corps of Britain and Ireland, the Royal Air Force and the Royal Navy. The commander that Sunday morning was Lieutenant Ivor Milne, R.N. Under the direction of MRCC, Valentia Radio (which is to North Atlantic shipping what Shannon is to flight) began broadcasting the last reported location of the *Emperor Kanishka* — 51°N, 12°50′W — requesting ships in the area to converge for a search. At 8:52, the Irish patrol ship *Aisling* (pronounced "Ashleen"), some fifty miles off shore at 51°18′N, 11°29′W, received the call and immediately headed for the site. Another ship, the *Laurentian Forest*, had already picked up the signal and was on its way.

At 9:00 came new evidence that the plane was down. A commercial aircraft flying the same track as Air India en route to London picked up the signal of an emergency locator, a device fitted to self-inflating lifeboats for planes and ships. Transmission is automatic, triggered by contact with salt water.

The operating assumption of all the rescue units was that there had been massive failure resulting in a downed aircraft. The rescue units steeled themselves for a heavy death-and-injury toll. But there was still hope, at 9:00, of finding survivors.

That hope ended by 11:05, when the first ship, the *Laurentian Forest*, arrived at the site and reported the sad, vast, floating debris of empty liferafts, torn-up airplane parts and human bodies. They reported that there were over a hundred bodies bobbing in the sea. The *Aisling* arrived shortly after noon and became the "On Scene Commander," taking charge of all co-ordination at the scene, relaying all information to the MRCC and the U.K. Coastguard. The *Aisling* immediately established radio contact with an RAF Nimrod patrol plane. The plane called to the scene helicopters, which were to winch the bodies out of the debris-clogged waves.

Although the *Laurentian Forest* had arrived about an hour earlier, Ivor Milne in the *Aisling* was the first official rescuer on the scene. That first day, floating wreckage from the 747 was confined to a three-mile area. By Monday it would spread over seven miles. On Sunday, just hours after the break-up and the plunge, the lighter, plastic parts from the jumbo's interior still floated buoyantly. Milne noted the large numbers of seats — their legs viciously buckled — and tables and lifejackets riding the waves. Some of the lifejackets seemed at least partly inflated, though most were still folded neatly. None of the lifejackets had been put on.

The rescuers were relieved that June 23rd was a bright, calm, northern summer day, just about the longest and brightest day of the year. The search teams needed every minute, for in high-seas recovery work there are no second chances. Bodies float for only a short while. Weather may change, wind and currents may scatter the evidence; and sooner or later there will be sharks, always. This time it was sooner. The searchers knew that bodies recovered on-site, at first contact, are likely to be the only ones recovered. As it happened, that first day Milne's joint-command retrieved eighty-eight bodies. On Monday, despite a predawn start and a helicopter sweep, only wreckage, personal effects and one body were taken aboard.

At the height of the operations on Sunday afternoon, all available Irish and British naval vessels, twelve helicopters and three commercial ships, the *Anstel Norman,* the *Laurentian Forest* and the *Kortgstein,* were on the scene. Thanks to the High-Seas drilling platform eighty miles to the north, the helicopters were able to be refuelled on the spot. Eight Sea-King and two Chinook helicopters of the MRCC were joined in the search-and-retrieval operation by two American

helicopters from Shannon. The *Laurentian Forest* was desig-
nated landing-site and temporary morgue. The skies above the
Laurentian Forest were roiled with heavy helicopter traffic. No
sooner were recovered bodies set down on the decks than other
helicopters picked them up for transfer to Cork. In the first
day's recovery, most of the eighty-eight bodies were retrieved
by helicopter-winching. But there were diver-teams working
the waves, too, and search teams in inflatable lifeboats scanned
the crowded, debris-choked waters.

Royal Navy Lieutenant Commander Roderick Cox was a
winch operator aboard one of the helicopters. He began the
search for bodies at 2:00 P.M. One man had to be winched down
into the water to secure the body-sling around the water-logged
body, then the retriever and the body were hoisted back to the
helicopter and ferried to the deck of a ship. That afternoon,
Cox picked up the bodies of three adult women and four
children.

Sean Murphy, captain of the Valentia lifeboat, had been
notified at 9:45 A.M. that a plane had gone off radar and that an
all-out search was on. He had mustered his crew by 10:10 and
headed for the crash scene, and was able (with his crew) to
recover the bodies of one man, three women and one young
girl. Murphy and his men returned with the bodies to
Knightstown Pier on the island of Valentia.

The bodies bobbing and floating were mostly those of
women and children. Many of the bodies were naked. Often
limbs were wrenched out of alignment. Among the sailors,
those who were very young and very new were stunned by the
nightmare they were witnessing.

At three o'clock, the MRCC received the report they'd most
dreaded. Sharks had been spotted. Bodies were still adrift, and
now the sharks were racing to them. There was no longer the
time for slow and careful one-body-at-a-time winching operations. Now three-man inflatable Gemini lifeboats were lowered
into the water, each of them powered by a forty-horsepower
outboard motor, each capable of carrying six bodies. Now the
divers jumped into the ocean to literally fight the sharks for
possession of the bodies.

Petty Officer Mahon, with his three-man (boys, really) crew — Doyle, Hyde and Coughlin — dived into shark-treacherous waters that Sunday afternoon. (Mahon and two others, Able Seaman Brown and Leading Seaman McCarthy were promoted for what they did that summer Sunday.) Mahon and his crew described how desperate the fight had been.

The sharks were six-foot blues. The sailors had lowered themselves into the sea in the middle of the sharks' feeding frenzy. They hadn't stopped to think of the danger. There hadn't been time to think or to dread. The horror at what they had seen came later. That horror, they said, would always be with them. What Doyle and Hyde and Coughlin would remember forever was the smell of the water, the smell of the aviation fuel coating the sea. Even now, they said, the smell of kerosene can make them throw up, suffer bad dreams and black moods.

They remember the faces of the dead, not the sharks. They still remember the bruised faces.

"Sometimes the decompression had flattened the bones. Sometimes you looked into the face and it was only...like a shell. The eyes were gone, the back of the head was gone. You looked in the face and you saw blue sky behind..."

When Mahon and his young men returned to the spot the next day, all they found were dozens of dead sharks, victims of the frenzy.

The MRCC's recovery at sea was only part of the overall Major Accident Plan. Soon the focus would shift to the problem of co-ordinating hospital, police and diplomatic services.

Sergeant Bill Williams of the Garda Siochana (the Irish Police) was duty sergeant in the Communication Centre at Union Quay, Cork, on the morning of June 23rd. At 11:14 he received a call from Marine Rescue at Shannon confirming that Air India Flight 182 had gone down, with unmanned inflated liferafts, 160 miles to the west-southwest. It was Sergeant Williams's responsibility to put the Major Accident Plan into operation formally. The decision about which hospital was to handle the bodies and all related service was made by the

Irish government in Dublin. At 11:15 Sergeant Williams called the Accident and Emergency Department at Cork Regional Hospital and told them to prepare for receiving bodies, and maybe a few victims. Then he notified the nearest police detachment, the Cork Fire Brigade, the Army Barracks in Cork and, finally, the Department of Posts and Telegraphs.

Eleven-fifteen, or three hours after the explosion, corresponds to 6:15 A.M. on a Sunday morning in Montreal, Ottawa and Toronto. The CBC News at five, then at six, had carried sketchy details, but only a few people had heard them. Some chose not to believe, others took brief comfort in a small confusion over flight numbers: 182 was reported down, but Toronto passengers had left on 181, which of course had changed its number after leaving Montreal. Most of the families started receiving calls shortly after seven that morning, from friends and family, all beginning with the question, "Did you have someone on last night's flight?"

Garda Inspector J. B. Long at Union Quay, Cork, received the Major Accident alert from Sergeant Williams at 11:30 on Sunday morning. He continues the narrative.

"On the instruction of Superintendent McQuinn, who was then in charge of Garda Operations, I went to Cork Airport at 12:30 P.M. I made arrangements there for the reception of the bodies, and that included medical attention and the conveyance from the helicopter to the airport mortuary.

"And I made arrangements for the allotting of a number to each body, in sequence of their arrival and their conveyance to Cork Regional Hospital under Garda custody in each case. Landing arrangements, and a landing office where transport was facilitated was arranged in an area close to the mortuary.... The allotting of numbers to the bodies was carried out by Garda James McKenna and Detective Garda Michael Cottrell of Union Quay Station, under the supervision of Sergeant Burke of Togher Garda Station.

"The Mortuary was not capable of holding a large number of bodies, and we decided to devise a system where we took a number that would fit, generally five to seven, and after they had been allocated numbers in sequence, they were despatched to the Cork Regional Hospital in Army vehicles, lorries and that. A Garda accompanied the bodies in a lorry, where the bodies were situated in the rear, and it was accompanied by a Garda escort on motorcycle or motor car."

Though no Irish or Indian or Canadian government official had publicly alluded to sabotage, the Gardai acted on the premise that the plane had been downed by criminals or terrorists, and took charge of the bodies. Forensic autopsies might reveal clues. The Gardai wanted to take no chances with tampering of wreckage parts and bodies.

The Press was less discreet in its speculations. (Conjectures about a collision with Soviet space debris or an encounter with Soviet submarine lasers appeared in some of the earliest articles.) Journalists from Britain, Canada and India, as well as from Dublin, settled in a grim corner of the Cork Airport and watched the smalltown Gardai manage a big-time crisis.

Between 3:00 P.M. of June 23rd, and 12:30 P.M. of June 24th, the 88 bodies that had been recovered by winching operations, and the 5 that had been taken aboard the Valentia lifeboat, and the 38 aboard the *Aisling* that were taken to Haulbowline, several miles from Cork — a total of 131 — were all brought to Cork Airport, bagged and tagged by the Gardai, and driven under police escort to the Cork Regional Hospital. The 132nd body would not float free of airplane debris for another three months.

CHAPTER 4

Thomas P. F. O'Connor, a plastic surgeon, and Deputy Director of the Cork Regional Hospital's Accident and Emergency Department, was at home on that morning of Sunday, June 23, 1985. His phone rang at 11:30. He listened to the monstrous details (that over a hundred bodies were floating in the sea) and to the ominous speculations (that very likely there would be no survivors). He agreed to be the Registrar of Accidents. He was instructed to come to a meeting of key co-ordinators at two o'clock that afternoon in the office of John Martin, the Hospital Administrator at Cork Regional Hospital.

Privately, neither the hospital nor the Gardai expected any Air India passenger to have lived through the prodigious descent into the sea. A Major Accident Plan, however, must prepare itself for surprising contingencies; so Bantry Hospital was chosen as the site for receiving the injured, and a mobile control ambulance sped an emergency team of four doctors, three nurses and a consultant to Bantry, a coastal town sixty miles west of the City of Cork.

O'Connor and Martin assumed that the mobile medical teams would need to be deployed in a more significant way at Cork Airport, where the bodies, plucked from the sea, were to be brought in by helicopter. So they dispatched a second mobile medical team to Cork Airport. (As it became sadly certain that this crash, so sudden, so total, would have no survivors, the medical team initially rushed to Bantry was sent back to the Cork Regional.)

In the meantime, the Gardai were receiving the bodies as they were flown in by helicopter. Although no official noises had been made yet about terrorist bombs or sabotage, the Gardai were clearly in charge. They tagged and labelled each body, noting physical identifiers, shredded bits of clothing, odd pieces of jewellery. Each body was numbered according to its time of arrival at the airport.

The Gardai then passed each body on to the mobile medical teams from Cork Regional Hospital. The mobile medical teams conducted their separate examination, recording all traumas, injuries, scars, bruises, marks. The Gardai placed each tagged body in a bodybag and stored it in a small, temporary mortuary facility at Cork Airport. In batches, and under Gardai escort, the bagged bodies would be transported by helicopter, or by Army trucks escorted by Gardai vehicles to the hospital.

No public official leaked suspicions about Khalistani commando-sponsored terrorism to the reporters who began to rush in from Dublin, London, Toronto, Delhi. But the journalists, tracking convoys of Army trucks and baby-faced winch operators still in shock, saw and smelled violent, newsworthy Death in the June greenness of County Cork.

At two o'clock in the afternoon of Sunday, just hours after the Major Accident Plan had been put into operation, six men and two women crowded into the small, modest office of the Hospital Administrator to plan an efficient way to cope with the storing and processing of the massive numbers of bodies that were to be trucked and helicoptered into its parking lot. Besides O'Connor and Martin, the men who attended the planning session that afternoon were Dr Michael Molloy, a consultant in the hospital's Rheumatology Rehabilitation programme, Professor Cuimin Doyle, a consultant pathologist, Captain Brian Phelan, the hospital's Chief Ambulance Officer, and Mr Denis Dudley, the Chief Executive Officer of the Southern Health Board. The two women members of this planning and co-ordinating group were Mrs Sheila Wall, Unit Nursing Officer, and Sister Thecla, Matron.

At two that Sunday afternoon, no bodies had yet arrived at

the Cork Regional Hospital. The message had come through, though: there would be many, many bodies, and they would arrive soon.

The Co-ordinating Group needed to find a large space that could be converted quickly into a mortuary for the post-mortem work to be done on the bodies that the Gardai would soon start to deposit. The Major Accident Plan provided for the appropriation of the gym in the Physiotherapy Department, but the Group guessed from the bulletins coming in from the airport that it would have to find a still larger mortuary facility where pathologists could work undisturbed for as long as necessary (since the pathology reports would establish the crash's criminal origin, if any). This temporary mortuary was best located away from the bulk of in-patients and their visitor traffic. Some of the bodies were likely to have been savaged by wind, waves, airplane metal and plastic. (Professor Doyle was later to describe one such savaged body at Coroner Cornelius Riordan's inquest: "She had dark black hair, which was matted around a twenty-three-centimetre-long metal bar, and it was marked "ASSY BOEING and NO. 60B50016 — 7' that was matted in the hair. It was towards the back of the head, and the body was naked...." The woman, about twenty-four, must have been standing when the plane dropped into the sea. There were "patterned abrasions" on her back, from her shoulders all the way down to her buttocks, and "gaping lacerations of the right buttock, natal cleft and left flank." Something had cut through the muscle and bone of her left leg, in the area between thigh and knee.) These grim visuals of disaster were what the hospital committee hoped to spare its regular patients.

The Co-ordinating Group considered different sites — the School of Nursing, the hospital's chapel — then finally settled on the recreation room of the Psychiatric Unit. It was an inspired choice. The recreation room, like the gym, was in the East Wing of the hospital, which meant that local visitors and bereaved relatives of crash victims could be kept separate from the bodies and from the harsh process of storing, examining and identifying. Since the recreation room was also close to the Accident and Emergency Department, the Army trucks and Gardai vehicles would have easy access to the Hospital Ring Road and to a huge parking lot. The hospital's helicopter pad was, naturally, situated near the Accident and Emergency Department. By consolidating the sites for the reception of bodies and for their X-raying, post-mortem examinations and embalming in the East Wing of the hospital building, the Group would also be helping the Gardai run its round-the-clock security of bodies without frightening patients and visitors in the West Wing. That the Gardai intended to guard the bodies at all times meant that government officials in India, Ireland and Canada were acting on the assumption that Air India 182 had been blown out of the sky by terrorists.

Each member of the Group assumed a special responsibility. Dr Molloy, for instance, was to be the hospital's Press Liaison Officer, which meant he was to keep journalists (who were arriving, some with TV crews) informed without allowing them to harass medical staff, patients and bereaved relatives. Mr Dudley was to work with the Gardai and governmental authorities. Captain Phelan was to co-ordinate the hospital's transportation requirements with the resources of the Airport authorities, Transport Services and with the Army and Naval Services.

The hospital's Senior Registrar, Dr N. R. Mulve, an Indian Muslim, was brought into the Group so that he could explain cultural mysteries and help put the bereaved relatives, who would arrive soon, at their ease. (John Martin and the hospital staff worried about having to cope with perhaps two hundred foreign "screaming relatives.") The Group agreed to meet at least once a day. Then it was time to prepare for the arrival of the first batch of bodies.

Four bodies arrived at 4:00 P.M. Later, there were more. And still more. All afternoon and night, until darkness grounded the helicopters. By 1:30 A.M. on Monday, June 24th, the Gardai had brought in eighty-seven bodies.

The hospital had permanent refrigerated facilities for holding ten bodies. It rented five refrigerated containers, increasing its holding capacity to forty bodies. The maintenance staff, working straight through two nights, fitted the containers with wooden shelves they had built. They made wooden steps for the containers so body-movers could deposit and remove bodies without straining. A local refrigeration firm installed cooling systems in the two temporary mortuaries at very short notice.

Everybody in Cork was involved somehow. Maintenance men, plant workers, housewives, schoolboys. There were even housewives from distant counties who wrote in, offering to put up relatives of the victims.

When a body arrived, the hospital fixed a number to it. To prevent confusion, the hospital number was made to coincide exactly with the number the Gardai had assigned the body. The medical team, made up of a doctor, a nurse and a clerk, labelled the body, and made notes on sex, estimated age, clothes still attached to the body, jewellery, old scars, fresh wounds, vaccination marks, birthmarks, repaired birth defects, unerupted wisdom teeth — nothing escaped notice.

The Technical Forensic Branch of the Gardai then photographed the body. Some photographs shock: bodies with shattered bones, twisted limbs, waterlogged skin.

The Gardai fingerprinted each body. They placed the personal effects in plastic bags. Then they wheeled the body into the makeshift mortuary in the gym in the Physiotherapy Department or in the Psychiatric Unit's recreation room for autopsy.

While all the examining, photographing and moving went on, normal hospital operations still had to continue. But the movement of bodies — so many bodies, bodies they heard but didn't see — upset the patients in the Psychiatric Unit. They had stayed confined to their units all Sunday, and on Monday, June 24th, the director of the unit had requested that they be transferred to St. Stephen's, a smaller hospital six or seven miles outside the city. There were fifty patients, a manageable number for relocation. The hospital's administration arranged the transfer quickly, so that not only the recreation room, but also the small consulting rooms in the Psychiatric Unit could be freed for eventual viewing of bodies by dazed, grieving relatives. Eighteen near-functional patients were discharged and the thirty-two who remained were moved to St. Stephen's.

Apart from the emptying of the Psychiatric Unit, however, the hospital did succeed in maintaining its normal services of patient care throughout the spectacular tragedy. John Martin and his staff were particularly pleased about that; they had not abandoned their own people under the klieg-lit scrutiny of international TV. There had been minor curtailments, of course: for the first three days after the arrival of the bodies, minor accidents and emergencies were sent to other city hospitals, and since the post-mortem and associated operations had to be housed in the Physiotherapy Department, out-patients requiring physiotherapy had their appointments rescheduled for the following week.

At first, when the body count was still manageable, the bagged bodies were laid out on tables. But as Sunday mid-afternoon darkened and cooled into evening and the bodybags kept coming and the available tablespace kept vanishing, the maintenance men were instructed to lay down polyethylene sheets on the vast floors of the recreation room and the gym. The men worked quickly.

The laying of polyethylene would cut down the chances of infection spreading from the bodies to the living. (Later, days later, after all bodies had been identified and removed from the hospital grounds, the hospital would repaint many rooms to rid them of the germs and the stench of collective death.) After the floors had been covered, the bagged bodies were laid out directly on the polyethylene sheets. That way it was easier not just for the space managers, but also for the pathology teams. Placing bodies on tables was a civil, not a medical, rite; such rites had been engendered in a world and in a time when no one dared scheme mass murders of housewives and children. Now, with the wet, heavy bodybags all around, the virtues of common sense and adaptability seemed more important than sentimentality.

The post-mortems had to be meticulous. The pathologists knew that their findings — the presence or absence, say, of burns and chars — would be pounced upon by governments and lawyers, who would, over the next many years, have to calculate rage, loss, desolation in dollars or rupees. And at the same time, the examinations had to be done quickly. The relatives that Martin's Co-ordinating Group had worried about were rushing the border.

The pathologists said they needed a week. And more bodies were still arriving. On Monday morning one body came in from Cork Airport, and thirty-eight more from Haulbowline, where the *Aisling* had chugged them in. And another five from the Valentia lifeboat. They had 131 bodies to work on.

The hospital recruited three pathologists — Dr G. Laoi, Dr J. Lucey and Dr R. Tait — from nearby hospitals to help Professor Cuimin Doyle and his regular staff. Dr John Frederick Austin Harbison, the State Pathologist and an expert in medical jurisprudence, took charge of the post-mortems. One of the pathologists had done post-mortems on explosives victims before this. Terrorism and its medical corollary — forensic autopsy — were not entirely alien here. But none had experience in aviation pathology. Dr Ian Hill, a well-known British expert, was brought in for that. The "odd man theory" was Dr Hill's. One body with burns could establish the presence of an explosive device on the plane, and that lone body could be among the 198 still at the bottom of the sea.

From Sunday afternoon through Thursday morning the pathologists worked in teams, listing in precise medical vocabulary the ghastly desecration of bodies. There were seven teams. The days were hot, and in spite of the recently installed cooling systems, the air was stuffy in the crowded, makeshift mortuaries.

The bodies that Dr Harbison and his teams examined were grievously damaged. The body of a middle-aged woman who in Toronto had kept proud house for her husband and teenaged children, who had worked part-time at a local store, now lay on the polyethylene with skull bashed and face mangled. Dr G. Lee, the pathologist whose job it was to conduct a post-mortem on this body, recorded the findings in detail.

EXTERNAL INJURIES: There was a massive laceration from the corner of the nose obliquely upwards to 4.5 cms above the left eye, this penetrated maillary antrum. There was laceration of the right ear. There were minor abrasions on the chest. There were striae and minor abrasions on the abdomen. There was a massive wound of the left buttock with the femur visible. There was a ripple effect on the back. There were multiple abrasions of the right forearm. There was a massive laceration on the left leg extending to the buttock. There was laceration of the right heel. There were multiple bruises over the femur. There was laceration of the sole of the right foot.

BONY INJURIES: There was a compound comminuted fracture of the left humerus, fracture of the right humerus, a compound fracture of the left femur, and fracture of the lower third of the right tibia and fibula with a compound fracture below the knee. There was extensive lateral fracturing of the base of the skull and the atlanto-occipital joint appeared dislocated. The manubrium sterni was fractured. Ribs 2−7 on the left side showed compound fractures internally, ribs 2−6 on the right side were fractured. T2 vertebra was fractured. There were bilateral fractures of the pelvis. Pleural spaces contained a small amount of blood. The oesophagus and trachea were ruptured. There was severe laceration of the right lung and the posterior surface of the left lung was lacerated. The pericardium was normal. There was a small laceration of the front of the heart which was otherwise normal. The ascending aorta was ruptured. There was laceration of the left and right lobes of the liver.

Such injuries are consistent with both flail, which occurs when the body is subjected to the violent twists and turns of a free fall, and decompression, which causes all the oxygen to be sucked from the blood.

Dr Harbison worked on a petite, young female body, whose nails were still painted a fashionable pearl grey. But the body's head had split open from the bridge of the nose to the occiput, and the brain had floated away. The brain stem and cerebellum were left, but "the floor of the anterior cranial fossa" was missing and the nasal cavities were exposed. Both eyes had been punctured. The bones had cracked, especially the collar bone and the ribs. The heart had been grossly lacerated. From a large wound in the lower left abdomen, hip, groin and thigh, a loop of the large intestine had popped through. The woman might have died instantaneously, except that Dr Harbison found evidence of bleeding in the central chest tissues and in the mesentary, opening up the possibility of two distinct episodes of injury. He could not confirm that there had been two separate incidents, because there appeared to be no tissue embolism in the lungs. But he could not ignore the possibility either. Had the poor young woman with the bright, pearled nails died at once? Or had she experienced a second episode of pain? The distinction would matter: to relatives, and to lawyers and insurance companies who have their own measures for reimbursing suffering and pain.

There was another body that interested Dr Harbison, a body that, too, could lead to hot courtroom debates. It was the body of a male child, young enough to be still getting new teeth where the gums were inflamed. The small body had its share of cuts, breaks, pits and gashes. The pathologist probed the wounds, looking for foreign objects, for shrapnel or for plastic. There appeared to be none, not embedded anyway. The upper thoracic spine and the first ribs had cracked. The boy had bled a lot as a result. There was subdural blood in the superior surfaces of the cerebral hemispheres and in the cranial fossae. More blood in the left frontal lobe and in the mastoids, a mist of blood in the left auditory canal. And blood, considerable deposits of it, along the oesophagus and the root of the neck. And, intriguingly enough, though the lungs had not been externally lacerated, the lung tissues were streaked with blood. The trachea was not dusted with soot or other telltale evidence of explosives, but it was stained with liquid blood. And the liver had bled. The boy had died of shock and hæmorrhage. But the moistness of the lungs, and they "were moister than normal,"

Dr Harbison recorded, suggested a medico-legal complexity: the boy might have drowned. Dr Harbison looked for more signs of drowning. The lungs were not hyperexpanded, however; nor was there froth in the airways. All the same, drowning remained a possibility. If the boy had drowned, he had hit the water while alive. He may have been unconscious at that point, but in the context of lawsuits, his being "alive" brings up the question of possible consciousness, and the chance that he had suffered unimaginable pain during the seconds of descent.

The wounds were grotesque, and occasionally mysterious enough, or the bleeding troubling enough, or the wetness of lungs pronounced enough, to warrant additional forensic scrutiny of blood and tissue. The forensic pathologists would look for carbon streaking and for evidence of explosive substances. In all, despite other injuries, seven bodies were determined to have drowned, though no suspicion of consciousness attaches to that conclusion.

Meanwhile, the seven pathology teams worked at an heroic and exhausting pace. The pathologists and their assistants moved methodically from body to body laid out in numerical order on the mortuary floors. The gym floor had just enough space for sixty-five bodies. The rest were set out in the recreation room. On Monday, June 24th, the teams finished eighteen post-mortems. Tuesday and Wednesday were heavier days: forty-nine on Tuesday and forty-eight on Wednesday. And the final sixteen post-mortems took all morning the next day. In the end, the pathologists finished by twelve noon on Thursday, June 27th. They had worked this fast because the relatives, kept out of Cork until the bodies could be fully processed, were confused and bitter and angry that they were being kept away from their dead.

The pathologists at Cork Regional Hospital would be asked to do one more post-mortem. Months later, another body, number 132, would wash up. The body would be dressed in good-quality clothes. Blue-grey slacks, white belt, Givenchy tie, fancy black socks, hand-waxed Daks shoe with buckle on the right foot. There would be no left shoe in the plastic bag of retrieved personal effects, which would include a goatskin wallet, a credit card, a social insurance card and a driver's licence. There would be no left shoe, because the left leg would be so spun out of alignment that the left foot would reach up to the left shoulder. From the back of the left thigh, so brutally wrenched out of place, pathologists would pick loose a three-centimetre-long chunk of steel-bright metal.

After a body was given a full post-mortem examination, it was hefted by trolley to the Radiology Department for X-ray. John Martin's Co-ordinating Group sanctioned the building of a special ramp so that the Gardai did not have to wheel the trolleys through halls crowded with patients. The radiologists made notes on bone fractures and bone age. And they looked for shrapnel.

The X-rayed body was returned to the mortuary, only this time to a corner reserved for the embalmer, William O'Connor, and his assistants. William O'Connor is a stately, silver-haired man, who, with his brother, owns The Jerh. O'Connor Funeral Homes in Cork and in Wilton. The business was established by Mr O'Connor's father, who had sailed to New York on the *Lusitania* and become an American citizen, who had fought as a conscript in France, then after the War had gone to embalming school and set up business. He had come back to Ireland for retirement, and had been Commander of the American Legion in Cork. The family business had grown; it had spread out to include limousine services; and it had joined the Kenyon Group, which was handling the repatriation, freighting and disposal of bodies for Air India. It was the Kenyon Group connection that had brought him to the gym in the Cork Regional Hospital on the morning of Tuesday, June 25th. And he had brought with him his son, Kevin, then twenty-four years old, as his special assistant.

What Mr O'Connor worried about was the presentation of the body to the family. His problem was one of æsthetics.

"Considering the distance they fell," he said, "they were in quite good condition. Only one wasn't identifiable, by my standards."

The women were beautiful, he thought. And the little children, there wasn't a mark on some of them. What the children had was damage to the tummy from all that spiralling.

Mr O'Connor set up a temporary office in the gym. He had ten teams of two working Tuesday through Friday. The teams started at 8:30 in the morning and finished at 7:30 in the evening, with only a half-hour off for lunch. They did repair jobs, embalming, and when the relatives began to show in Cork, they took cremation requests and booked cremations in Dublin. Sometimes Mr O'Connor worked till two or three in the morning.

For William O'Connor the week was both sad and heartening. He was struck by the loss, especially the loss to families that had had little children on the plane. But the disaster had brought the people of Cork together. Everybody — pathologists, nurses, the coroner, the Gardai — had co-operated. Men like Mr Martin had given him their private home phone numbers. Cork had acted as one big team.

After the embalming, the bodies were photographed again. These were photographs that could be shown to the relatives. The bodies were now presentable, with bashed or missing parts wrapped discreetly in fabric. The embalmed bodies were coffined, and the coffins numbered, again in accordance with the numbering by the Gardai and the hospital. The coffins were stored in a tent on a grassy stretch beside the parking lot, and watched over by the Gardai. Some of the second batch of photographs were sent on to the Air India office in London, where many relatives were waiting for word from Cork that the processing of bodies was finally done.

CHAPTER 5

The first fifteen relatives flew into Cork on the 26th of June. One of them, a middle-aged mother who had lost her only son, had sat since the morning of Sunday, June 23rd, on the sofa in her Toronto livingroom, bags packed and dressed for travel, waiting for word that she could come. She wanted to be with the body.

A man, Kamal Saha, whose brother had been a flight attendant on the downed plane, had caught a flight from Calcutta to London within hours of hearing the news. He said that he had not waited to change clothes, not even sandals. He had heard the news on the radio in Calcutta, and he had somehow made his way to Dum Dum Airport, and somehow he had found a seat on a London-bound flight about to leave. "I could not think of anything else. I wanted to be with my brother. From the moment I heard, I could not eat, I could not sleep."

Just being in Cork was a relief. Just being together with other relatives, with mourners who could really, intimately, share their grief. On the flight over, the relatives had told each other family stories. They had shown each other photos of their loved ones. Death wasn't real to them yet. The dead weren't yet bodies that were already autopsied and X-rayed and repaired and embalmed. The dead were glossy-haired, black-eyed, expensively dressed wives, daughters, sons. They got off the plane, anxious to get to the hospital, to locate and sit with their lost ones.

John Martin's Group had made plans to receive the two or three hundred relatives. The Nurses' Training School was on holiday, and so the Group had chosen the Nurses' Residence in the West Wing as the site for holding the bereaved through the long, tormenting hours or days that it took them to identify their dead. The West Wing entrance was the main entrance to the hospital, the entrance through which local visitors entered and left.

The relatives would need places to stay, and so the Group had asked Tony Dawson of the Cork-Kerry Tours, a representative of Cork's Tourist Board, to find them rooms in hotels. Cork isn't a city with huge tourist resources, but Tony Dawson had arranged with seven hotels, all within thirty miles of the hospital, to put up the bereaved. One man from India arrived with so little money that he couldn't squander his dollars on hotel bills, so Dawson took him in. He organized car pools for getting the relatives to and from the hospital, and coach trips to Bantry Bay, the landmark nearest to the spot where the *Emperor Kanishka* had hit the chill, swirling sea. Always, the numbers were staggering.

Martin's Group had had to make other practical arrangements before the relatives flew into the city. Even in grief people must eat. There would be two to three hundred extra people to feed at every meal in the hospital's dining room. It would have to stay open all day, all night. And there had been telephone lines to install. The fifteen direct lines at the hospital switchboard could not cope with the new volume of urgent calls by the Gardai, Interpol, the government's press office, the foreign diplomats and the journalists. The Group had asked Bord Telecom to put in new lines, which they did right away and free of charge. Finding space, equipment and personnel for the processing of bodies had tested the Group's administrative skill. The relatives, crazed by grief, unprepared for the brutalities of disaster-victim identification, would test its soul.

The relatives were met at the airport by the Gardai, and by hospital-trained counsellors, who were mostly nuns. The diplomats were there, including Mrs Razia Doshi, the wife of the Indian Ambassador to Ireland.

Kiran Doshi is a career diplomat with previous postings in

Pakistan, Hong Kong and Washington. He is now the ambassador to Libya. Given India's primary role as the owner of a plane that had crashed in international waters, he became the link between Irish rescue services and Air India.

His wife, Razia, is a physician. She's lively, organized, demonstrative. Between them they embody a contemporary Pan-Indianism. She is Muslim, he is a Jain Hindu; they met in Bombay, though she did her medical training at Vellore in the south of India. During their week-in-hell of body identification, the families all felt, somehow, that Razia Doshi understood each of them, no matter where they had come from in India. Along with the kindly Irish came the Doshis, with a familiar word, home-cooked Indian food, an open house and, in the case of some early arrivals from India, an open pocketbook.

"As far as an Embassy's role is concerned," Ambassador Doshi said later, "it's not that there is any drill laid down. It is left to your common sense really. You have contacts. You know people whom you have to defer to back home. You know people in the country where you are posted. Essentially what you try to do is to help people in getting what they want. And more often than not, it's a question of your assistance which will make all the difference.

"It was roughly at 11:30 in the morning that they were sure there was a very small likelihood of survivors. They had started to pick up bodies. In such matters it has to be an ad-hoc decision...what all your training and your background and your experience has prepared you for. All that suddenly becomes useful to you.

"So once they told me that the base was to be Cork, I informed the Indian government and Air India to rush their teams over. The first available team came from London. We have a very small office here. There are only five of us in the embassy in Dublin. The Canadian Embassy is, maybe, the same size.

"As the shock of actually seeing the bodies started wearing off, the appallingness of the tragedy sunk in. This was hundreds of tragedies rolled into one, though each tragedy was unique in itself. It touched all of us here at the time, whether from India or Canada or Ireland.

"I must say that the Irish understand grief much better than we do. Maybe they have seen so much of their own."

Razia Doshi remembers that there were thousands of telephone calls and letters from ordinary citizens. People would come up to her and ask if she needed to put relatives up in their homes or if they could help out with food and clothing. Even the children asked to help.

But the Canadian officials hung back, so far back that many relatives assumed they hadn't come. The invisibility of Canadian consular staff in those first desperate and confusing hours in County Cork angered some relatives. They felt abandoned. Even in their grief, they felt they had been shunned by their adoptive country.

Canada's ambassador to Ireland, the long-time Liberal Cabinet member Edgar Benson, had retired and returned home only three weeks before the crash. The Canadian Embassy in Dublin was without an ambassador. Without a credentialled head, and lacking India's clear legal role in the tragedy, Canada took several days to assert its presence. It probably never caught up. Many bereaved families from Canada felt abandoned by their country, both at home and in Cork, and stated so publicly.

Matters were not helped by the fact that officials from the prime minister on down were slow to acknowledge Canadian responsibility for the Air India disaster. Prime Minister Mulroney had telephoned his condolences to his Indian counterpart, Rajiv Gandhi — an act that was based on a fundamental misunderstanding of who, exactly, had been victimized, and who, in fact, was to blame. India had lost a plane and a crew, but over 90 percent of the passengers were Canadian. That call helped estrange the Canadian public from the enormity of its shared loss, and worst of all, it denied communion to a segment of Canadian citizenry in their hour of indescribable pain.

A similar detachment was expressed by Transport Minister

Don Mazankowski, defending his ministry in Parliament in the wake of the numerous security failures that had contributed to the disaster. He would not admit that Canada was in any way accountable. Indeed, seizing on the incident of the three suspicious bags in Montreal, he charged Air India with a serious dereliction of duty. If Transport Canada security had been notified, he told reporters, then the plane would have been grounded until *all* bags had been taken off the plane and re-examined. In other words, he implied that if Air India had done its job in Montreal, the tragedy would still have been avoided.

It was an appealing statement, and it got the Minister off the immediate hook. However, some hours later, an official of his own Department contradicted the statement, saying that under the circumstances described, only the suspect baggage would be removed.

In Parliament, the Minister was later forced to amend his statement according to the following formula: Since there was a special security request by Air India, extraordinary precautions had been taken. But since there had been no specific threat made against this *particular* Air India flight, the plane had not been held in Montreal for a thorough search.

From an official Canadian perspective, the chronology went something like this:

Sunday, the crash. Staff at the Canadian Embassy in Dublin calls Bob Hathaway, the Counsellor left in charge of the embassy. (He is in Waterford, where he is to address participants in the Eastern Canada-Ireland Week.) Bob Hathaway drops everything, gets into his car, and drives through a bad storm to Cork. He checks into Jury's Hotel. He doesn't remember seeing any Indian Embassy officials that night, though he's sure they must have been there. He picks up what news he can about how many people were on the plane that went down, how many bodies have been found, where the bodies will be temporarily kept. The information is sketchy and confusing. He keeps in touch with his staff in Dublin and his colleagues in London. The embassy grasps the magnitude of the disaster. "But what we were going to do about it," Bob Hathaway remembers worrying, "was an unknown."

Monday, more staff, including Mike Phillips, the Minister-Counsellor, arrive from the Canadian High Commission in London. A task force has been constituted in Ottawa quite early on Sunday morning, and the task force has cabled London, instructing the London mission to liaise with Dublin because of the size of the disaster. "Ottawa thought that we might have to provide some assistance to Dublin in the consular area [issuing travel documents]," Mike Phillips recalls now. "Of course, it was a consular problem at the time."

Those were not easy days for the relatives or for the Canadian staff. The Canadian officials were certainly there in numbers by mid-week (by the middle of the week, one Ottawa-based official noted that Cork was now the largest Canadian embassy in all of Europe), but the cause of grief was extraordinary and their mode of comforting alien to the New Canadians. The relatives perceived the Canadians as cold, stiff, unfeeling; they reserved their love for Razia Doshi, who was quick to hug them and sit with them all day in a hospital room, to open her residence to them, to cook curries for them.

Mike Phillips blames the relatives' physical isolation — of being stuck in small hotels in the Irish countryside without a car — for their initial bitter (and often public) outbursts against the Canadian mission.

"Another frustration," he recalls, "were all the forms they had to fill out here in Cork, and the interviews they had to give. Kenyon's, the London-based undertaking firm, had had their field people in Canada and India take detailed information on Monday. Some of these relatives had sat down and filled out forms for hours. Then when they came to Cork, the Gardai asked them to do it all over again."

Bob Hathaway remembers the difficulty of merely establishing a proper list of passengers from the flight-manifest. Sometimes they worked with a list that said only "Singh" or "Sharma" with no other initial, and with no sex or age on it. He and Mike Phillips were very aware of what must have seemed to the relatives as callousness: sometimes they would drop in on a distraught family to solicit help in identification and discover that they had not come to the right family in the first place.

"And then," said Phillips, "there were the appalling tragedies. All we had at the start was a list of names, a printout. And as we worked through it, all of a sudden we realized, my God, a whole family has been wiped out. It wasn't clear on the face of those names, but after you have looked at the material, and collated it, you realize that there was a whole family missing. And we had to pick up the phone and call the RCMP. In Halifax there was one family…it just came to us that there was a house in Halifax that nobody was ever going to come back to."

The Canadian diplomats also marvelled at the Irish handling of so much human grief. Gar Pardy, Director of the South Asia and Southeast Asia Relations Division of External Affairs, and who was also in Cork for the week, recalls, "Though the citizenship might have been confused, it didn't matter to them in terms of the way they treated the people. Everyone was treated with the greatest of humanity." (The Irish had a consistent difficulty — on a continent where ethnicity and citizenship are usually one and the same — conceiving of the victims as Canadians and not Indians. But then, so had the Canadians, who even today persist in referring to the victims as "Canadians of Indian origin.")

And Mike Phillips continues the thought, "In terms of having a place where this disaster had to be dealt with, it couldn't have happened in a better place. I mean if it'd happened in London, for example, it would have been handled very efficiently and with compassion, but it's too big a city to be able to cope with that. And religious differences meant nothing in either direction, it seemed to me. There were nuns at the airport talking to the people as they got off the plane, and there was real empathy there. There were always two or three nuns waiting with us."

The nuns, the other counsellors, even the Irish Gardai were

there to hug, to listen, to look at photographs of happy families. And the Gardai were not at all like policemen back home. They were big, caring fellows who weren't afraid to show their feelings. And the counsellors were special, acutely sensitive to their grief, not like white Canadians. The relatives talked. Right there at the airport, they showed their colour photos to the nuns and to the Gardai.

The counsellors listened, and while they listened, effortlessly they broke the sad, big, faceless group of the bereaved into mini-families: each relative was surrounded and buffered by his or her own counsellor and policeman. They stayed intact throughout the horrifying body-identification visit.

CHAPTER 6

At the Cork Regional Hospital, the relatives were let off at the main entrance in the West Wing. Some local people were in the lobby; patients' visitors, nursing staff, ordinary citizens moved by the tragedy. The counsellors escorted the relatives through the lobby — a short walk — to the stairs leading up to the Nurses' Residence, and upstairs down a corridor lined with glass cases of plaster models of human parts, cases now draped so their contents would not upset the bereaved, to the hall where special Gardai detectives were to talk to them.

The detectives explained the identification process. First, each relative would have to fill out a pink Interpol identification form with the help of the policeman assigned to her or him. Then the Gardai would try to match the physical characteristics listed on the pink form with their own photographs and lists. If the Gardai found a match, the relative would be led away to another room and shown a selection of photographs. If the relative made a positive identification in this photo gallery, the mini-family of mourner, counsellor and policeman would make the long walk to the East Wing. There the relative would be taken into a room and shown a plastic bag of wet, ripped clothes and jewellery. If the relative recognized the washed-up debris, then and then only, would he or she be led into another, smaller room and shown a coffined body.

The Gardai announced the procedure. The bodies were in their care, and they had to be sure that the right body went to the right relative. Besides, that first day, with the first batch of relatives — it was Wednesday, June 26th — the pathology teams were still working on the retrieved bodies.

The relatives thought they would get to see the bodies of their loved ones right away. They thought they would, at least, see the photographs. They thought they would arrive, claim their dead and try to make sense out of abominable tragedy. They didn't know what they thought. There were no rules on how to behave well in circumstances like this. Nobody they knew had gone through what they were going through. They knew one thing: they were angry. They didn't want to fill out more forms listing shape of nose, length of playground scars, shade of black hair. They had already done this back home while they'd been kept waiting by the authorities. Agents for the Kenyon Group, the undertakers and the local police, had gone over all that with them. The men had lifted fingerprints from textbooks in neat, suburban homes. Those men had come with Yellow Identification Forms. Pink forms, yellow forms. The relatives wanted to fill out no more forms; they wanted to grieve over bodies.

The counsellors calmed the relatives. The Gardai were patient, sympathetic. They had to be sure, they said. Having the relatives on hand made the filling out of the Pink Identification Forms much easier. The relatives allowed themselves to be comforted. Like them, the Irish were family people, emotional and god-fearing. They filled out the Pink Forms. Separate agencies had their separate forms. The Yellow Forms, not handled by the Irish, were lost, they suspected.

They waited. They told each other how and when they had heard the dreadful news. One man's nephew, a studious immigrant, had been cramming for college exams with the radio on and he'd heard at four in the morning. Nobody had believed the nephew. You fell asleep, they had scolded him.

The counsellors encouraged the relatives to talk. They saw an extraordinary bond forming within that vast, mournful body in the hall of the Nurses' Residence. The bereaved comforted each other. The bereaved accepted solace from other bereaved. More arrived. From India, Canada, the United States, Britain. Here were the nearly three hundred relatives, but they were not screaming; they were demanding nothing. They were private, and noble, in their terrible grief.

The Gardai, the counsellors, and beefed-up staff from consul-

ates and embassies met each flight at Cork Airport. So did TV
and print journalists. The Press followed the relatives to the
hospital. Do you believe the plane was sabotaged, they asked.
Are you satisfied with the hospital's arrangements? How well
have Canadian officials handled this tragedy? On camera, one
or two men blew up at what they perceived as consular
callousness or white-Canadian coldness. "Where are those
bastards?" one relative demanded. "Are they sitting tight in
cozy chairs?" Back home in Toronto his astounded teenaged
son witnessed his father's grief on TV. He had never heard his
quiet, hard-working, very correct father use the word "bastard."

The Gardai read through their records. They had 131
bodies. One hundred and ninety-eight bodies were in the
plane's wreckage at the bottom of the sea. Most relatives who
had come to Cork would have no body to grieve over or to cre-
mate. The Gardai had to be careful. They called in a relative as
soon as they felt there was a fair chance of match-up. The
relative called in felt "lucky." (Afterwards, John Laurence, the
father of the young dancers, said, "Can you imagine how
topsy-turvy those days were? We thought we were 'lucky' if the
police came in saying that they thought they had a body for
viewing!" His two daughters were beautiful. He had photographs of them, eighteen and sixteen, in their splendid dance
costumes. Their bodies were not brought back in bodybags to
be rephotographed in mutilation.)

In the photo gallery some relatives had trouble recognizing
the marked faces and bloated bodies. These were not the faces
of the people they had hugged at Pearson International Airport
or at Mirabel in Montreal. They had an easier time recognizing
the photographs of friends and neighbours. The Gardai was
glad of that help. Whole families had been lost on that plane.
This was a tight community. The mourners in Cork remembered
what departing friends had worn for the vacation trip to India.
Those who could identify the pictures went on to the East
Wing for the rest of the sad, grim procedure. The others came
back to the hall to wait for a change in "luck."

In the hall relatives who had flown in from India had a hard
time filling out the forms. Two women, both wives and

mothers, both naturalized Canadians, had gone on to India ahead of their families. They did not know what their loved ones had worn on the plane when they had taken off on Saturday. The Indian relatives of Canadian families that had perished without survivors had the hardest time. They had come to identify and mourn brothers or sisters they hadn't seen perhaps in years. The faces had thickened or maybe thinned; many of the women had cut their hair. The infants they had cradled years ago had grown into teenaged math whizzes and dance instructors. Some India-based relatives could not speak English and had a harder time still with the identification.

So the relatives helped each other. Do you remember any birthmarks? Did they write you of any surgery, any illnesses? They felt very close.

Some of the relatives from India had horror stories about the Canadian High Commission in New Delhi. They had tried to get visas to go on to Canada after Cork, so they could at least help look after a devastated brother or sister for a few months. The Canadian High Commission, some said, had not only refused them visas but had behaved badly, had treated them with unnecessary rudeness. They said that the Canadian visa officers had acted suspicious, as though this were not family rallying in time of monumental tragedy, but just one more immigration scam to sneak into Canada.

There was a lot of waiting around in the hall where the Gardai detectives had given their procedural talk. To make the wait a little easier, the Friends of the Hospital, a volunteer group, set themselves up in a corner of another hall. They poured tea, cut cake. Some relatives fell sick during the waiting, and four had to be treated — for assorted ailments such as hysteria, diabetes, bad heart — in the hospital.

The relatives waited and asked each other deep questions about Fate. What if their families had been booked to fly on an airline other than Air India? Would the 329 people on that Air India Flight 182 have all died precisely at the ordained moment on the morning of Sunday, June 23rd? Many had originally reserved tickets on other airlines: British Airways, Kuwait Airways. Some had planned to send their families a week

earlier or a week later. Why and how had it happened? The
journalists were full of stories of sabotage. The journalists
played phrases by them: Sikh terrorists, bag-bombs. (The
refinement of phrase from "Sikh" to "Khalistani" would be
slow.) Was the destruction of family life, which meant their
lives in Canada, the lives they had worked so hard and saved so
hard for, caused by the individual wills of *saboteurs*? In those
early days, when the pain was real but the loss not yet felt, the
Hindu relatives consoled themselves with thoughts of Destiny.
When one has fulfilled one's mission on earth, one is recalled
by God. Atman, the individual soul, dissolves forever into the
Brahman, and the cycle of reincarnation is stopped. This
happy fusion is promised to "pure" souls. And their loved ones
on that plane had been innocent, pure. They had hurt nobody.
The children, in fact, had done good. Many were carrying back
money from their piggy-banks to give away to the Indian poor.

Thoughts about Fate consoled the Hindus in Cork. And this
fatalism was a temporary boon to government and insurance
companies. Angry relatives making emotional remarks about
Sikh-Hindu conflicts to the Indian press could set off dreadful
communal riots. Delhi had gone through such communal riots
the day Mrs Gandhi was fatally shot. The plane crash, the
Indian officials suspected, was an act of Khalistani terrorist
revenge — innocent blood for innocent blood — for those very
riots. The Canadians and Air India were thankful for the
fatalism of these New Canadians, which delayed any ferocious
complaints to the Press about Canadian laxity in securing its
major airports.

The relatives who were still without bodies tried their best to
change their "luck." One man, an engineer, shaved off his
mourner's stubble and spruced himself up. "My wife wouldn't
go out with me if I didn't shave," he told his nephew who had
come from Toronto to look after him in Cork. "I haven't shaved
since I heard the news. Who knows, if I shave maybe she'll
show up." And his wife's body did. The engineer found the
bodies of his wife and son. The son didn't look mangled. His
father was told it would be better if he didn't look at the wife's
face. He didn't find the body of his teenaged daughter. And he

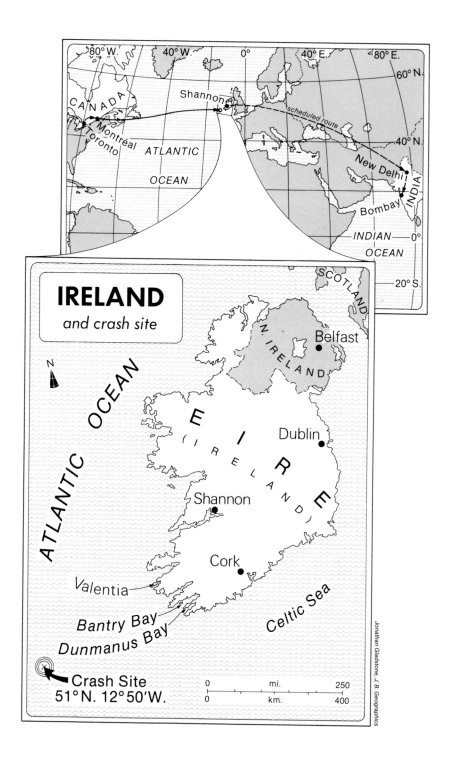

80°W.   40°W.   0°   40°E.   80°E.
60°N.

CANADA   Shannon
Montréal   scheduled route
Toronto   40°N.
ATLANTIC
OCEAN   New Delhi
                                              INDIA
                                    Bombay
                                    INDIAN   0°
                                    OCEAN
                                              20°S.

IRELAND
and crash site

N

ATLANTIC   OCEAN

SCOTLAND

N. IRELAND
Belfast

E I R E
(I R E L A N D)
Dublin

Shannon

Cork

Valentia

Bantry Bay
Dunmanus Bay   Celtic Sea

Crash Site
51°N. 12°50′W.

0   mi.   250
0   km.   400

Jonathan Gladstone, J B Geographics

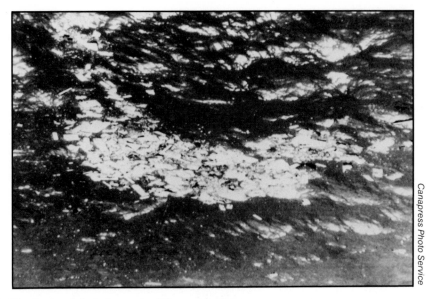

Canapress Photo Service

The first aerial photograph of the crash site.

Toronto Star, David Cooper

An Irish soldier carries a young girl's violin case which was recovered from the flight's wreckage.

Police investigators in Japan sift through Narita Airport's luggage area for clues after baggage on the flight from Vancouver exploded in the airport. The blast killed two baggage handlers and injured four others.

Two tickets purchased at the same time by passengers identified as L. Singh and M. Singh. One ticket is for Air India 182 (top) and the other for the Canadian Pacific Tokyo flight.

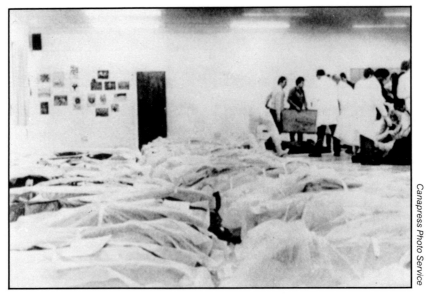

Bodies of victims, recovered from the sea off the Irish coast, laid out on the floor of the Cork Regional Hospital.

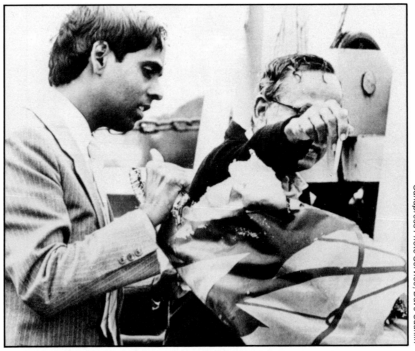

Air India officials examine part of the wreckage showing the Air India logo.

Meena Sarangi carries a rose given to her by Mother Teresa after she and her husband Raju, in the background, met privately with Mother Teresa over the loss of their daughter Lita.

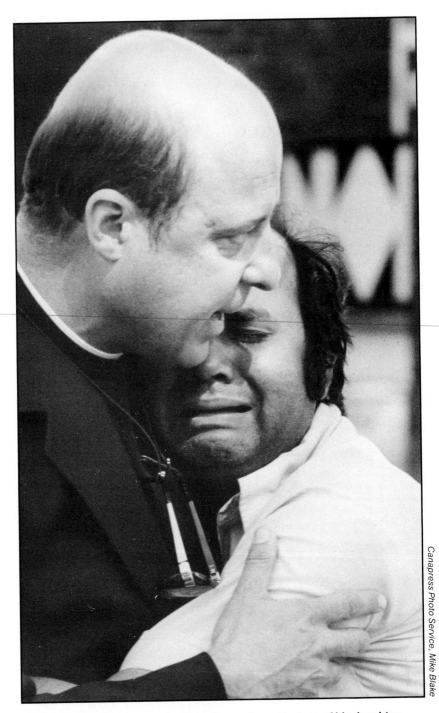

Father Brad Massman consoles Raju Sarangi over the loss of his daughter.

Reshaw Cheema (left) is comforted by Dilraj Cheema as she mourns the death of her son.

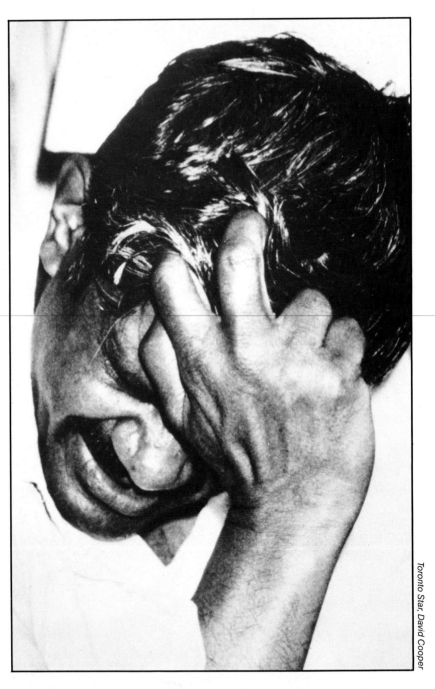

Murthy Subramanian holds a note from his eight-year-old daughter Veena, reminding him to pick up some books at her school. Hours after first reading the note, Subramanian learned that his wife and daughter were killed in the crash.

thought to himself that if it is God's will to take a life, then it is also God's will to save life. "Why a miracle can't happen and save her?" he said to his nephew. He remembered what the Gardai had said about ocean currents bearing bodies, very possibly, towards Spain or France. Why not, he thought. Maybe, by a miracle, the daughter was alive. (In India, where he went from Cork, two astrologers assured him that his daughter was still alive. So did a Canadian astrologer when he got back to work. Water was a miraculous medium. He had heard a story of a man drowning in an Indian river, and then returning home alive to his family a year later. There were other stories. He liked especially the one in which a man died in a plane crash in Kashmir, and then two years after the "death," the man walked in the door of his house as though he'd never died in the crash.) He had posters made from his daughter's picture — posters as for a Missing Person — and a year after the crash he went to Málaga, Spain, and put the posters on walls.

The engineer was not the only one who believed that a daughter had survived the terrible fall. One mother brought dry clothes to Cork for her two missing girls. The girls were excellent swimmers. They would swim ashore and need clothes. The daughters were not retrieved by the rescue squads, and for a long time, for months in fact, the mother believed that they had made their way to an island and were waiting to be found.

For some relatives the process of identifying bodies of loved ones they had seen off cheerfully in Toronto just days before was grimly swift and grimly smooth. The young parents of a teenaged dancer rushed into London as early as Monday the 24th, and, dazed, located their daughter's photograph in the Air India office at Heathrow Airport. Their inconsolable grief made gut-wrenching international headline news.

They arrived in Cork, sped through the police identification process and had the body released to them. Their daughter had loved Toronto. Toronto, not India, had been her home. Toronto was where her soul should rest. The parents wanted to fly back with her casket right away. But the Air India office in Cork had its own cost-effective casket-freighting schedule. The parents were advised to fly home by themselves and wait for the body, which would be freighted into Toronto separately within three days, maybe four. But they would not part with their daughter a second time. They tried Aer-Lingus; they would fly Aer-Lingus if Aer-Lingus could fly the casket and them on the same flight. Aer-Lingus had its own problems; in the middle of this swell of disaster traffic, the local airline was grounded by a strike.

The parents tried the Canadian Embassy as a last resort. Many relatives perceived the Canadian officials as insensitive to their grief and as unhelpful. These officials were correct, but how could they know what was needed. The Canadian Embassy did have an office on the second floor of the hospital, however, and that's where the determined parents went. The Canadian officials served these parents coffee, and confided that they had instructions from External Affairs to get in touch with Ottawa as soon as the family arrived in Cork. The parents sat in that second-floor office while the Canadians called, first Ottawa, then on Ottawa's advice, the Canadian Forces base in West Germany, so that space for the family of living and dead could be freed that evening on a Hercules transport aircraft.

Months later, in Mississauga, the father recalled the soothing words of the Canadian official. "The diplomat said to me, 'The Hercules will be at the airport by 7:30. Get ready. But please don't tell anyone. There are a hundred and fifty other Canadians out there. We can't help anyone else. Let's go. Please get in my car and I'll drive you back to your hotel.' So he took us to the hotel, and he packed up my little suitcase. Then he took us down to the airport, to a small room where nobody could see us, and he waited with us until the Hercules came. Our daughter was lucky. We knew she would have fame, and she did. Her picture was in the papers. She was treated special."

The relatives whose loved ones' descriptions had not yet been matched with photographs of bodies spent many hours by the shores of Bantry Bay. Tony Dawson arranged coach trips. By island standards, Cork to Bantry is a longish way. The mourners left early in the morning and got back to their hotels late in the evening. The ocean calmed them. They felt close to the people they had lost. The water at the bay was still, still enough for good swimmers to stay afloat. They couldn't visualize churning seas or sharks, and the sailors who had plucked or winched or hefted mutilated bodies had been instructed not to talk; at least not about the gory part of their heroic job. The Laurences spent their most peaceful hours at the coast. They remembered their daughters had loved roses. One girl had loved red roses, the other white. They wanted to offer the sea red and white rose petals. There were gardens with rose bushes in Bantry, so they asked the owner of one garden, could they please pluck a rose. And the owner and her neighbours told the Laurences to take not one, not a bunch, but gardensful. In spite of the horror, these were radiant times. Thank God the plane went down off Ireland, the Laurences said. The Irish were sincere people. Anywhere else, in London or Toronto or Delhi, for instance, the same grief would have been unbearable.

But when they came back to Cork, to their hotels, the loss became nightly more real. And there were pictures to see, descriptions to listen to. Just in case. The relatives and the Gardai wanted to be sure, absolutely, positively sure, before they let a relative leave Cork. The Laurences looked through ninety pictures.

One of the relatives, Dr Bal Gupta, a calm, methodical man not known to be emotional except for one outburst at the invisibility of Canadian officials, had lost his wife in the crash. He came back from Bantry Bay on Saturday evening and found a message from the hospital. The Gardai thought they had a match for Mrs Gupta. He took the bus back to the hospital at once.

He had left his older son in Toronto, and brought with him his younger, a thirteen-year-old who'd suddenly, mysteriously, developed an ulcer. The boy, though sick, had come to Cork to look after his father. Father and son had arrived on Wednesday night. On Thursday Dr Gupta had filled out forms. Friday had been a nightmare of waiting, but the waiting hadn't been the hospital's fault. He praised John Martin's Group for its generous-spirited management of the mammoth disaster. He praised the counsellor and the policeman who had stayed with him

through the long, slow days of ordeal. He praised Kiran and
Razia Doshi, the official and the unofficial Indian ambassa-
dors. He had no praise, however, for the staff representing
Canada.

"Up through Thursday," he said, "we didn't see the Canadians' faces, nobody's. . . . What happened was on Thursday night
all of us were being bused back to our hotels from the hospital.
It was very late, and I was probably the last one to come out. I
came out and reporters surrounded us. I don't know if they
were local TV crews, or CTV or what. They kept asking
questions, such as 'Are you satisfied with the arrangements?' I
told them that I was disappointed that more bodies could not
be identified that day but that I understood why the Gardai
had to be slow and meticulous. But when they asked me about
the Canadian representatives. . . I don't know, I just burst out. I
used some very unparliamentary language right there on tape!
That night some Canadian official called me at the hotel, and
the next morning, Friday morning, some Canadians came and
apologized and said that they were working behind the scenes."

Saturday he and his son had gone on the bus to Bantry Bay.
He had prayed on the ride over — he was a licensed Hindu
priest back in Toronto — and he had prayed at the shore,
tossed flowers in the water and prayed, and prayed again on the
ride back to Cork. And in Cork there was the message: come
to the hospital.

Dr Gupta left his sick child in the hotel and rushed to face
whatever alien ordeal. This is how he remembers the rest of
Saturday night:

"First of all they [the Gardai] sat down and read from the
post-mortem report. There were some discrepancies: the height
was off by an inch, and the weight was a little different. But
those things were all right, I thought, because of water
absorption, etc. The description was about right. The clothes
they described sounded the same as the *kurta* and *salwar* she'd
been wearing. She'd dressed in a long *kurta* dress and tight
pyjamas. The design seemed the same. Then the Gardai
brought me a bag of effects. They showed me ornaments. I
said, 'They don't belong to my wife. She didn't own those.' And

they said, 'Well, anyway, we may as well show you the picture.' Then they showed me the picture. I said, 'This isn't my wife. This is my friend's wife. This is Mrs Sharma.' The Gardai said, 'Well, it hasn't been a waste then. At least a body has been identified.'

"So we — the policeman and counsellor and I — came back up to the hall in the Nurses' Residence in the West Wing. They told us to wait. They said they would call us one by one. There were others waiting. What they had done was put the pictures up in a room, and they were asking people in small batches. Then all of a sudden, I don't know if somebody goofed or what, they opened the door and we went in and we looked at the pictures.

"#2 was Mrs Sharma. #40 was the Sharma's elder boy. #96 was Mrs Radhakrishna. And then #97 was my wife's picture. I had no difficulty in identifying. The face was in reasonable shape, except for a cut. We identified two of the Sharma boys. We had some doubts about the third.

"Then I went to the policeman, and I said, 'That's my wife's body.' It was the same policeman. That was very good, you always dealt with the same policeman.

"Around seven or eight in the evening, they came to us and took down our description. Then they led us downstairs [to the East Wing] and showed us a bag of belongings. There were two rings, nothing else. There was no clothing.

"Then they showed us the body. The bodies were very well kept. The Gardai were identifying first through pictures, then they were bringing in the body from the morgue.

"If you requested they would leave you alone with the body in a little room. Otherwise, there were nuns there all the time.

"Then there was a lot of paperwork involved. I made a declaration about my wife's body. Then about the other bodies I'd identified. They made notes. We finished around eleven o'clock. Probably I was the last one to leave the hospital.

"I phoned home that night. I have a brother in Toronto. My brother's opinion was that if the body has been found, it should be taken to India for funeral rites. He said that he would call India and let my in-laws know.

"On Sunday the hospital organized a mixed service in the chapel. It was very beautiful. The Laurences read from the Bible, I read from the Gita. There were Muslim prayers. After that we had to do paperwork for the transportation of the body. I spent the whole of Sunday on the paperwork, and still it wasn't completed. The body could only be released by the police authorities. And the police authorities had to make sure that the body could be released. I was told to come back on Monday. I was making all the arrangements for the Sharma family, too. I phoned Sharma's brother in India, but the brother was already on his way to Ireland. Sunday night I had to take care of my son. He had fever, and I gave him antibiotics. I finished my wife's paperwork by lunchtime on Monday."

There were only two cases of initial misidentification. One husband matched memory with photograph and identified his wife's body, but the dental records on his wife's Yellow Form did not match the dental records from that body's post-mortem. Another body, misidentified and shipped on to London, was recalled in time for correct identification. One man, who had lost his wife and two small children, found his wife's body fairly quickly, but not those of his children. He remembered a year later that towards the end of the identification week when only a few bodies were left and he was hysterical with grief, the nuns had let him into a room so he could view the unclaimed bodies of children. He remembered (or misremembered) the nuns urging him to take two bodies as his own. He peered into faces, but the faces were alien. In the end, all the bodies retrieved were positively identified. This is unique in the history of air-crash disasters of this magnitude.

But some identifications took a long time. The identifications, for instance, of Ms Rama Paul's brother's family. The whole Bhat family — mother, father and two daughters, Bina and Tina — was wiped out. Rama Paul is a nurse at the Princess

Margaret Hospital (for cancer patients) in Toronto. Soothing people in pain and in fear of death is her job. She is a remarkable person, remarkable in the Toronto Indo-Canadian community for her energy, her frankness and her ability to live a happy life on her own as a single woman. In this community, women in their forties are invariably wives or widows. Rama Paul devoted herself to her brother's family and to her patients at the Princess Margaret Hospital. She was so devoted, and so capable, that she had packed the Bhat family's suitcases the night before the Air India flight and labelled each one with waterproof markers: BHAT, DOWNSVIEW, ONTARIO. She'd told the family what to wear before they'd driven to the airport: the suit he had graduated in for her brother, bridal red for her sister-in-law and smart Canadian clothes she herself had bought for her nieces, who slept over more often in her apartment than they did in their own. When tragedy struck — and she had had premonitions strong enough and recurrent enough to urge her family even at the airport not to go — she became an excellent filler of the Pink and Yellow Forms. She knew what each member had worn, what object was in which part of each suitcase. With her nurse's memory for minutiae, she knew about birthmarks and scars. But she did not want to go to Cork as soon as she heard the dreaded, pre-intimated news.

"Air India wanted me to go when it happened," Rama Paul said. "They told me how many bodies had been found. I said to them, 'What guarantee can you give me that of the 329 who died, I'll find even one from my family. No, I don't want to go.' But I told them I wanted them to keep in touch with me. So they used to ring me up. They were very good about that.

"Then one Sunday morning, at about a quarter to five, the phone rang. I thought it was probably my sister in Australia. She sometimes calls. I get up at five on Sundays. It's a work day for me, and there aren't that many buses, so if I miss my bus I have to wait another half-hour. It wasn't my sister on the phone; it was a policeman from Cork. He said that he wanted to ask me some questions. I said, 'Look, I'm going off to work. I have to get ready to catch my bus. I'll be late if I answer your questions.' But he kept on asking questions: what was your niece wearing, and so on. I told him.

"He said, 'Miss Paul, we want you to fly immediately to Cork.'

"I said, 'No way. I'm not flying to Cork. I am going to work.'

"The policeman said, 'You have no choice.'

"I said, 'Look, Monday is my day off. I can fly on Monday.' But he wouldn't agree to that. So I warned him, 'I'm going to work now, and don't call me at work.'

"It was my bus time already, and I hadn't brushed my teeth or had a wash. I just slipped on my uniform and rushed to catch that bus. When I got to the hospital the nursing officer could tell that I was in a panic. In no time there were five calls from Cork, and three from Air India. The girls on the floor were really worried, because the callers identified themselves as police officers and kept asking what kind of passport does Miss Paul hold? I think between 7:30 and 9:30 that morning there must have been ten calls.

"Around twelve noon a man from Air India brought me a ticket. And early that evening Chandra's brother and I were off to Cork.

"When we got to Cork, we were treated like VIPs. We were the last relatives to arrive, you see. There were a lot of people there, because they were putting on a big ceremony. A very beautiful ceremony. I think that's why they were rushing to identify bodies."

Rama Paul found three bodies in Cork. She had Kenyons air-freight those coffined bodies to India. At least the souls would finish the trip home.

Of the 132 bodies recovered from the sea, 60 were shipped to India, 13 to Canada, 2 to England, and 1 to the United States. There were 52 bodies cremated in Dublin, 2 bodies buried in Dublin and 2 buried in the serene, green city of Cork. Many had to leave the bodies of their loved ones on the ocean bed. Some day, they promised themselves, they would rent a ship to carry them to the exact spot where the *Emperor Kanishka* had torn through the waves. They would chant the final prayers for their lost families from the ship's deck, and in that way, calm their own bereft, bewildered souls.

PART THREE

CHAPTER 1

These winding streets of middle-class Toronto suburbs, Etobicoke and Mississauga, the areas east of the Don Valley, north of the 401 and off the Queensway, bearing names like "Brendangate," "Wildfern" and "Morningstar" should never have known such tragedy. These are suburban developments of split-level houses and double garages, fenced yards and quiet streets studded with stop signs. Tricycles stay out at night, neighbours barbecue and talk over the fences. Here the nature of a new Canada is taking shape; the faces and names are oriental, Caribbean and Indian, pictures in the school yearbooks go on for row after row without a "traditionally Canadian" name or face.

These are now the dark houses on active streets. These are the houses needing paint and a trim of the lawn. The insides are quiet and dusty. On weekends ("Saturdays and Sundays are the hardest") the men sit in white cotton pyjamas, drinking tea. They call one another, and sometimes they visit each other and just sit, saying very little. One man, aged fifty-two, credit manager of a clothing factory, a man who lost his wife and only child, the top boy in his collegiate, 98 in all five subjects, d.j. on the school rock station, tells us: "Even now I pass his bedroom and tell myself, 'He is tired. Let him sleep.' I make tea for myself and sit here and think, 'It is 9:30, they'll be out soon.' It is hallucination, I know."

They are a new kind of family, those who have been through the ultimate tragedy a man or a woman or occasionally an intact, childless couple, can suffer. They keep tabs on one another: who has "accepted" and who has not. Who among them still has trouble eating, sleeping, working. "What is there to plan now? The enthusiasm is gone. Soon they will ask me at work if I will step aside, take a lateral appointment if I am lucky. Release me. I don't care."

The pattern seems to be universal. Denial. Acceptance. Reconciliation. Eventually...though none have arrived there yet, despite a spate of adoptions and remarriages... reconstruction.

CHAPTER 2

We are sitting in an Indian restaurant in a shopping mall in Toronto with Parkash Bedi, a forty-five-year-old engineer who works for American Motors. Mr Bedi is a lithe, emotional man. "We are so wanting to talk!" He weeps into a wadded bit of tissue. "That wanting to talk is in all of us. We are all in that condition, we who have lost our entire families. We have nothing left except talk."

Parkash Bedi lost his wife and two children in the crash. The daughter, Anu, and the son, Jatin, aged fourteen and nine when they died, had both been born in Canada. He himself is a Canadian citizen. He came to Ontario from Punjab in 1967, when it was still hard for an Indian engineer to immigrate. He has worked in both Sarnia and Detroit. He has gone wherever American Motors has sent him. Borders are fluid to him; family was all.

Mr Bedi wants his family remembered. He is afraid that for all their tough public stands on terrorism, Canada and the United States have done nothing to remember the victims of the Air India crash. A year has passed, a year — he complains — in which not Ottawa, not the Ontario government, not even the mayor's office in Toronto, has organized any *official* memorial ceremony. Canada has left the remembering exclusively to temple societies and ethnic cultural clubs.

This is not a bereaved man's paranoia. We have just come out of a memorial service organized by a Hindu religious society in a Toronto school auditorium. Most politicians invited to this memorial ceremony, for instance, the prime minister of Canada, Cabinet-level ministers, the premier of

Ontario, the mayor of Toronto, have not found it politically
expedient to show up in person.

Parkash Bedi and his fellow-mourners feel totally alone as
they struggle to keep the dead remembered. Mr Bedi has set up
a "Jatin Bedi Soccer Tournament" in his son's school because
his son loved soccer. He's thinking of putting up a hospital in
India. He's talking to architects and politicians in Toronto to
have a monument built. The monument is to be 329 feet by 182
feet, and will include two halls and an eternal flame. The
living, as well as the dead, need this memorial.

Mr Bedi's gentle face clouds over, and he pushes wavy hair
back from his forehead with agitated hands. "When you say to
a politician, doesn't matter Conservative or Liberal, what have
you people done, they say, why, the government set up a relief
fund. The relief fund was a program that entitled every family
to a hundred dollars and to visits by social workers who could
help them fill out forms. So I say to these politicians, do you
think that the Indian community is so poor that we need your
hundred dollars? Let me remind you that the Indian community has done very well even though you people don't recognize
us as Canadians but only as 'immigrants.' We don't need their
money and their bureaucratic support system. We need to be
treated in a caring way. We need to be made to feel that we are
first-class citizens."

There are other kinds of bitterness, too. He feels betrayed by
friends who stay away because they do not know how to
console him in his enormous loss. "What do these so-called
friends think?" he demands. "One doesn't have to go to a
school to learn consolation etiquette!"

He plays with his coffee spoon. He hasn't touched the coffee
the waiter brought him an hour ago. He can't eat. He can't
sleep. His life has been derailed.

The owner of the restaurant comes in through swing doors
from the kitchen. He is a Sikh, traditional enough to wear a
turban and steel bracelet, but nonobservant enough to keep a
well-stocked bar for his patrons. The owner joins three other
turbaned Sikhs at a table close to the bar. They are four loud

men in their thirties, enjoying a weekend night. We worry about the effect of their boisterousness on Mr Bedi, newly wifeless and childless.

Mr Bedi is quick to sense our anxiety. "It's all right," he says, forgivingly. "If I had known this place was owned by Sikhs, I would not have entered it. But now that we are here, let us stay."

Until last June he had felt no fear of, nor revulsion for, Sikhs. He had been born in Punjab, into a family in which interfaith marriages between Hindus and Sikhs were common. In Punjab the family worshipped in *gurdwaras*, as well as in Hindu temples. In fact, his father had raised money to build a *gurdwara* in Delhi, where his father's portrait still hangs. His eldest brother is now an officer in that Delhi *gurdwara*. Parkash Bedi married a Hindu woman. In Detroit the Bedi children therefore prayed in both *gurdwaras* and Hindu temples.

The intimations of Sikh-Hindu strain in Detroit came to Parkash Bedi gradually, over the first five months of 1985. There were some nasty, humiliating incidents inside the *gurdwara* in Detroit. The worst of these incidents happened one weekend in May, about a month before the crash. That weekend Parkash and Jatin went as usual to the *gurdwara*. And, as usual, father and son sat with the rest of the congregation in the *langar*, or dining hall, to be served food that had been specially blessed. The food-servers, carrying heavy, steaming bowls and ladles, went around the dining hall three or four times, and filled worshippers' plates. But that day in May the servers suffered from a vicious blindness. On each round they missed the empty plates of short-haired diners, heaping blessed food only on the plates of turbaned men, especially of men rebaptized into *khalsa*, men known for their loyalty to the Khalistan movement. Each time, they walked, deliberate, slow, unseeing, past the conspicuously empty plates of Parkash Bedi and his nine-year-old boy.

"It was so humiliating!" Mr Bedi remembered. "And it was

very scary. I couldn't figure out why they were doing that to us."

After that incident in late May 1985, the Bedis stopped going to the *gurdwara*.

Now he regrets that he stopped attending the services. If he'd continued, he thinks, he might have seen the anti-Air India posters on the *gurdwara* walls and heard the rumours of boycott and sabotage. He learned, too late, from Sikh friends in Detroit and Sarnia, that all spring such hate-posters had been up in the bigger *gurdwaras*, especially in the *gurdwara* in Malton near the Toronto airport. He suspects now that some of those friends even knew the targeted date for the bombing of an Air India aircraft.

Memories of telltale signs of his Sikh friends' foreknowledge of the disaster flood back to Parkash Bedi these days. He remembers that a Sikh friend had wanted Mrs Bedi to carry several letters to Delhi for his family. The friend had arranged to meet the Bedis at Pearson International Airport well before Flight 181's departure time, so he could deliver his letters. The friend, however, didn't show until long after the Bedis had gone through the final security checks and vanished into the Passengers-Only area.

Instead of looking for Mrs Bedi in the airport, the Sikh friend went straight to the British Airways counter and handed his mail to another Sikh man waiting in line to check in.

"I saw this so-called friend march over," Mr Bedi says, "and suddenly I noticed something strange. I noticed that there were a whole lot of Sikhs in the British Airways line. There were many, many more in that line than there had been in my wife's Air India line."

So he confronted his friend. "Why are Sikhs crowding the British plane?"

The friend answered, "Don't you know that Sikhs have boycotted Air India?"

"You're telling me now?" Mr Bedi lashed out, in despair. "You're telling me after my family's gone and I can't call them back!"

Bitter, confused, Mr Bedi says, "Now I think I know maybe

why this Sikh didn't give my wife his letters to carry. Maybe he knew something. The word in the *gurdwara* was that anyone who travels Air India is the enemy. Anyone who doesn't attend the *gurdwara* regularly is sacrificeable."

Now, in this Toronto restaurant, his voice almost drowned by Punjabi muzak, Parkash Bedi says, "The thing really hit me when I heard why the Sikhs were in the British Airways line. I thought right away that something would go wrong."

The intransigency of Fate now staggers him. He had initially reserved seats on British Airways for his family. But he had cancelled those reservations in March 1985, because he had heard from a friend that Air India had started a Toronto-Delhi flight, and that it was cheaper, more convenient, than the British Airways flight.

Fate plucks those whose mission on earth is done.

Parkash Bedi recalls other bad omens, omens he did not heed, because until June 22, 1985, he had considered himself a modern man, a man of reason and logic, a believer in science, not in signs. Mr Bedi's mother should have been on Flight 182 with Mr Bedi's wife and two children. Mr Bedi had bought her a ticket, too. But Fate intervened. The older Mrs Bedi fell and hurt her backbone badly just days before the flight, and her doctor refused to let her leave.

But the most troubling sign had not been supernatural. The last passenger that Mr Bedi had seen go through security clearance at the airport on the night of June 22nd had been a *nihang*. The *nihang* are considered a particularly fierce sect within Sikhism. They are traditionally the temple guards, known for their reckless, even violent, mode of guarding and for their fondness for dope. The *nihang* that Mr Bedi saw rushing through airport security that night was carrying a huge picnic hamper, and he was very old.

"I don't know why, but the thought immediately came to me," Parkash Bedi says, leaning across the table, "that the *nihang* was sneaking in a bomb inside that basket. I saw him in his *nihang* robes, I saw his beard and his special turban and the big hamper he was carting, and I thought there was something fishy. He was real old, so old he was sacrificeable. I turned to my nephew who was with me and I said, 'I know it. That fellow will die and he will take everyone on the plane with him!'"

In the first weeks after the tragedy, the dazed father shared this intuition about the aged, basket-toting *nihang* passenger with the Canadian authorities — with consuls in Cork, with policemen and RCMP in Toronto, with anyone who would listen.

"The diplomat types told me they did not want to know," Parkash Bedi recalls. "I don't know if the RCMP did any follow-up work."

For Mr Bedi's generation, India continues to be the heart's core. India, perfected by nostalgia, is where the successful immigrant returns again and again for vacations or where he sends his young family. The children are more ambivalent about their roots.

"My son didn't want to go to India." The father sobs openly in the restaurant. "*I made him go*. I wanted him to get to know India. I told him, 'Jatin, you like fireworks, don't you? Well, here they don't let you set off fireworks whenever you want. But you go to India and I've arranged with your uncle to give you fireworks displays every day. Every day you can have fireworks, son. In India everything is available.'"

Filial love and guilt torment Mr Bedi. "I was too strict," Mr Bedi says, still sobbing. He was an Indian-style father, an "immigrant" father, he confesses. On Friday, June 21st, the day before Jatin boarded the deadly flight, he had scolded the boy for losing a soccer game at school.

"I told Jatin that he didn't play good; I gave him a hard time because he lost the game," the father says. "Now I cry why was I so strict. My son said, 'Why, Dad, we did the best we could.' And I still kept at him. I said, 'No, honey, you could have done better.' And then tears came into Jatin's eyes, and he said, 'Dad, everyone can't be good at everything.' He was so wise."

We look through Jatin's school essays. He was in a program for gifted children. One essay we read is entitled "What Is

Life?" Another "What Can Man Buy?" Like many of the eighty-four children on the sabotaged plane, Jatin Bedi was aware of the contrast between his own New World affluence and the poverty of millions in the country of his roots. Like those others, he had a social conscience and a strong impulse to charity.

"You know something," Mr Bedi confides. His body heaves; his sobs are dry and soundless. "I get up in the middle of the night and read my boy's essays. Nothing consoles me as much as his writings. Not the Bible. Not the *Guru Granth Sahib*. Not the Gita. Only my boy's words renew my faith in an after-life. Sometimes it seems to me that Jatin's brain was not a child's brain. How could such wise thoughts come from a child's brain?"

To Parkash Bedi, Jatin was a highly evolved soul sent down to earth to complete a mission and be withdrawn when its work was done. The body is a temporary shell for the soul.

In Cork Mr Bedi identified his son's and his wife's bodies. He accepts their deaths. He did not find the body of his fourteen-year-old daughter. In his mind, Anu remains a missing person who might someday be found.

Anu was very beautiful. Pride and regret come through as Mr Bedi talks of his daughter. He didn't praise her enough. He didn't tell her she was beautiful. On the drive out to the airport on June 22nd, his daughter had looked so stunning in a new jumpsuit that he had had a hard time not staring at her.

Was it premonition that he would never see her again, he now wonders, that had made him say to his daughter in the car, "Boy, that looks nice on you. Did you buy it in more colours? And those new shoes, they're nice. Did you buy them in more colours?"

Her body hadn't been lined up with the other recovered bodies in the Cork Regional Hospital. Her stylish new jumpsuit hadn't washed up. Nor the new shoes. Perhaps she was alive and still wearing the jumpsuit and the shoes. The hope of reunion with her — and the plans for the monument and the hospital — keep Parkash Bedi going.

"You know how I spent my last birthday?" Mr Bedi demands.

He laughs a stony laugh. "I went to see two psychiatrists. Two. My wife and I used to be the pillar of strength for our friends. If anyone had any kind of trouble — marriage trouble, children trouble — they ran to us. You know how we people worry about bringing up girls in this date-crazy culture. My wife and I always solved people's problems. Now my wife is dead. And I'm knocking on the doors of shrinks on my forty-fifth birthday."

CHAPTER 3

Like Parkash Bedi, Sam Swaminathan, an engineer, lost his entire family — his wife, his fifteen-year-old son, his two very young daughters — in the crash. And he lost two other relatives: a brother-in-law and a sister-in-law. All six were on their way to India to perform prescribed Hindu funerary rites for Mrs Swaminathan's father. Mrs Swaminathan's father had died the year before in the split-level house in Detroit's suburbs where Mr Swaminathan now lives alone. The house is in a newish development, within easy driving distance of schools, fast-food strips and a shopping mall. This is a dream-come-true sort of neighbourhood, where no homeowner has trouble meeting the monthly mortgage or making payments on the boat or the four-wheel drive stored with the family sedan in the garage. There are trail bikes left in driveways and family-sized washes hanging up to dry in treed, tidy backyards.

We arrive at Mr Swaminathan's house while he is still at the supermarket buying fruits, cookies and crackers, to serve us. This is a gracious community, even in the face of monumental grief. Before the tragedy, shopping, cooking and cleaning house had been shared and pleasurable family activities; now they are the survivor's lonely tasks.

Soon Mr Swaminathan swings into his own driveway, shopping sacks bunched in the back seat of his car, and lets us into a house cozy with memorabilia. There are family photographs on the diningroom wall, plush animals on the top shelf of an expensive wall system, chess books and chess sets stacked on the TV stand's rack. This is a house still warmed by family presences. Any minute now the Swaminathan children will bounce home from a neighbour's and start a game of chess or cuddle a stuffed bear.

Was it Fate? Philosophy is what fascinates Mr Swaminathan now. He reads books on all religions. He debates fine philosophical issues by phone with relatives, with fellow-mourners, with men in his car pool, with secretaries at his office. He debates even with a Jehovah's Witness, who has taken to showing up at his house every Sunday. Was it part of God's larger plan that his wife and children be blown out of the sky and plunged into the sea?

Sam Swaminathan has gone through a crucible experience. He has been melted down, ground up, then restored into a new person. "I feel I have been transformed." He says this very modestly. "I feel I have packed in more thought, more growth, into the last six months than I had into the preceding ten years."

Hinduism comforts him, but he stays away from holy men with cult followings. Why did innocent children die so brutal a death? The answer seems clear to him: reincarnation. The sins of one life may be punished in another one.

"There is one *niti sloka* in Sanskrit," Mr Swaminathan explains. "It explores the question of why there is an inveterately but inexplicably malicious relationship between certain creatures or people. The *sloka* goes like this: for the fish, there is the fisherman; for the deer, the hunter; for a good man, a bad man. It is a very difficult question. I try to be tolerant."

Hinduism allows Sam Swaminathan to stay in control of his grief. In September he will change jobs. He will head the international division in the design and development of axle products for a large engineering plant in a different city. He expects to function well in the new high-pressure job. "I have pondered these questions from both the ethical and the guilt points of view. I don't have guilt feelings. I eat; I do a lot of things. I may some day get resettled. In Hinduism, whether the dead ascend or descend, they go on into a different level. We continue to care for them, of course. We continue to suffer. This problem, of caring, is ours."

Mr Swaminathan's voice breaks and his eyes shine. He has not rearranged a single book or toy or piece of clothing in his children's rooms. His wife's saris still hang in her closet in the master bedroom. In another month he will have to disturb the nostalgic orderliness of the unused closets and the unlived-in rooms. He has already sold the house. For now he is peaceful in this split-level suburban mausoleum. He has been visited, he tells us, by his late wife. He was asleep when she came in and sat on their bed. "I feel my wife is aware of my life down here," he says. "She made me feel very serene."

In the meantime, he comforts others. He begs his mother in India not to worry about him and make herself sick. He writes long letters to the Montreal law firm that is handling his settlement suit, applying what he calls "the principle of finite element and compound synergism" to his post-disaster problems.

This is what he writes:

Discussion: The cultural aspect of the Indian way of life is very important in assessing the pecuniary loss suffered by the dependent as well as in evaluating the damages inflicted on the dependent arising out of the loss of human lives in the Air India tragedy. There are several interesting questions.

Question no. 1: What is the pecuniary loss sustained by an earning parent in the death of a child? Putting it differently, is a surviving parent like myself truly dependent on his non-earning child within the scope of the law? The answer you will find is that in the context of the Indian way of life, [children] are at least as important as would be a spouse to a husband, or a parent to a child. A parent is dependent on his child (in the Indian context) for all the intentional purposes of the law and therefore the dependent should be entitled to compensation that are in conformity with the said relationship. *In other words, there should be no difference between the treatment of the death of a child and the death of an adult in the granting of damage and pecuniary loss awards.*

Discussion: There is a mutual dependency which tran-

spires between the parents and the children from the time
an Indian child is born. There is an unwritten contractual
agreement which exists between the parent and the child
which is culturally, socially and continuously practised
over thousands of years in India. Some of the aspects of
those unwritten contracts are valid in the Indian courts.
This conceptual agreement, while not on paper, implies
that the parents make considerable sacrifices in their
working lives for the sake of their children, and their children take care of the Indian parents when they get older
(parental sacrifice is far greater than among most Western
parents). It is for this reason that Indian children do not
"fly out of the nest" when they finish schools. Also, these
children are helped until they are college-educated, and in
many cases, even after they are married. What this means
is that a parent is willing to borrow or sacrifice his entire
life savings and is personally willing to devote his time and
effort toward the upbringing of his children. What a parent
really is doing is that he is investing in his own children's
future, which is also his own future. This is a unique insurance system, which is culturally binding and is socially
enforced in our system. In return, the children consider it
their moral duty to conform to the unwritten contract
mentioned above. These practices are easily evidenced by
several facts unique to the Indian way of life: most Indians
have joint-family system; most marriages, including mine,
are arranged marriages; invariably parents live at last with
one child and children take care of the total needs of their
parents (this is a potential pecuniary loss). It is because of
this close and life-long relationship in many instances as I
have contemplated to do, the parents and the children
form a business.

An Indian emigrates to a Western country purely with
the economic motive in mind. Pursuit of political or
cultural freedom had hardly been the reason for emigrat-
ing from India. The parent most often sacrificed a stable
job or cultural surroundings, and now spends a dispropor-
tionate sum of money in initially establishing new roots in
a foreign country. This a parent does, not for his own

comfort alone, but essentially to provide a better future for his children. He fully knows that his children are his caretakers in his older years....

In this Indian way of life, continuity of family tree, including every branch of it, is very important. Therefore, children are given the greatest importance in life....In our system, the only way a parent gets spiritual salvation after his death is when the children perform the funeral rites. In a situation like mine where all of my children were destroyed, theoretically I cannot attain salvation. The only recourse under the Hindu religious practices will be that I adopt a child and employ somebody to take care of this adopted child. In Western terms, one can dollarize the cost of adoption and raising charges. In my opinion, this is potential financial loss and is very real.

Writing the long letter to his Montreal lawyers makes Mr Swaminathan feel good. He has demonstrated one of the ways in which Canada's "cultural mosaic" works. He may be a Westernized sought-after engineer with an expensive car and house, but he has not forgotten his roots: "What I really want to say to them is, will a million dollars bring back even one of my children? But the only pain that courts here understand is one that can be counted up in dollars and cents."

The human heart may grieve heedless of the gender and the age of lost kin, but Canadian courts of law are gendrist in toting up reimbursable suffering. The loss of a well-employed husband rings up a dramatically higher figure than the loss of an underemployed wife and unemployed kids.

There isn't enough bullion in the bank vaults of the universe to recompense the loss. Immediately after the crash, no bereaved relative wanted to collect on damages or on life-insurance policies. Then the numbness began to wear off. Now many are demanding a share of the settlement money that is owed them. This is their way of expressing rage at politicians who have been slow to label the crash the work of terrorists.

Among themselves, the bereaved accuse their Canadian law firms of race-related apathy. They are convinced that white Canadian lawyers would have sought loss reimbursement for 329 white Canadian victims with more alacrity.

"Their attitude is that these people are immigrants; they aren't used to money," complains one bitter relative. "They think we'll take anything. They think we don't have to be compensated in the same way as mainstream victims."

His bitterness may be unjustified, but it indicates a mood swing.

The U.S.-based relatives would have preferred to sue in U.S. courts, because settlements in Canada have traditionally been petty. But there are only weak legal grounds for prosecuting in the U.S. courts an Indian airline flying out of Canadian airports with lax security. Besides, the pressure to sue in bulk was hard to resist. To sue as individual plaintiffs would be to compound the delay and the legal fees.

Only one mourner has been a maverick. "I was totally dissatisfied with the bulk handling," he snaps. He claims that official investigators at the crash site have withheld facts about sabotage from the relatives. He has hired his own very expensive aviation expert to get at the truth of this tragedy.

This new rage should be seen as a sign of health. The bereaved return to high-stress jobs. They make the best of traumatically reduced families or marry new, ready-made ones. One couple plans pregnancy, another couple adopts. Most widows ignore their relatives' pleas to return to India; they stay on, declaring quite firmly that they are Canadian citizens and Canada is where they belong. They argue among themselves whether they should remain celibate or whether they should remarry.

The widows are generally in their late thirties, the men in their mid-forties. Most of the men, conscientious emigrants from an overpopulated country, have undergone vasectomies. The widows think of themselves as too old to really start over, but too young to withdraw from society like nuns. Not one of the widows has yet remarried. After the damage settlements, the widows will come into minifortunes.

Two widowers, however, have remarried. They say that they

gave in to family pressures in India, where they went straight from Cork for cremation rites. Their Indian relatives convinced them that a middle-aged man stuck in an alien continent needs a wife to cook and keep house in familiar, companionable ways. One of the two men has married a widow with a child of her own. This man said that he intended to be a generous provider for his new family, but that he could not accept as his own a child he had not fathered himself. He acknowledged that he was too old to father more children. His new bride and he were two wounded people propping each other up in the face of a herky-jerky destiny. There could be no question of a *new* start or a *new* life, he said. He, too, had died on Flight 182.

Most widowers see their desire to mourn their lost wives and to prolong their unplanned celibacy as a possible mark of their North Americanization. An engineer in Toronto said in his only burst of anger during a sorrowful afternoon, "I am not a rebel. My eldest brother in India is the head of the family, and I've always listened to him. But not about getting remarried. Not about this, no, I shall not listen. He wants me to remarry for my own good. Who will look after you in your old age? my brother says. Who will be mother to your poor children? I have told him I shall bring up the children myself. I have made a beginning; I have learned to cook."

The engineer has made a compromise with his family. The family has sent over a niece to keep house for him and his young children.

Another widower, also a Toronto engineer, confesses that he would like to remarry. "When something awful like this happens, one can finish oneself off. Or one can condemn oneself to loneliness and singlehood. Singlehood isn't the life for me. Singlehood isn't for anyone who wants to rebuild." He wants to wait until he has married off a surviving college-age daughter before he looks for a bride for himself.

Sam Swaminathan also wrestles with the problem of remarriage. "If I remarry, I will choose a bride who is handicapped — a blind woman or a lame woman, a woman suffering from some physical deformity — because this time around, I will be marrying to purify my soul and not to raise a family." He doesn't expect to be ready to remarry for a long time yet. He had loved his wife, who had been found for him in a "traditionally arranged" marriage. It is to the topics of spousal love and spousal loss that he keeps coming back.

"Do you know that quote from Shakespeare's Bassanio?" he asks. "Bassanio is in *The Merchant of Venice*. He is given one line that is simply beautiful. Bassanio says, 'With much more love.' That is how I feel. A man is nothing if he loves his wife because she is a prize he has captured, because she is valuable goods. Like Bassanio, I say, 'With much more love.' With much, much more."

Mr Swaminathan's pain glints like a shard in the afternoon sunlight seeping in through the livingroom's picture window. To calm himself he talks about literature. Always literature has consoled him. He recites from Milton and Matthew Arnold and Rabindranath Tagore.

"With so much, much more," he says.

For some the tragedy has led to self-transformation. A woman who lost four members of her family confesses, "I have become more outgoing. I call up those I know are still hurting. I visit them in their homes. And they feel more comfortable with me than when I had my own family. They drop in without calling. They know I don't have to worry about fixing family meals or putting children to bed. They feel comfortable with me because I am alone."

This woman's wonder is replicated by many of the family-less men. It isn't the money that keeps them here, they confide; it is their New World sense of self and their new feeling of "liberation." They may have arrived ten or fifteen or twenty years ago as economic strivers, pursuing the dream of the golden life for their children, but they stay on because they cannot see themselves fitting happily back into their old lives and their old personalities. What they think about, what they talk about, what they want out of life: all this, they feel, would seem strange, even alienating, to people they left behind in the old country.

One widower describes this "liberation."

"The tragedy has freed me to help others, and in ways that I could not back in India," he says. "I can talk to the grieving women with a frankness I could not there — there I might have been misunderstood. For instance, the other evening I was talking to a woman, a widow, on the phone — my phone bills are staggering! I said to her, 'Let us suppose that you and I were to marry. This is just a supposition. But if you were to marry me and move into this house, would you expect me to remove all photographs of my first wife?' And this widow said, very firmly, 'I shall not allow you to display her photographs.' Then I confronted her. I asked, 'What is your objection? I wouldn't object to you keeping photographs of your late husband. If I don't object to his photos, would you still object to mine?' And she said that she would.

"Then I tried another area of discussion. I said, 'I have kept all my wife's saris. There are many, many of them, and at least twenty-seven of them are Benarasi silks with gold thread. They are saris my wife has worn probably just once. I bought them for her, because I liked giving her things. Would you wear her saris?' And this widow said, 'No, I wouldn't. The only reason that I might wear your wife's saris is if I felt that was the way to win your heart.' I said then, 'I don't mind if you bring his things to my house. You can bring his shoes, and little things.'

"We kept on talking like this, talking very freely. And we discovered that neither she nor I had washed our late spouses' clothing. We helped each other by talking. That is my point."

But always, after they hang up the telephone or see the visitor out the front door, comes the dread moment of unsharable loneliness. A widow, greatly admired in the community for her Hindu stoicism, sits on a rock by Dunmanus Bay, in Ireland, and thinks how much easier it would be if she were to slide off the rock and walk into the seductive waters and join her loved ones.

For another widow, loneliness and hysteria alternate. She had warned her husband and her daughter not to take Flight 182 on June 22, 1985. She had warned them against that flight, because she had heard Khalistani women in her office tell each other that that flight would be bombed. She had begged her husband not to board that flight. But he had been stubborn. If he cancelled his tickets because of women's rumours, he would look like a coward. He had travelled on June 22nd.

This widow was visited by the RCMP, who brought her mug-shots to identify. The RCMP linked the sabotage with a man they considered its chief perpetrator.

The children on Flight 182 were truly bicultural children. They were bright synthesizers, not iconoclasts and rebels. Every day at school, where mainstream kids chatted around them about drugs and dates and at home where parents pressured them to study hard and not let go their Indianness, they negotiated the tricky spaces of acculturation. These were children with the drive and curiosity of pioneers, but they were also children who took family love, family support and family dependence for granted. They switched with ease from Calvin Klein and Jordache to saris or *salwar-kameez* brought over by doting grandparents, aunts and uncles. They ate pizzas with friends in shopping malls, and curries with rice and unleavened breads at home. They were smart, ambitious children who won spelling bees in a language that their parents spoke with heavy accents; they were children who filled high school chess clubs and debate clubs, who aced math tests and science tests, who wrote poems and gave classical dance recitals while they waited to go into engineering, medical or law school; they were children who pleased their old-country parents by avoiding school proms and dances where kids misbehaved, and above all, they were newly affluent children with purpose and mission, who organized benefits for Ethiopia and Bhopal and projects closer to home.

Some of the children had premonitions. One fourteen-year-old girl wrote to her closest friend that she expected to die very shortly, and she packed her Hindu rosary of *tulsi* beads into her flight bag instead of in her suitcase, which would have to be checked into the plane's cargo hold. Another girl, an eighth-grader at Woodlands School in Toronto, made her peace with

God and destiny in a poem she wrote ten days before she boarded Flight 182.

This is Jyothi Radhakrishna's poem, "The Leader of All":

> I look into your eyes
>   and what do I see?
> I see you looking back at me
>
> Without pain, without sorrow
> Your lotus eyes make me follow
>
> Through the doors, through the halls,
> Over the bridges, under the walls
>
> Lead me forth, lead me on,
> Lead me to where the sorrow is gone
>
> Take me to the promised land,
> Come, let us go hand in hand
>
> I will follow your footsteps true,
> Lead me to the world so new
>
> Lead me on the true right way,
> Our destiny is where we will stay
>
> To the land of good, never bad,
> Where all are happy, never sad
>
> We will stay and stay forever,
> Where my love for you shan't die ever!

CHAPTER 4

"Dear Mr and Mrs Laurence," writes George W. Bancroft, a professor at the University of Toronto's Faculty of Education and a former senior advisor on multicultural policy development to Ontario's Ministry of Citizenship and Culture. "Words cannot describe the shock and profound sense of loss I felt when I saw the photographs of your gracious and talented daughters, Krithika and Shyamala, as being among the victims of the crash of Air India Flight 182."

George Bancroft had seen the teenaged Laurence sisters dance in Toronto's St Lawrence Centre in mid-October of 1982. He remembered the sisters as "attractive and sweet young ladies," their execution of *Bharat Natyam* as "brilliant."

The Laurence sisters — Shyamala Jean and Krithika Nicola — were loving, diligent, bicultural young women. They were honour roll students and tutors at Applewood Heights Secondary School, winners of civic awards and Canada Council grants, holders of the *Natya Visarad* (Great Dancer) title. They were young Canadian high-achievers featured on the CBC program *Going Great*. Over the last four years of their young lives, they gave more than 300 *Bharat Natyam* recitals in school gyms and civic halls and church basements, and through dance brought home to suburban families (in soothing, even flattering, ways) the multicultural reality of the nation.

Children wrote them fan letters on graph paper:

Dear Dancers,
I really liked your dance, you performed good. Thank you.
Love Allison

Dear Dancers and mother,
We really liked your dance we liked your peacock feathers
and costumes. We liked the way your mother made the
costumes. I liked to hear the bell ring on your feet.

Krithika Nicola finished school on Friday, the 21st of June,
and the sisters left the very next day for India. This summer they
were to perform for hard-to-please Indian audiences instead of
taking lessons from their familiar dance *guru*. They lived for
dance, and though they were Canadians — outsiders — the *guru*
had judged them ready to win over the locals. This was the
tricky space between cultures that the sisters called home: in
Toronto, wearing their pretty peacock feathers and their belled
anklets, they were outsiders of sorts; in Madras, they were rich
expatriates who had to prove their expressiveness and grace.

At the airport, their parents, Saroj and John Laurence, calm,
gentle, soft-voiced people, saw the girls and their friend, Lita
Sarangi, a fourteen-year-old dancer also from Mississauga, go
through security. They waited around for a while, chatting with
the Sarangis and with Dr and Dr (Mrs) Nadkarni of St Catharines,
Ontario, parents of two boys who had also stepped through the
arches of metal detectors and vanished out of view. After a
while, John and Saroj went home.

Saroj heard the phone ring early next morning. It was six-
thirty and a woman friend who'd come to see the girls off at the
airport was sobbing on the phone. "Saroj, my husband wants to
talk to your husband." She knew at once that it was about her
daughters, and that it was bad news.

The friend's husband said, "Turn on the TV or radio. We
don't know if it is a hijacking or what."

Saroj and John prayed that it be a hijacking, not a crash. They
still believed in the goodness of people, even of terrorists. They
thought no one could kill in cold blood women and children
who'd had nothing to do with the raid on the Golden Temple.

As she reached for the radio, Saroj remembered that her
niece had broken a glass — a bad omen — the night before and
that her brother-in-law had lost his way back home from the airport — another bad omen. The omens didn't lie. John called the

travel agent, a Mr Muller, who had arranged tickets for nineteen passengers on Flight 182. The travel agent, distraught himself, took away all hope. The Air India jumbo jet had crashed into the sea an hour out of London. It was a crash, he was certain.

John called Raju and Meena Sarangi. Lita was on that flight because the Laurence girls were on that flight; Meena and Raju hadn't wanted Lita to travel to India alone.

This is an emotional community, which is at its best, at its most cohesive, in disasters and crises. Friends began to arrive almost at once. As did journalists. Your daughters were dancers? Can you spell that name again, please? Do you think it was a bomb? Are you angry with Sikhs?

"We thought right away it was Sikhs," John says now. "There was too much coincidence. We knew in our minds it had to be Sikhs. I am sure there are good people among them, but why don't they come out and speak out against the extremists?"

Like the Sarangis, the Laurences went to Cork as soon as Air India and the Irish government would let them. Lita's body was found, but not the bodies of Shyamala Jean and Krithika Nicola.

"We can thank God it happened in Ireland," John says. His wife is Hindu, he is Catholic. "We feel the crash happening off Ireland made it so much easier to bear. We can't imagine it happening in India or in Canada. In Canada they would have been businesslike. Ireland had a human touch. You need the human touch."

The house in Mississauga felt too big, too empty. They put it up for sale. Their real estate agent was a Canadian Sikh.

"Our whole life was centred around the girls," Saroj says. She is a pretty woman with bright eyes and luminous skin. "Everything was going like clockwork. From the time we came to Canada, everything went smoothly. We made plans, and the children co-operated fully. They were very much into our culture, but at the same time they were very Canadianized. They knew about sports, music, art, politics, you name it."

But the girls, who were eighteen and sixteen, didn't go to parties to which boys were invited. "They didn't date," Saroj explains proudly. "They knew we wouldn't have liked it. We didn't have to tell them not to date. We just told them that problems could arise from mixing two cultures. Sometimes they went to school dances, but then they would tell us afterwards what had happened. We didn't hide things from each other. They came into our room, and we talked, we argued, and all of us always came out of the room happy."

Since the girls' bodies were not retrieved from the deep, for months Saroj believed that they were alive and had swum to an island or shore. She had no proof of their deaths. A mother's duty is to have hope.

Her unsinkable hope did not please the social workers and the psychiatrist who made it their business to manage the relatives' grief. "These people came to us and they were very keen that we attend their meetings. But, to be honest, I didn't like their approach. They had their medical patter. And I had my hope — I was clinging to hope as any mother would do.... We preferred to heal ourselves in our own way. We kept up our hope for as long as we could. Then we accepted it. We accepted the girls' deaths."

On the coffee tables there are stacks of books on reincarnation and after-life. Studies on resuscitation methods fascinate the Laurences. They read case histories of people who claim to have died and been brought back to life, people who have had out-of-body experiences.

John says, "At the start, we were very, very angry with God, whom we'd trusted so much. He seemed to have let us down. But little by little we have begun to understand that He is not out there preventing one individual from loading a bomb onto a plane, or preventing some other individual from holding up a store."

God doesn't rush around saving or destroying bodies. Destinies are planned to affect souls, not bodies: that's John Laurence's point. The destiny of each soul is planned thousands of years in advance; soul-span is distinct from life-span. This is the lesson the Laurences have learned from a *swami* they were taken to in Orissa by Saroj's sister. This is the lesson that has given them most peace — and their tranquillity as they describe their life before and after the tragedy is astonishing.

"The crash was no accident was what the *swami* said," Saroj says. "The *swami* spent a whole week with us. He came every evening and stayed two or three hours. One evening he said, 'It looks fantastic that 329 could all have the same fate, that they could be gathered together in a plane on a continent so far away. But it was planned long ago, thousands of years ago.' The next evening he came back and said, 'Your children had a very short mission to accomplish in this world. They finished their mission, and it was time to leave.' So I said to him, 'Do you mean that if I'd taken the girls off that plane that Saturday, they'd have still died?' And the *swami* told me, 'You could have pulled them off that plane, you could have locked them up, you could have done anything, but you couldn't have stopped them from dying that day. Their mission was fulfilled.' And we believe that."

The Laurences have their faith and their memories; they have given away Shyamala's and Krithika's dance wardrobe to another young *Bharat Natyam* instructor. They have moved to a smaller house. They have gladly attended the memorial services organized by the girls' dance students in Toronto and by the Irish government in Dunmanus Bay. But the best memorials come from kids who still send notes on graph paper:

Dear Saro antie and John uncle,
Shyamala and Krithiga are the best people in the world and everyone loves them!!!
Love Rajani

CHAPTER 5

In a big, new house with a grand, spiralling staircase, Meena Sarangi watches her daughter dance and re-dance on the VCR. The daughter, Lita, is stunning to look at, and graceful, and, on the screen, eerily animated.

"I was only eighteen when Lita was born," Meena Sarangi says. She is wearing blue jeans and a pink sweater. Her face is still round and girlish. "My father was very conservative, very strict. I wanted to be a doctor. I wanted to be a dancer. But anything I wanted to be, he wouldn't let me be. My father wouldn't give me the chance to do what I wanted, be a somebody. I was so depressed when I was growing up, I thought what a failure I am. But Lita was doing everything. Her father and I were so proud of her."

Lucky, her energetic seven-year-old son, squirms upright on the sofa beside her. He is a lively kid who smiles a lot. He points to the screen. "Look! I like the next bit."

"I was Lita's mother," Meena Sarangi continues from deep inside a world of unshakeable grief, "but before she left we'd started to wear the same blouses. We shared clothes. I used to brush her hair, paint her nails. She was my daughter. She was my friend. She was my dream. She was my life. She was my everything."

She collapses on the sofa. The sofa is new. All the furniture in the house looks, feels, smells new. The house itself is so new and the household so disrupted by tragedy that some rooms on the main floor are still unfurnished. This was the house that Lita would have come back to. When she left for India, the Sarangi family had been about to move here from a smaller house in Rexdale.

Raju Sarangi, the father, leans forward in his cozy armchair. He is an electrical engineer who has worked for Domtar for over seventeen years and owns a small consulting agency. He is a self-made man. He has done very well in Canada, he has provided well for his family. Until June 23, 1985, this success had made him happy. Now his life feels empty.

"In the beginning, Lita didn't want to move from our old house," Raju says. "Then we explained to her that we were building the new bigger house for her. We wanted her to have a proper dance studio. We wanted her to have enough place for sound equipment, professional lights, professional everything. She had a dance school for little kids. She was only fourteen, and already she was earning $1,400 a month from her dance activities! She was God's gift."

Raju Sarangi wants to show us the basement where the dance studio is. We follow him downstairs. Lucky sticks close to us. Father and son point out where the stage will eventually be, and where the audience will sit. He is building an auditorium. There will be a separate kitchen downstairs, and an area for post-recital buffets.

"We had so many plans," Raju says, breaking down. "Now I am finishing it for the use of the community."

We come back up to the main floor, where Meena is still reviewing tapes. "Why did this happen to Lita?" asks Meena. "She was so good! This time she was carrying a stethoscope to give to a doctor in a free clinic in my hometown, and money to buy medicine. And she was wearing a locket with a picture of Lord Tirupati. So why did this happen to her? Sometimes I have so many questions I want to ask God."

The screen darkens. Meena Sarangi turns to us again. "She was going to be a film star," she says.

"To tell you the truth," Raju continues, "I still don't understand why God did this. Sometimes I grow weak and I ask myself is there any other alternative to this life? Is there any consolation? Sometimes I lose faith. She was such a good girl, but *nothing worked out!* I have never hurt anyone, stolen from anyone, then why did this happen?"

Luck and Fate: the mother wonders about the relationship between these two forces. She had thought her daughter very lucky until Flight 182 crashed. She had won a few dollars a couple of times playing Lottario. She even got a letter from an Indian film star who was notorious for ignoring his fan mail. Lita had mailed him a photograph of herself. She must have known she was an irresistible sight, in sari or in blue jeans. Right away he had sent her his autographed picture. He expected her, he had written, to become a film star herself.

Luck and Fate.

Lita had not wanted to go to India in June 1985. She'd wanted to spend the summer with her friends, have them stay over in the new house, go with them to Wonderland, an amusement park north of Toronto. She begged her parents not to send her to India, but to buy her a Wonderland season's pass instead. Meena insisted that she go to India. The Laurence sisters were going on Flight 182 on June 22nd, and so Meena felt safe sending her fourteen-year-old daughter with them. She thought that the time on the plane would be the safest phase of the trip. "I thought," she says bitterly, "what can happen on a plane?"

Raju breaks in, memories flushing out other deeply hidden memories. "Even at the airport Lita said, 'Daddy, I don't want to go. I want to go home. Mummy is making me go, but I want to stay.'"

Hysteria washes over us. "I killed her!" Meena sobs. "Oh, God, I killed her! God, why don't you take my life instead? I didn't know that Lita had said that. God, why did I send her away?"

Raju tries to comfort her, but he is tormented by memories himself. He says that he no longer believes in saving and planning. "Life is just rolling on," he says. "What is tomorrow? What is planning? Just day to day we are living."

A terrifying irony — the irony that besets all the victim-families at one time or another — is not lost on Meena Sarangi. These indulgent, doting, fiercely proud parents had wanted the best of both cultures for their children, and now that biculturalism had caused Lita's death. She remembers now how Lita had cried and begged to stay. India was supposed to be their talisman of innocence, their security in a threatening new world.

"Lita cried and cried," she says. "And I told her, 'Don't cry, because this is the last time I'm sending you for a while. You're growing so big that I shan't want you to go alone after this trip.' But she just kept on crying. And I said, 'Lita, we're just like sisters. I promise that when you come back from India, we're going to sleep together in the guest room on Friday nights, and we'll watch Hindi movies together. And I'll get a babysitter for Lucky, and you and I will go downtown for shopping.' My husband is always so busy with his work, you see."

"Oh no!" says Lucky, screwing up his baby face in mock terror. "Not a babysitter. Mummy, you wouldn't!"

We are watching Lita's dance recital on Raju's professionally mounted videotape. They recount Lita's triumphs on stage and talk about the funds she had raised for Bhopal victims the last time she'd danced. In her memory they have created a Rajsri (Lita) Sarangi Memorial Fellowship at the Ontario College of Art. They show us the room she would have filled with all her teenage bric-a-brac if the bag-bomb had only been detected, somewhere. Lita's books, essays, poems are in bureau drawers. Her cosmetics are ranged, ready for use, on the dresser. Her boutique-sharp clothes and her dance costumes hang in the closet.

Raju picks out a precious item. It's a Maple Leaf pin. When he and Meena had boarded the plane in Cork, with their sad baggage, a Canadian General had scooped the Maple Leaf pin off his own jacket and pinned it on Raju's lapel.

The room is a museum.

"The plane got bombed, you know," Meena explains from near the door of the closet. She says that in Toronto she was afraid to open the casket and look at Lita's face. But they did open the casket. Visitors came to the house to see Lita. The face was still beautiful. The long hair was still black and silky. Only one tooth looked chipped.

"We took a picture of her." Meena walks up to the bureau to look for the picture, then changes her mind. "She was not the same, she wasn't our Lita. She was black.... Her face was black and swollen. She'd been in the water."

"It's all right, Mummy," Lucky soothes her. "You still have me. Poor Laurence uncle and auntie have no kids left."

CHAPTER 6

The story of Vijaya Thampi is a special story, a story about love and dread and self-discovery in the New World.

Vijaya was born in Bombay in 1957 into what she thought of as an unhappy family, and grew up a lonely, diffident girl. Marriage, she assumed, was her only way out. When she was sixteen her older brother brought home a friend, Venu Thampi, a dashing, adventurous young man, whose family, like hers, had come to Bombay from the South. She fancied herself in love. She had no idea how beautiful she was, nor could she gauge the impression she had made on Venu Thampi.

It took him two years to get up enough courage to ask for her hand in marriage. She was eighteen, very much of marriageable age. He was a handsome and ambitious young man from a progressive and well-to-do family that already had two sons in Canada, and he was an Economics graduate with a bright future as a civil servant, the kind of groom that Vijaya's parents hadn't dared hope for. Her parents agreed without fuss to this "love match" in a country where most marriages were still arranged by relatives or marriage brokers. Venu's parents fell for her beauty and her docility, and so did not hold out for a richer girl. Venu and Vijaya were married right away, and Vijaya moved happily into the Thampi house.

"What I liked about her in those days," Mr Thampi recalls now, "was her adaptability. She had an immense ability to adapt and adjust." It is spring 1986. We are sitting on a plush sofa in the livingroom of his split-level home in suburban Markham, outside Toronto. It seems vast. The house is starkly but expensively furnished. Venu Thampi is a short, bearded, intense man of thirty-two. He has a showcase house, a responsi-

ble job with the *Globe and Mail,* a demure six-year-old
daughter. But we have come to meet him not because of what
he has, but because of what he has lost.

In Toronto, his name is Vern. They were Vern and Viji Thampi.

Vijaya, the adaptable bride, settled into the Thampi household
routines very fast. She was quick, and she was brave. And she
was grateful that Venu Thampi had got her out of her family
house. Her husband told her that to him his mother was the
most important woman in the world, and, a good Hindu wife,
she accepted that she was the second-most-important person.
Her husband told her that he wanted her to speak better English
— English is still the language of upward mobility in post-
colonial India, and he was a customs agent with a promising
future — so she signed up for lessons at once.

Vijaya liked Venu's Bombay better than she had hers. She
liked to dress up and he liked her to dress up when he took her
out. She liked the perks that came with her husband's job: the
movie and theatre tickets, the cars that businessmen sent over
to chauffeur them places. She even liked her husband's mother
— something of a rarity in India — who taught her, with
patience and humour, what her husband did and did not like.

Sensational smuggling cases came Venu Thampi's way. More
than any city in India, Bombay drew smuggling high-rollers
from all over the world. The bays and coves were full of
modern-day pirates. Sometimes the pirates tried to bribe the
bearded young customs official, but Venu Thampi arrested
them and seized the contraband goods. He was getting famous.
He had a future in government. And he had a beautiful wife,
whom he loved.

All the same he felt discontented. There were no causes he
could pin down and root out. But surely there had to be more
to life than power and luxury gifts. One thing he knew about
working the Indian docks: sooner or later, the bribe will be
offered that you cannot refuse. And then you will wind up like
all the others, hypocritical and dishonest.

One evening he went to a movie by himself. His wife and

mother were doing something together, and in any case, this was a disaster movie, *The Towering Inferno*, the kind that a delicate girl like Vijaya would not have liked. But he loved blockbusters; he loved American movies with lavish budgets. They enlarged his own circumscribed world.

Afterwards, instead of going straight home, he jumped on his Vespa scooter and rode around for a bit. The Vespa zoomed him past the Princess Docks, and, always the suspicious Customs official, he swung in just to check out what action there might be. No smuggler would be fool enough to dump a boatload there in broad daylight — but what if . . . in the dark of the night? With the high tide coming in . . . ?

Venu Thampi, the cowboy on his Vespa, charged in. Dockworkers waved. "Hey! *Dariwalla* [bearded guy] *Sahib!*" they yelled. He was popular with the workers because he was civil and fair (bureaucratic rank in India not only has its privileges — it often condones odious behaviour towards one's inferiors). They liked his flash and boldness, his Bombay-film looks, and because, like them, he was South Indian. "Hey, there! *Chokra Sahib* [young gentleman]!"

He waved back and kept going until he found himself on Sand Walk, where a truck careened towards him. Men he didn't recognize scattered. He looked over their heads and saw a fishing boat dumping out goods, and a man picking up the dumped goods, and other men, many men, running. He shouted to the foreman to help. The foreman and the Tamil dockworkers surrounded him. "Don't worry, *Sahib*," they shouted. "We're with you. We won't let them kill you." But Venu Thampi, superhuman with adrenalin (he looks on it now as the "sheer courage of innocence, like Daniel in the lion's den"), hurled his Vespa into the fishing boat, took over the helm, brought the boat into the wharf and called his superior right then in the middle of the night from a dockside office.

His superior cursed and swore. "You bastard!" he screamed at young Thampi over the phone. "You don't do this! Do you know what you did?"

"I said, 'No, aren't you happy I got the case?' "

"He said, 'Not at the cost of your life.' "

He says now it took him two years to understand the intricacies of that night. He feels that if you're honest you never have to feel unsafe, because even the smugglers respect you. But if, once, you "show your hand" (meaning the palm of the hand held outward for a bribe) and play smart with them, they will beat the hell out of you. That's exactly the life he saw for himself in India, the impossibility of remaining honest, his superior's assumption of his corruptibility.

That's why Venu Thampi came to Canada. He was an idealist and an enthusiast. The profound corruption on the Princess Docks sickened him.

He wrote to his two brothers in Canada. One lived in Toronto, the other in Winnipeg. The brothers agreed to sponsor him. In 1976, he left his young wife in the care of his mother, and landed in Toronto to look for a job and find a place to live.

"I didn't come here for the money," Mr Thampi repeats. "I came for the lifestyle. I'd heard from my brothers that in Canada you could be who you wanted to be. You didn't have to take abuse from anybody." For a moment nostalgia glows through grief.

Then he recovers. Softly he says, "That night on the Docks, I didn't have a clue as to what my boss really meant. I was very innocent. I just leaped into the boat; I didn't stop to worry that I didn't have a revolver on me. Now I know more about life's intricacies."

For a South Asian, Toronto in the late seventies was a heartless city. It was a time when even decent men and women forgot ordinary decencies. It was a time of not being served in stores, of being bounced out of mid-town hotels, of being sent to the end of the line by Voyageur bus drivers and of being churlishly treated by Air Canada flight attendants, of being threatened by bullies in subway stations.

It was to this Toronto that Mr Thampi, chasing golden dreams, arrived in 1976. He rented a room. Every day he circled ads and set up interviews; every day smooth-talking personnel managers in clean, well-lit offices told him, "No, we can't hire you because you don't have any Canadian work experience." In their offices he held his head high as he had when he had been the dashing young *Dariwalla Sahib*, leaping like Errol Flynn or Rajesh Khanna into a contraband-laden boat. But every night he held his head in his hands in a pokey, loveless room, and wept.

His wife and mother knew nothing about these bad times. He wrote them cheery notes. To settle on the golden continent and fail was unthinkable. There was no going back. His brothers offered to lend him money to bring Vijaya over. They offered him floor space so he wouldn't have to spend money on room and board. But the man who had made criminals quiver in Bombay gritted his teeth and bore his pain. He worked a string of dead-end jobs for impossible hours; he laid aside his bitterness and lived for the future; he saved obsessively. And by November of 1976 he was able to send Vijaya her one-way Bombay-Toronto ticket.

Through the thick glass wall of the Customs Hall at the airport in Toronto, Venu Thampi watched Vijaya float towards him. She was a knockout. He had forgotten how beautiful she was. She was wearing her wedding sari and all her bridal jewellery. The red and gold dazzled him. The past six months of despair slipped off him like snakeskin. He felt as though he were a groom again, that good times were starting to roll again.

"She was so trusting," Mr Thampi recalls now. He plays the night of her arrival over and over again in his mind. "She didn't realize what I had gone through. She'd always thought of me as very strong, and I didn't want to spoil that for her. She didn't realize anything at all except that she was joining me, and that together we were going to throw ourselves into the wonderful North American lifestyle for which we had given up everything."

For a while the young, handsome Thampis played at keeping house and were happier than they had ever been. There were no relatives, no servants, no nosy neighbours. From the beginning, the Thampis were slightly apart from their fellow-immigrants, fundamentally different in the nature of their marriage and in their response to Canadian life. They were not, in those first couple of years, obsessive savers; they spent, they enjoyed.

Sure, the husband had to leave for work very early every morning but they had all evening, every evening. All day the wife cooked. She cooked him curries that she knew he'd like; but, later, she tried out recipes — lasagna, pasta, burritos — from women's magazines. He took her to shopping malls and loved to watch her spend his money. She bought herself Canadian clothes. In pants and sweaters she looked like a movie star. She didn't look Indian, most people said; she looked Italian or Greek. On weekends they splurged on fancy meals at French restaurants. He bought her flowers. He took her to the movies. He arranged vacations in New York and Washington, D.C. On her birthdays he threw her surprise birthday parties. In winter, they took skiing lessons.

"We enjoyed the Canadian way of living," Mr Thampi says. "We didn't lose our traditional values, of course. But our lives, our perceptions of ourselves, changed in this country. Viji so loved it. We had all kinds of friends here, not just Indians. She adjusted to this life enthusiastically."

This determined responsiveness to Canada is what distinguishes the Thampis from many Indian-born couples. In this community, most had chosen to forget why it was that they had left the old country. This was where the "new life" meant savings accounts and money market funds and real estate investments — external signs of success — but not a porousness of spirit. Westernization of the soul was to be guarded against.

The Thampis appeared conspicuously acculturated. The community sensed the Thampis' growth and change. The men noticed, for instance, that Viji didn't shrink from handshakes as their own wives did. Wives did go out to work in this community, but it was usually for defineable goals: reducing the mortgage, building a college nest-egg — not spirited self-reliance.

The first months couldn't have been happier. Then Vijaya became restless. *The Price Is Right* lost its charm. She had too much time to experiment with recipes. She wanted to do something. Her husband advised her to go back to school, but no, she felt she wasn't the bookish type.

"Try *Bharat Natyam*," he said. There were excellent teenaged dance instructors in Mississauga and Rexdale. No, she said, she couldn't practise Indian dance in an apartment without getting complaints from the tenants below.

"I want to go and get myself a job," she said. "I bet I could get a job."

Vern Thampi didn't doubt that she could. Her English, he felt, was more fluent, more Canadian, than his. She was an adaptable Indian wife; she had applied her adaptability to learning Canadian English. But at first he couldn't take it seriously. "You want to waitress at a McDonald's or a Burger King?" He didn't quite like the idea of his wife working outside the home.

"What if I did? Would that bother you?"

He pretended it wouldn't, and the next thing he knew she had gotten herself a job at McDonald's. The community disapproved of a respectable married woman running around in a McDonald's uniform wiping tabletops and tidying up garbage. But Mr Thampi backed his wife fully. For four months she worked part time and banked her money. Then she quit, because she knew that waiting tables didn't really amount to being a new woman.

Keen to improve herself, Vijaya enrolled in secretarial courses at Seneca College. She was an excellent student, better than most others in the class, and she was competitive. After dinner, she would ask her husband to dictate letters so she could work on her shorthand. Her excellence scared her. When she was through with the courses, she felt she had to decide between looking for a serious job and having a baby. The Thampis decided on having the baby.

Their daughter, Nisha, was born in 1979. "Life was getting a little bit easier," is how Vern Thampi remembers that time. "And the money was building."

He worked at the time in the *Globe's* Circulation Department. His was a high-pressure, but satisfying, job. A diligent provider, he put in ten- and twelve-hour shifts while Vijaya looked after the baby and the home. But it was hard for the young mother to bring up an infant without help from devoted and experienced women relatives. She especially missed being fussed over by her mother-in-law. She took baby Nisha to Bombay for three months. Most of that three-month period Vijaya spent with Venu's family, who cooed over Nisha, an adorable baby in adorable baby clothes, and admired the new self-reliant person that Vijaya herself seemed to have become. Her picture in a McDonald's uniform became part of family lore. Her own family she avoided as much as she could; they were quick to find fault, slow to show affection and annoyed by her Canadian ways.

When Nisha was not quite two, Vijaya announced her plans to work full time. She told her husband that she meant to check for vacancies at the offices of the *Globe*. Mr Thampi wanted his once shy and diffident wife to keep growing and becoming her own person. But he wished she wouldn't do her growing at the *Globe*. He did not want her to discover the tensions he faced every day. "She liked to think of me as a strong, fearless man. She believed that my career went straight up, that it had no downs. In our community, everybody talks about the ups and nobody talks about the downs. She didn't know there were both."

Within days Vijaya Thampi found herself a full-time job at the *Globe*'s afternoon competitor, the *Star*. She began in Circulation, taking calls, sending out the route-men. She found a good babysitter. She loved her job at the *Star*; it fulfilled her in new ways. After a few months, she enrolled in management courses at Seneca College; soon she was brought into the personnel offices as an assistant. She'd been in Canada five years, and had already become a superwoman.

"She was so thrilled about going to work every morning," Mr Thampi would reminisce later. "It was as though she'd found a new meaning in her life. She used to be the traditional, submissive, obedient Indian girl, but then she blossomed. She started to believe in herself. Her self-confidence gave me great satisfaction. Because you know how it so often is with our people: the husband dies and the widow is totally dependent because she's never had to make decisions or deal with the real world."

Viji's ballooning self-confidence meant that she was no longer reluctant to disagree with Vern and to speak her mind. In this community, where most marriages are still arranged by parents and where the wife looks up, and gives in, to her husband, where a word like "love match" is salacious, suggesting heartache and lack of control, the Thampis' relationship — their squabbling and their sweet making-ups — seemed too Canadian. In their community, even the word "relationship" itself was troubling and alien.

"Yes, we quarrelled sometimes. Never in front of Nisha. But we quarrelled. There were days when we didn't speak to each other. But we never let a quarrel last through a Saturday. If we were still mad at each other on Saturday morning, we'd fix Nisha her breakfast, and then we'd say, 'Let's go upstairs and talk,' and we'd go upstairs to our bedroom and we'd make up and everything would be back to perfect.

"We didn't have anything much to fight about. I'm very good with money. I had my priorities. I used to say that first we have to pay off the mortgage and put aside money for Nisha's private school. Nisha must go to a private school. She's in French immersion right now, she's totally bilingual, she has her mother's gift for languages. I used to say that by the time Nisha's ready to start school we must bring the mortgage down to $30,000. And Viji would say, 'Let's go on a vacation.' She didn't have my head for money. She'd grab money from me for her TTC fare, for dresses. I didn't mind, of course. I think it is very important to dress well. You have to dress right for work. She had a terrific wardrobe, business suits, dresses, *salwar-kameez* combinations ...we really enjoyed life!"

In her sharp clothes, Vijaya attracted attention, not all of it wholesome. One evening, on her way home from work, she got off the bus at Steeles Avenue and was whistled at by cruising teenagers. The whistling and catcalling frightened her, and she burst into tears. After that incident, Vern always met her at the bus stop, and when he was travelling, he arranged with a friend to meet her and drive her home.

In 1985, before Vijaya Thampi made an impulsive decision

to visit her parents, the Thampis were doing very well. They had bought a house in a brand-new development just north of the 401 Highway, a little east of the city, for $100,000 two years before. They had saved the $25,000 for the down-payment in the four years since marrying, another $8,000 thousand had come from federal and provincial incentives. Their double-income was going entirely into the house, even as its value sky-rocketed.

"We were doing great. We had the house. We had Nisha. Viji was coming up so fast. She wanted to get into personnel management. She loved her work and her colleagues at the *Star*. For that matter I loved my work, too. Life isn't always roses, but I never had problems. I am the only East Indian in that position, and I go all over the country, Calgary, everywhere, representing the *Globe and Mail*, and I make my presentations. I face these guys in these new places and I say that, all right, I have my accent, but that they have to put up with it. As long as I'm in command they have to try and understand what I say. Viji used to get so anxious for me. One time she came to my presentation — she told my assistant that she wanted to see how I do it — she came to the presentation and she was so proud of me. We weren't just traditional husband and wife, like other couples in the community. We had a relationship. A real relationship."

Then, out of the blue, Vijaya made up her mind to go by herself to India for four or five weeks. She wanted to confront her parents, force them to see how far she had come in life, and she wanted to make peace with them.

Mr Thampi tried his best to talk her into delaying the trip for a year or a year and a half. "Let's wait until all three of us can go," he pleaded. "Let's not waste so much money on a trip now. Let's use the money more efficiently."

But Vijaya Thampi, no longer the meek, shy girl she used to be, would not listen. She said, "I can pay for the trip without your help. I have my own savings."

The spiritedness hardened into stubbornness. "It was as though she was driven," Mr Thampi would reflect later. "And the main reason that I didn't want her to go was not the money;

it was superstition. I didn't want to rock the boat when life was going so great for us."

The Thampis quarrelled long and hard over her going. Finally, Mr Thampi gave in. "Okay, go if you feel you have to," he said, "but don't expect me to help you with your gift shopping."

"Okay," Vijaya snapped back at him. "You don't have to help me."

She called a travel agent and settled on a date: June 15th, a Saturday.

"Good," Mr Thampi said. "I'd like you to be back in time for Nisha's birthday." Nisha's birthday was on July 29th.

"I'll be back in time," Vijaya said.

"Aren't you forgetting something?" he asked.

"I know what you're thinking," she said, laughing. "Our tenth anniversary." So she rescheduled her flight. Her new departure date was June 22nd, another Saturday.

Every weekend Vijaya took the family car and drove off to the block of Indian shops and restaurants on Gerrard Street. No Indian-born Canadian goes back to the hometown without bringing a Samsonite bag filled with gifts. People have been known to stuff suitcases with personal computers, colour televisions and VCRs, as well as small items like transistor radios, steam irons, blenders, hair dryers, pocket calculators, watches, gold jewellery, and, of course, Japanese chiffon saris. The stores on Gerrard Street carry 220-volt appliances, and the right valued-in-India brand names. To bring back a bagful of gifts is to prove to the people left behind that, in terms of dollars and cents, immigration has been more than worth it. And, even more than that, it is to prove that the gift giver hasn't forgotten his or her Indianness.

Vijaya Thampi went into a frenzy of gift buying. She bought for all her relatives. She bought for all the servants. She bought for all the children of all the servants.

Friends watched in awe as she shopped. The Ramaswamys, who had once lent the Thampis their new Parisienne so they could vacation at Daytona Beach, told him to reconsider and help her with her Gerrard Street shopping on weekends. But

Vern Thampi remained hurt and angry. "She wants to shop, so let her shop," he told the Ramaswamys. "She has the car. She has enough money. She can do what she wants. She knows I don't want her to make this trip."

His pigheadedness in their last weeks together would bewilder him later. "I don't know why I didn't help her," he would say, weeping. "We used to do all our shopping together. Every Thursday we used to buy something for ourselves and something for Nishi. But the gifts — I didn't even look at the stuff she bought on Gerrard Street."

A few nights before she was to leave, she finally asked him for help. She couldn't pack what she had bought into two suitcases. They were huge suitcases, but not huge enough for all the things she wanted to take back for her family in India.

Mr Thampi surveyed the luggage. "How are you going to haul such heavy bags?" he demanded.

Vijaya Thampi started to fill a third suitcase.

"How are you going to get all this through Indian Customs?"

"I bet the Customs people still remember you," Vijaya retorted. "Anyway, it's not your worry."

The Ramaswamys' teenaged daughter, Janaki, was to take the same flight as Vijaya, so Vijaya decided that, since Air India allowed only two bags per passenger, she would ask Janaki to check in the third suitcase. It was a very neighbourly community in that way, and to Janaki, Vijaya — so young, still, but married and a mother and working at the *Star* — was a bit of a role model.

On Sunday, June 16, Mr Thampi's brother and his wife came over for dinner. The brother brought along his movie camera. He'd never taken pictures of the Thampis' new house, and he thought that Vijaya could carry the film back and show it to Mrs Thampi, Sr., in Bombay. He got his camera rolling. He caught the family walking around the big, comfortable house, sprawling on the expensive sofa, cooking in the hi-tech kitchen. Vijaya made a batch of *chapati* bread while the camera rolled. Then she looked straight into the camera and spoke for almost half an hour. That night the Thampi brothers and their families had their dinner outdoors. The dinner, too, is on film. Mr Thampi is grateful that the film didn't get sent back with Vijaya. He has the film now. At least he has that film.

On June 18, Mr Thampi arranged his last "surprise" for his wife. He told Vijaya that they were to meet with the principal of a private school for Nisha, but instead he whisked her off to an expensive French restaurant. She loved going to dances and eating out in gourmet places. When she realized that he had planned a special night for their tenth anniversary, she hugged him tightly. "May you plan many more surprise anniversaries!" she kept saying.

On Saturday, June 22nd, Vijaya dressed all in white for the trip to Bombay. Vern Thampi was stunned by her beauty and elegance. "Don't go, Viji," he begged her. On the way to the airport to drop her off, he lost his way. She laughed at him. "You just don't want me to leave you," she said.

The area around the Air India counter at the airport was loud with giggling children. Nisha and her two cousins raced each other. Janaki Ramaswamy checked in Vijaya's extra suitcase. Friends swirled around the Thampis and the Ramaswamys. A Hindu woman said to Vijaya, "Why are you wearing all white?" White is the colour for widows. Vern Thampi ignored the woman's question. But he noticed that his wife had taken off her *mangal sutra* (a necklace that married women from his village don't take off until they're widowed). She said the gold and black beads were in her purse, but that she'd wear it for his family when she got off in Bombay.

One of Vijaya's cousin's ran up to Vijaya. "Auntie," the boy said, "please don't go. Nobody wants you to go."

"Come on, you guys," Vijaya joked, "don't give me a hard time. Don't make it so tough on me."

All too soon it was time to go through security. She kissed little Nisha. "You must look after Daddy for me," she said. "Don't leave him alone."

To her husband, she said, "I'll worry about you not eating enough. Please don't eat junk food. I've made a whole week of lasagna for you. It's in the freezer. Just put the lasagna in the microwave. And if you can't do that, then go over to your brother's place. I'll worry about you."

And then she walked through security's metal arches.

Hinduism and its theory of reincarnation does not give Vern Thampi solace. He sighs. He weeps quietly. "God is unfair," he says. "Even God didn't prevent the incident."

His daughter is his whole life now. His real job is that of being a single parent. Five weeks after Vijaya's death, he made a party for two for Nisha's birthday. He got a cake and candles. On her birthday Nisha asked her father a riddle. "How do you get to heaven, Daddy?"

"I don't know, Nishi," he said. "How do you get to heaven?"

"You take an Air India plane, Daddy."

For a while Nisha had nightmares about crashing planes. Now she thinks that if she and her father look happy, then *ammah* will see them from heaven where she is and be happy herself. She doesn't want *ammah* ever to cry. And because *ammah* told her never to fight, she doesn't intend to fight the men who put a bomb inside her *ammah's* plane. She forgives those men.

Mr Thampi twists and twists in his grief. "I can't pardon the men who did it," he says now. "I know there are good Sikhs, of course. But I tell you, I feel not too thrilled to see a turbaned guy. I hope I don't ever find myself in a situation where a Sikh needs my help, because I may not be able to give it."

"I want the crash properly investigated," he says. "I am not saying this out of revenge," he goes on. "Revenge isn't the solution. But did Viji die because some man made her disappear like an exterminator working on pests?"

Vern Thampi looks after his six-year-old daughter, and she, in turn, looks after him, just as *ammah* had instructed. "My ambition is to be a responsible parent. I want Nisha to know what a great woman her mother was, how much she made of her life." So Nishi will know and remember and learn from

Vijaya, he has edited the home movie that his brother made that last Sunday when the family was whole and the present was perfect.

PART FOUR

CHAPTER 1

On June 24, 1985, even as pathologists were beginning to work on the bodies, crash investigators from Canada, Britain, India, the United States and Ireland concluded among themselves that a bomb, somehow carried on board the *Emperor Kanishka* and concealed in its nose or cockpit, had caused the catastrophe. What they needed to find most urgently was Flight 182's "black box" — consisting of a Fairchild A100 Cockpit Voice Recorder (CVR), and a Lockheed 209E Digital Flight Data Recorder (DFDR) — which was housed in a spherical unit in the aft pressure bulkhead. Both the CVR and the DFDR were fitted with Dukane underwater acoustic beacons, so that in the case of emergency situations at sea, they could be counted on to send out signals for up to four weeks.

The wreckage, the investigators decided, had to have come to rest on a continental shelf 6,000 to 7,000 feet below sea level. Retrieval of the wreckage from such depths would make history. It was a project to excite both government air safety board researchers and keenly competitive salvage firms.

The excitement at the uniqueness of the salvage operation and the frustration with the limits of available technology were underscored by Gerry McCabe, the Irish investigator at the scene, and by Art Laflamme, Senior Aviation Accident Investigator of the Canadian Aviation Safety Board (CASB). They did not want the media to generate melodramatic hopes about the salvors' capacity to retrieve the wreckage. And, they warned, even if the black box was recovered, it was not guaranteed to yield satisfactory explanations.

In the first panicky days after the crash, the researchers worried publicly about ocean currents that might force the debris to drift out of the reach of salvage operations, and about the porous ocean bed, which might totally entomb the aircraft parts.

The Indian government, which had the primary responsibility for, and the authority over, the retrieval of Air India property in international waters, initially hired a British firm, Gardiner Surveys, to find the black box. Gardiner Surveys dispatched to the wreck site a survey ship, the *Gardiner Locator*, which had impressive experience of salvaging in depths of about 1,000 metres. The company seemed very confident that it could locate and bring up the black box. The survey ship was expected first to locate the exact position of the recorders through sonar soundings and then to lease a remote-controlled mini-submersible to haul the recorders to the surface.

While the *Gardiner Locator* sailed towards the site, floating wreckage — suitcases, seats, doors, part of a wing, cabin fittings, a Cabbage Patch doll, a teddy bear — came to rest by Irish and Welsh shores or were plucked out of the sea by the alert crews of Irish patrol boats.

The recovered fragments were rushed — under police escort because neither the Indian government nor the Canadian government ever really doubted that they were investigating a criminal misadventure — to O'Driscoll's Boatyard near the drowsy little village of Calligalin, about three miles from Cork. In the boatyard, the pieces, the biggest of which was no larger than 1.8 metres by 2.4 metres, were tagged and numbered with the same grim meticulousness as the recovered bodies in Cork. Then the multinational team of crash investigators scrutinized them for signs of mechanical defects and metal fatigue and, more importantly, for the scratches and fractures that might reveal the in-flight presence of explosives.

From the start, Dr V. Ramachandran, a high-ranking Indian naval officer, co-ordinated the separate and complex aspects of the salvage operation. The recovery of the black box was assigned to Canada. The salvage was a technologically sophisticated and very expensive project, which eventually cost the Canadian government nearly $20 million.

The Canadian team enlisted the help of a hydrophone, two

SCARABs (the name stands for Submerged Craft Assisting Repair and Burial) and several vessels, especially the Canadian Coast Guard ship, *John Cabot*, and the Irish Navy corvette, the *Aoife*, in a race to find the black box before the weak signals it was emitting gave out.

The private firm, Gardiner Surveys, saw itself in direct competition with the official Canadian investigators and the salvage teams that Canada had hired. There were accusations of weak Indian leadership, and counteraccusations of self-promotion. Within the first three weeks of the frantic search for the black box, India replaced its co-ordinator in Cork, and Gardiner Surveys pulled out.

Meanwhile, representatives from six countries hunted for the black box. The initial five who were directly involved had been joined by France when the French cable-laying vessel, the *Leon Thevenin*, was brought into the search. The *Leon Thevenin* housed SCARAB 1, a remarkable submersible without which verifiable data on the cause of the crash would have been lost forever.

The story of SCARAB 1 is the heady story of pioneering technology. It was designed by an American firm to assist in the laying and repairing of underwater cables as deep down as one nautical mile. Though its beginnings were prosaic, in the first two weeks of July 1985 this 3,000-kilo submersible bristling with clawed arms and looking like a prehistoric beetle that had strayed off the sets of a Space Age horror movie, had captured the popular imagination.

The SCARAB cost $5 million, and was owned by an international consortium that included AT&T and Teleglobe Canada. It was leased by the Flight 182 salvage team to survey the ocean bed, map the site of the crash, photograph the wreckage and retrieve selected targets. The SCARAB was equipped with sonar, two TV cameras with zooms and one 35-mm still camera. It was also fitted with intense lights that lit up the ocean as it glided along the firm, sandy seabed on its skids.

SCARAB 1, attached to the mother-ship by a cable three kilometres long, was dropped off the side of the deck, then controlled by an operator on the mother-ship. Working on a grid pattern, it mapped the site and sent back film to be analysed and interpreted by experts on the deck of the *Leon Thevenin*.

On two separate trips to the ocean bed on July 10, SCARAB 1 located and retrieved with its mechanical claws the Cockpit Voice Recorder and the Digital Flight Data Recorder. Marine salvaging history had been made.

The Indian co-ordinator in Cork took possession of the flight recorders and dispatched them at once to India for analysis. The flight recorders might yield valuable confirmation of the weeks-long rumours of a terrorist bomb. The Indian government, fearful of communal riots if information contained in the flight recorders fell prematurely into public hands, and fearful of lawsuits citing negligence, controlled access to what the SCARAB had so astonishingly recovered from nearly 2,000 metres below sea level.

India's decision to strictly limit access to the tapes disturbed many members of the multinational crash investigation team. The British complained bitterly that India had imperiously excluded them the moment the black box had been found. And, in a pale show of neocolonialism (which the Indian government resented), Britain complained that the Bhabha Atomic Research Centre (BARC) in India did not have the equipment or the expertise to assess the material they had found.

"This isn't the first time that we have analysed flight data recorders," snapped H. S. Khola, on behalf of the Indian government.

It was left to Ambassador Kiran Doshi to establish with firmness and civility the primacy of India's jurisdiction over the tapes. "Our people seem to be absolutely confident that we have the capacity to conduct this investigation," he told journalists. But privately he showed less patience with the arrogance of some Britons.

In Montreal, the International Civil Aviation Organization (ICAO) clarified that the Indian government was required by international law to conduct an inquiry into the crash of Flight 182, and that under Annex 13 of the Convention on Civil Aviation it could invite another country to aid in the process of investigation. Because of the large numbers of Canadian

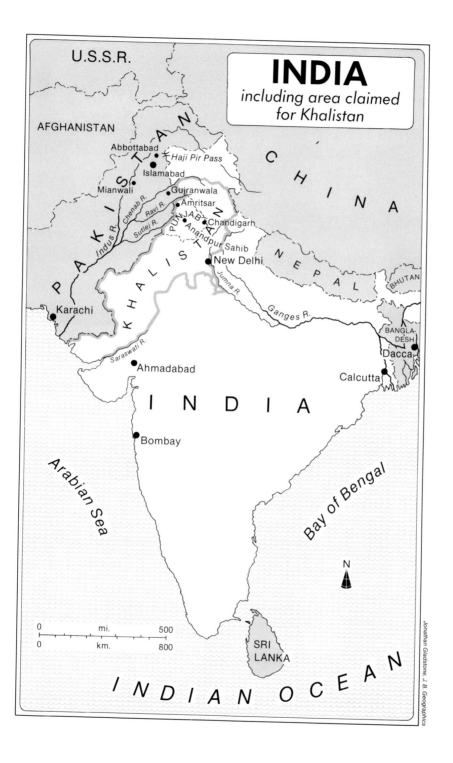

INDIA
*including area claimed
for Khalistan*

U.S.S.R.

AFGHANISTAN

Abbottabad
Haji Pir Pass
Islamabad
Mianwali
Gujranwala
Amritsar
PUNJAB
Chandigarh
Anandpur Sahib
New Delhi

PAKISTAN

CHINA

NEPAL

BHUTAN

Indus R.
Chenab R.
Ravi R.
Sutlej R.
Jumna R.
Ganges R.

KHALISTAN

Karachi

Saraswati R.

Ahmadabad

BANGLA-DESH

Dacca

Calcutta

INDIA

Bombay

Arabian Sea

Bay of Bengal

N

SRI
LANKA

INDIAN OCEAN

| 0 | mi. | 500 |
| 0 | km. | 800 |

Krithika (left) and Shyamala (right) Laurence.

Mr. Sam Swaminathan and
Mrs. Indira Swaminathan with
their daughter Ramya (left),
son Anand, and daughter
Padma (right).

Vern and Vijaya Thampi and their
daughter Nisha.

Mr and Mrs Thampi.

Mr Parkash Bedi and Mrs Saroj Bedi with their son Jatin and daughter Anu.

SCARAB, an underwater robot, used during the investigation to retrieve the black box recorder from the crashed jumbo jet.

A door from Flight 182 floating in the sea off the Irish coast.

Photographs taken from the robot submersible a year after the crash. The plane's galley (top) and a section of seats still attached to a piece of the floor are visible, more than 6,500 feet below the ocean's surface.

The First Officer's seat and a piece of luggage both rest on the ocean's floor.

Wreckage of Flight 182, photographed by the submersible during the investigation into the crash.

The Air India memorial in Dunmanus Bay, Ireland.

Detail from the memorial.

Dunmanus Bay, Ireland.

citizens who died in the crash, Canada had a right to request to be allowed a role in the mandatory investigation.

In the end, the Indian government set up a one-man commission of inquiry, which came to be known as the Kirpal Commission. The Honourable Mr Justice Bhupinder Nath Kirpal's commission held its first pre-hearing on September 16, 1985 in India. Canada was given "participant status." The governments of Ireland and the United States and the government of India were also given "participant status." Because of the bomb explosion that had occurred in Tokyo's Narita Airport and that explosion's likely link with the *Kanishka* disaster, the government of Japan was assigned "observer status." The British government was not invited to participate.

Through June and July of 1985, investigators and the crew of search vessels located and retrieved the wreckage at the bottom of the North Atlantic, interpreted the tapes, retrieved selected parts of the wreckage, examined them in Cork, then sent them on to Bombay to the Floating Wreckage Structures Group for more tests.

From mid-July to mid-October, a second SCARAB operating from the Canadian Coast Guard ship, the *John Cabot*, videotaped and photographed the broken *Emperor Kanishka* on the ocean floor, making available about fifty videotapes and three thousand still photographs to the Kirpal Commission.

The entire search and retrieval operation revolutionized the conduct of all such future inquiries. For the first time, surface-based investigators had remote "eyes" enabling them to preselect only those fragments determined to be of forensic importance. At these examinations, other interested parties, such as V. J. Clancy, Boeing's aviation explosives expert, came to the same conclusion that Laflamme had: while no absolute proof of an in-flight explosion could be obtained, circumstantial evidence pointed strongly to it and certainly eliminated natural causes, such as lightning, or mechanical failure, such as faulty doors and metal fatigue. By such elimination, the conclusion that a bomb had caused the disaster, despite the lack of evidence of a bomb, was able to be officially sustained by the Kirpal Commission in India.

Retrieved segments of the fuselage, including doors 2R and 2L, a 35-inch piece of floor stanchion, lower skin panel from the forward cargo area, a foam-backed floor panel riddled with perforations, a peppered forward cargo door, scorch marks on the right wing root fillet, all bore damage marks suggestive of an explosion. The pitting and the punctures, the outward petalling around the punctures, the curling of metal flaps and lips, the fractures (which had a reverse slant) with spiked edges, the recovery of several hundred minuscule and moderately sized fragments of nonbrittle aluminium, all suggested that a bomb had gone off.

The Canadian Aviation Safety Board showed interest in an upper deck storage cabinet from the left side of the aircraft. Ironically, in the midst of such dramatically torn and twisted fragments, the interest focused on a large, gentle dent in the bottom inboard edge of this retrieved cabinet. The roundedness of the deformation seemed compatible, to the CASB, with "the spherical front of an explosive shock wave generated below the cabin floor and inboard from the cabinet." What the investigators sought were unusual modes of failure.

Boeing's V. J. Clancy observed about a retrieved segment of lower skin panel from the forward cargo area (called Target 362/396): "There were about twenty holes in the lower skin panel, clearly resulting from penetration from inside. In addition to the fact that perforation was from inside, there were certain features which suggested that they were made by high velocity fragments such as those produced by an explosion." The metal around the holes petalled outward and had toothed or spiked edges, but the petals themselves were free of scratches. One of these holes, identified by investigators as #14, looked like a "bullet hole," and clearly resembled holes punched out by high-velocity missiles.

At the request of the Kirpal Commission, this segment of lower skin panel, and other retrieved wreckage, were subjected to metallurgical tests at the Explosives Research and Development Laboratory in Pune, India, on November 30 and December 1, 1985. The researchers used plastic explosive (PEKI) and varying combinations of TNT and plastic explosive to simulate explosive damage. The amount of explosives varied from 60 grams to 100 grams. For experiments on damage to stanchion tubes, the researchers varied the quantity of explosives from 5 grams to 50 grams.

The experiments conducted at the Explosives Research and Development Lab confirmed that certain damage features — for instance, "twinning" of metal (which the Kirpal Report defines as "parallel lines or cracks cutting across the crystal"), and "pitting" or "peppering" of metal surfaces so that tiny craters with rolled-over lips are formed — are uniquely produced by explosives detonated at very high velocity (8000 metres per second, or more). Twinning and pitting — the proof of explosion — were discovered on the fuselage side that contained the 2R Entry door (Target 399) and on the lower skin panel section (Target 362/396), which was immediately below Target 399.

The metallurgical tests carried out in Pune also showed that in Zone E (the rearmost section of the plane) the underside of the floor of a retrieved segment which contained right-section double seats from rows 46, 47 and 48 F and G (Target 117) appeared to have been penetrated by shrapnel. Radiographs of this area did not pick up any metal chips.

The Kirpal Commission in its report dated February 26, 1986, officially concluded, therefore, that "there had been a detonation of an explosive device on the *Kanishka* aircraft."

In addition to the metallurgical confirmation of a bomb, there was some circumstantial, but intriguing, evidence. A red suitcase of plastic material with a tattered blue lining was plucked from the floating debris. The tatter-pattern was similar to the tatter-pattern on the lining of a suitcase recovered from a bombed plane in Angola. Plastic retains verifiable traces of explosives in spite of immersion in water.

The CASB's Art Laflamme holds the personal belief that a bomb was placed on board, that it was stowed in the Delhi-exiting cargo compartment that happened, coincidentally, to be very near the electronics bay, and it exploded at a time when the plane was expected to be on the ground in London. (The electronics bay, the first-class cabin area and the cockpit

— a section identified as Target 192 — were heavily damaged; this section was found upside down.) In an ideal world, he said, he would have preferred more exhaustive metallurgical study. He knows, however, that he was part of an investigation that rewrote the book on undersea wreckage retrieval and forensic interpretation.

CHAPTER 2

The last intelligible communication from Air India 182 to the Shannon Control Tower took place at 8:09:58. But the last actual communication was the 5.4 seconds of carrier wave, beginning at 8:14.

A carrier wave is merely unmodulated sound, an open microphone waiting for a voice. At first, it was not clear that the carrier wave had even originated with Flight 182. But after electronic filtering and comparisons with Air India's electronic "signature," the carrier wave was determined to have come from the cockpit, immediately after the initial incident.

No one knows how the microphone was turned on. As explained by the Chief of Shannon Air Control, Desmond Eglinton, "The microphone which created the carrier wave could have been the pilot's headset or it could have come from a hand microphone. If there was an explosion, a microphone could have been knocked from its position; something might have pressed against it and pressed the button, which caused the microphone to become alive."

Those who first listened to the carrier wave in the Shannon tower said, "There was a frightening feeling. We have never had anything like this before."

Early reports, including that in the July 8th cover story in *Maclean's* magazine, assert that the tape ended in a shriek or howl.

When scientists in Britain, Canada and India analysed the tape of the 5.4 seconds of carrier wave, they discovered 5.4 seconds of indecipherable sounds — beginning with an untranscribable "three or four words" according to the analysis by the Accidents Investigation Branch (AIB) of the United Kingdom's

Department of Transport. To the National Research Council
(NRC) of Canada, the series of short intermittent sounds
seemed, at first, to end in a human cry. However, after
subjecting the tape to spectral analysis and to comparisons
with voice imitations, the NRC decided that the sounds lacked
"human pitch harmonics."

Shriek or howl; no human harmonics. Even Desmond Eglinton
wasn't sure. "At the end of that wave, a noise — there was
something I could not know, but something. There was something
there. I could not hear. Other people say it was a screech or a
voice."

Perhaps the important thing is not what's on the tape, but
what the investigation shows about the limits of our knowledge
and our language in confronting unsurvivable disaster. It's
important to honour every attempt to reach out and analyse
the most fleeting bit of evidence. Three separate national
laboratories have studied the tapes exhaustively; three have
looked for and found different things.

And there is another concern. Call it the "Uh-oh" factor,
made famous in NASA's *Challenger* disaster. Two little syllables
can mean millions of dollars in liability, because in the face of
death, consciousness is defined as pain. And the consciousness
of death — or the trace of human pitch harmonics — can spell
political oblivion for anyone who tries to hide it. We keep an
open mind, noting only that Canada and India, the countries
with the most to lose, find no voices, and Britain, involved only
as a contributor to the investigation, initially assumes a voice,
though untranscribable.

Since this is the last communication we have from the plane,
here, in the language of the Canadian Aviation Safety Board's
report, is what the tape contains:

AI 182 was proceeding normally when the cockpit area
microphone detected a sudden loud sound. The sound
continued for 0.6 seconds, and then almost immediately,
the line from the cockpit area microphone to the cockpit
voice recorder at the rear of the pressure cabin was most
probably broken. This was followed by a loss of electrical

power to the recorder. The initial waveform of the cockpit area microphone signal is not consistent with the sharp pressure rise expected with the detonation of an explosive device close to the flight deck, but with the multiplicity of paths by which sound may be conducted from other regions of the aircraft, the possibility that it originated from such a device elsewhere in the aircraft cannot be excluded.

By correlating the oscillograph records of the CVR and the Shannon ATC [Air Traffic Control] VHF [Very high frequency] recording, it was estimated that the unusual sounds recorded on the ATC tape started 1.4 plus-or-minus 0.5 seconds after the start of the sudden sound detected by the cockpit area microphone and lasted inter-mittently for 5.4 seconds. It was felt that the closeness in time of the two noises indicated the 5.4 seconds recorded on the ATC tapes originated from AI 182. The ATC record-ing that followed the cockpit area microphone sounds appeared at first to contain a series of short intermittent sounds.... Irregular signals were observed over the last 0.27 inches of the DFDR (Digital Flight Data Recorder) tape. Laboratory tests indicated that the irregular signals most likely occurred as a result of the recorder being subjected to sharp angular accelerations about the lateral axis of the recorder, causing rapid changes in tape speed over the record head. This equates to an angular acceleration on the recorder about the aircraft's longitudinal axis in a left-wing-down sense. Therefore, these tests indicate that the digital recorder was subjected to a sharp jolt separate from any violent motion of the aircraft.

Inadequate phrases like "sharp jolt" are as unavoidable in this context as "extensive injury" in the pathology reports, or technical terms like "intense vertical loading" (i.e., an explo-sive, upward force) and "sinusoidal buckling" that assault the lay reader in studying the wreckage reports. The sharp jolt alluded to in the previous paragraph could be the explosion itself. Or it could be the sound of the aircraft breaking up in mid-air, the sound of seat-legs buckling, floors pulling from their moorings, wings snapping off, doors tearing and holes stretching around bolts like the stomach buttons on a fat man's shirt. A young aeronautical engineer, reading the report at our request, commented sadly, "A 747 isn't an F-16. It's not designed for stress like that."

A word like "flail," described as the violent tossing of a human body as it is flung "like a leaf" at high altitude and speed from a pressurized environment and subjected to winds as it hurtles to the earth's surface, fracturing every bone in the body, redefines the concept of violence itself.

"Human pitch harmonics" is an eerie concept, another fundamental reinvention in the mini-world of terminal agony.

The Accidents Investigation Branch of the United Kingdom, which confined itself to analysis of the CVR and the Shannon Air Traffic Control (ATC) tapes, was able to compare the CVR tapes with two other taped bomb explosions, one aboard a DC-10 and the other on a B737. The AIB analysis pointed out significant similarities between the sound on the Air India 182 CVR and the sound of explosive decompression on the DC-10.

These are some of the findings of the Accidents Investigation Branch, as summarized in the CASB report:

> ...Knocking sounds were also heard during the transmission. These were initially thought to be due to hand-held microphone vibration, but this was discounted because of the frequency of the sounds. Almost identical sounds were heard on the DC-10 CVR after the explosive decompression had occurred. Their source was not identified. On the DC-10, the pressurization audio warning sounded 2.2 seconds after the decompression. No such warning was identified on the ATC tape [because the microphone itself was affected by the explosion].

The CASB, analysing the AIB analysis, reports:

> The AIB report concluded that the analysis of the CVR and the ATC recordings showed no evidence of a high-

explosive device having been detonated on AI 182. It further states there is strong evidence to suggest a sudden
explosive decompression of undetermined origin occurred.
Although there is no evidence of a high-explosive device,
the possibility cannot be ruled out that a detonation occurred in a location remote from the flight deck and was not
detected on the microphone. However, the AIB report is
of the opinion that the device would have to be small not
to be detected, as it is considered that a large high-
explosive device could not fail to be detected on the CVR.

The AIB report touches on one of the most difficult and
most expensive parts of the investigation. How much explosive
material *does* it take to blow a 747 from the skies at 31,000 feet?
Obviously, this is an experiment that cannot be duplicated
under laboratory conditions. The CASB "regrets" (in the rather
strong diplomatic meaning of the word) the Indian government's "haste" in taking possession of the salvaged fragments.
The only way to determine the size and makeup of the bomb
and its location is to restage the bombing until the pattern and
depth of penetration of explosive particles (the "peppering"
effect) matches the original. There was some fear that India
would not go to such expense.

In the absence of the entire *Emperor Kanishka* (videotaped
and photographed evidence can be misleading, and only
selected targets were retrieved from the bottom of the ocean)
Japanese investigators have worked extensively with the metal
fragments recovered from the Narita baggage room. In that
case, a fairly accurate analysis was made, and the working
hypothesis has to be that the same kind of bomb with the same
explosive strength was used on Flight 182.

But even the AIB does not conclusively identify a bomb as
the cause of the crash. However, the Bhabha Atomic Research
Centre (BARC) of India does, and even attempts to measure
the explosion's distance from the cockpit by an analysis of
sound levels:

Channel 3 of the recording, which corresponded to the
cockpit area microphone, showed the first indication of a

rising audio signal. The signal level rises from the ambient level in the cockpit by about 18.5 decibels in approximately 45 milliseconds. [In terms of absolute sound, this is not an enormous increase. In the standard explanations, 0 decibels is considered the threshold of hearing, 10 decibels is virtual silence and even 70 decibels is loud conversation. The pain-threshold for sound, a jack-hammer, is pegged at about 110 decibels. However, what is important here is the sharpness of the rise, not the loudness of the noise.] The signal starts falling and stabilizes at a level about 10 decibels higher than ambient for about 375 milliseconds. The total duration of the signal is about 460 milliseconds [that is, nearly half a second].

The noise of the CVR was compared with an explosion that caused the crash of an Indian Airlines B737. In this occurrence, the explosive sound recorded on the cockpit area microphone showed a rise time of about 8 milliseconds. It was also determined that the explosion occurred 8 feet from the microphone. The report concluded that the rise time can be used to determine the distance from the cockpit area microphone to the source of an explosion. Hence, the exact location in the aircraft at which the explosion occurred is likely to have been about 40 to 50 feet from the cockpit, judging from the rise time of 45 milliseconds.

BARC concluded that the series of audio bursts on the Shannon ATC tape were most probably generated by the break-up of Air India 182 in mid-air. Analysis of the tapes, then, including those in the black box hauled up from about 6,500 feet, turned out to show relatively little. The suddenness of the event was confirmed, an explosion was identified as probably having taken place in the forward baggage hold, and the sound of a 747 accelerating to its disintegration was heard.

Valuable data, however, was revealed by the correlation of information on a passenger's assigned seating and on the nature and extent of her or his injury. Of course, no one can be sure that passengers actually occupied their assigned seats at the time of the catastrophe. However, it is known from the pathology reports that very few had their seatbelts on when the plane went down. Some may have been walking through zones C, D and E, visiting with friends; some others were freshening up for the transit stop in London. But there wasn't really much unassigned seating for the economy passengers to spill into and fill.

The passengers were crowded into zones C, D and E: 104 adults and 2 infants in C; 84 adults, 1 infant in D; and 105 adults, 3 infants in E. The passengers in the rear end, from zones C through E, especially passengers in zones D and E, suffered very severe injuries. Only 117 bodies were recovered from those three zones — 29 from C, 38 from D and 50 from E. (Wing Commander Dr Ian Hill, a British expert on aviation pathology, categorized the injuries sustained in the initial moments — as opposed to those added in the subsequent break-up or flail — as "mild," "moderate," "severe" and "cata-strophic," and submitted to the Kirpal Commission his finding that 26.8 percent of the passengers had suffered "severe" injuries and that of that 26.8 percent, 10.7 percent — the largest percentage — had been seated in Zone E.)

The first class was almost totally empty. Only one seat was occupied in Zone A, none in Zone B, and seven in the Upper Deck. The bodies of these eight occupants of the *Emperor Kanishka*'s luxury spaces were not found.

Of the bodies that were recovered, 23 bore marks of injury from a vertical force. Most of the bodies with vertical-force injuries were of older passengers seated in the back of the plane. The concentration of the vertical-force injuries in the rear, together with the evidence of damage to the aircraft itself, led one American investigator to conclude that the explosive device had gone off in the aft (rather than in the forward cargo container as cited by the Canadian investigators), and it encouraged Indian investigators to speculate that there might have been *two* bombs, not one.

Thirty children's bodies were recovered — they showed evidence of less severe injuries than the recovered adult bodies. Hypoxia (or oxygen-starvation) and decompression injuries were suffered by passengers seated at the sides, especially on the right side of the plane. Flail injuries showed up on the bodies of seven passengers and one crew member. Of the flail victims — that is, people who had been shot out of the plane prior to hitting the sea — two had been in Zone C, one in Zone D, 5 in Zone E, and the crew member may have been ambulating. Twenty-one passengers, of whom 11 were in Zone E, had their clothes blown off their bodies. The 49 cases of impact injury were very evenly distributed in zones C, D and E. Most significantly, none of the recovered bodies showed burn marks. However, to the aviation pathology experts, the absence of burn marks on the salvaged bodies did not rule out the possibility that the bodies at the bottom of the Irish seas carried evidence of in-flight fire and explosions.

From the pathology reports and from the scattering pattern of the wreckage, investigators concluded that the aft portion had very probably broken off from the forward portion of the aircraft before hitting the water. The forward cargo compartment blew up first, initiating the break-up sequence. The forward cargo door broke horizontally and was badly fractured and frayed. Cabin floors pulled away. Some seat legs buckled badly. Twenty-three passengers were blown right out of their seats, at least sixteen ejected out of the crack in the plane.

The forward portion fell into the water in a localized area about 0.8 miles north of the vertical and horizontal stabilizers, which strongly supports the conclusion that the aft portion separated before striking the water.

The aircraft's tail broke off and spun towards the ocean bed. The aft cargo compartment scattered widely in an east-west direction.

As the forward portion, up to and including the wheel-well area and wings, plunged towards the ocean in one enormous mass, flying debris struck the right side, especially the right wing and stabilizer, and "a heat source," to use the cautious phrase of investigators, scorched the right wing root interior area. The nacelle (or main) strut of the number 3 engine separated from the engine itself.

Major forensic evidence for the exact cause of the crash would have to rely on microscopic study of fragments lifted from over a mile below the water-surface. Never has aircraft wreckage been raised from such depth. That, along with the evidence from pathologists' reports on the bodies, stretched the limits of science. The rest was up to the police.

CHAPTER 3

The killers made one major mistake. In a general sense, they overreached, going for two planes instead of one, overcommitting their manpower and overextending their technical capacity. But the crucial, forensic mistake was in miscalculating the moment of detonation, or in underinsulating the circuitry of the Narita bomb against rough handling or tampering or extreme weather conditions in the baggage hold.

Premature detonation in the confined space of the baggage-transfer area permitted the Japanese police to reconstruct the bomb in its minutest detail. Over two thousand pieces of evidence were gathered, many of them lifted from the bodies of the two murdered handlers. When they were reassembled, police knew of "L. Singh," they knew the size and nature of the bomb and, most important, they knew the serial number of the AM-FM stereo tuner that had contained it. Sanyo Model FMT 611K. It was one of two thousand FMT 611K's that had been shipped to Canada for distribution during its three-year production run from 1979 to 1982. Furthermore, fragments of cardboard packaging and adhesive tape discovered in the blast indicated it had been recently purchased, presumably for this purpose. Japan is the wrong place to commit hi-tech murder.

Eventually, the evidence developed by the Japanese police, when added to the parallel efforts of the RCMP and other police agencies in Canada, would lead investigators to the doors of the chief suspects.

By reconstructing the scene in their own laboratories, using suitcases, tuners and Duralumin containers, and by duplicating the scale and pattern of damage, police in Canada were able to calculate the probable nature and size of the explosive charge.

Then they had to track down the store that had sold the tuner — a matter of dogged police work, under the direction of RCMP Inspector John Hoadley. By trial and error, by process of elimination, two thousand units up to six years old had to be accounted for, but the pool was finite and getting smaller by the day.

The RCMP were operating with a significant advantage: the bomb makers had not anticipated leaving any evidence behind. They probably had not exercised the normal caution of making a "double-blind" purchase using surrogates with fake names. Sooner or later, the RCMP would find what they were looking for: a recently purchased unit without a matching warranty card. As hundreds of dormant receipts were checked in Sanyo's Toronto headquarters and each unit painstakingly accounted for, the police were drawing closer to the one sale and the one customer that held the answer. And finally it happened. A unit matching the description was traced to the Woolworth's outlet in Duncan, British Columbia, and the clerk who had sold the appliance remembered the two Sikhs who'd purchased it and even produced the bill. The name on the bill was "Inderjit Reyat."

The terrorist cell had made several other careless mistakes. They had violated a simple rule of self-preservation: divide responsibilities, separate each step into component parts, assign each duty to a different individual. If everyone is kept ignorant of the overall plan, conspiracy is impossible to prove.

If the suitcase of "L. Singh" had been loaded onto Air India 301 in Narita as planned and if its contents had exploded somewhere over the seas or jungles of Southeast Asia, the worst terrorist act of modern times would likely have gone unpunished. No one would have known about "L. Singh" or about the Sanyo FMT 611K stereo tuner, and no one would have been able to trace its purchase to Inderjit Singh Reyat and the straggly-bearded young Sikh who had accompanied him. His bomb demonstration off Hillcrest Road on June 4, 1985, with Talvinder Singh Parmar and the same young Sikh in attendance would have been viewed as an isolated act, one entry among hundreds in the surveillance logs of the CSIS.

Parmar and his Vancouver cell of the Khalistani Babar Khalsa would not have been implicated. The existence of other Babar Khalsa cells and other conspiracies, including the Montreal cell's attempt to bring down a later Air India flight out of New York, might not have been detected. Pressure would not have been applied to the weakest link in the terrorist chain. The informer would not have come forward.

Even without the solid clue from Japan, however, the CP Air computer contained strong hints of a conspiracy to bring down two Air India planes. Consecutively numbered tickets had been issued to L. and M. Singh to Japan and Toronto, respectively. L. Singh's suitcase had contained a bomb; M. Singh's plane had held a bomb which exploded from the air. Neither man had taken his seat. *By paying for both tickets at the same time, the gentleman in the saffron turban with the salt-and-pepper beard gathered in a fine black mesh had linked two otherwise discrete, but obviously suspicious, events.* From that certainty flowed further recollections of CP Air clerks at Vancouver Airport (Jeannie Adams remembered the "jerk" who had demanded the interlining of his bag to Air India in Toronto) and the uncovering of the series of glitches and blunders in Toronto that permitted a lethal bag to get aboard.

The ticket purchasing in Vancouver stretched the cell's manpower beyond its capacity. The cell had been forced to "borrow" sympathetic outsiders, and one of those outsiders would later turn informer.

There is even suspicion about the saffron-turbaned ticket purchaser and his decision to change the names of the two reserved ticket holders from Jaswand and Mohinderbell to "M." and "L." Singh. Why would he do such a thing? Perhaps he did it out of a sense of bravado, tying what were planned to be spectacular acts of vengeance to the names of the only known fugitives, the failed assassins of Rajiv Gandhi, Lal and Ammand Singh. Secondly, it might have been to throw off the police pursuers: the RCMP had been combing Vancouver for weeks, acting on tips that Lal and Ammand were in the city.

The RCMP and FBI should have been watching Vancouver Airport for any sign of their attempted escape. Perhaps they were watching the ticket lines that day. Perhaps they took a good long look at "M." and "L." Singh and decided they were innocent tourists with unfortunately common names.

In the world of conspiracy and counterconspiracy, every clue has a possible double meaning, every actor a possible secret identity. At least that is the interpretation of Toronto *Globe and Mail* reporter Zuhair Kashmeri, whose provocative thesis is that the Air India crash was either an Indian government operation undertaken to discredit Sikhs or a Sikh operation they were fully aware of and permitted to happen. He claims the ticket purchaser was an Indian government agent (or acting under Indian government control). He claims unnamed police backing for the theory, but offers only one piece of evidence. After the explosions, the suspicious names on the passenger list were announced first by Indian authorities, not by CP Air, Air India or the investigating police. How would they know such a thing unless they had placed them there precisely for this purpose in the first place?

The RCMP has strongly refuted any suggestion of Indian government involvement.

The police case turns on three major breaks. The first is the Japanese contribution, particularly the discovery of the serial number on the Sanyo tuner. The second is the RCMP's tracking down of the purchaser of that same unit, Inderjit Reyat. The third is the contribution of an informer, himself a deeply implicated member of the original planning session, who has named the money-source behind it all.

As it stands now, at least four members of the Vancouver-based terrorist cell are known. The straggly-bearded young Sikh is also known. Very little, in fact, is not known: the problem lies in proving it in court, irrefutably. At $60 million and still counting, the investigation has turned out to be the largest in Canadian history. To lose the case on any kind of technicality would be a political nightmare.

The casual reader of this book or of accounts in the popular press can hardly be blamed for feeling the case is virtually closed. As early as February 1986, the Vancouver journalist Salim Jiwa enraged police forces across Canada by suggesting in his book, *The Death of Air India 182*, that arrests were imminent. He had jumped the gun.

On August 26, 1986, RCMP Commissioner Robert Simmonds stated that charges against "three conspirators" were very close to being laid. He was then on his way to India to "interview" some prisoners — illegal border-crossers from Pakistan — recently taken into custody by Indian police. Presumably, these would be the foot-soldiers, the couriers who had carried the fatal suitcases.

On December 4, 1986, James Kelleher, Solicitor General for Canada, stated to a Parliamentary committee that new evidence would "likely" lead to the filing of criminal charges against those responsible for the bombing. However, he, too, stressed the need for absolute certainty.

But consider the same case from a defendant's perspective.

Making a bomb is a very small crime in stump-blasting British Columbia. For his indiscretion off Hillcrest Road, Reyat has already been convicted and has paid a fine of $2,000. Making a connection between that bomb test of June 4th and the explosion that ripped through Air India 182 on June 23rd could be made to appear, in this era of terror phobia, an act of contemporary Sacco-Vanzettism.

Witnessing a detonation is no crime.

Driving people to the ferry or picking them up at the other end is perfectly innocent.

Purchasing a stereo tuner is no crime, nor is giving it as a gift. Having it explode in Japan three weeks later is a bizarre twist of fate. Not knowing the name of a house guest for whom you have bought such a present seems evasive, perhaps, but it is not illegal.

Picking up tickets and paying for them in cash is rare but no crime. Changing the names of the ticket holders in the process is odd, indeed, but not unheard of.

Requesting that a suitcase be interlined is done all the time.

Acceding to such a request is fairly common. Not claiming one's seat after making such a fuss is suspicious, at most. Even if the lowly courier is finally tracked down in Pakistan or India or Europe (if he's not already dead), he will argue that he had no idea what was in the suitcase.

What is more, there is no hard evidence that "M. Singh's" suitcase (or one that looked like it) on the plane that exploded even contained a bomb. Or — to stretch a legalism — that the bomb in his suitcase was the one that brought down the plane.

Consider a mild deviation from the scenario reconstructed so far: What if there were *two* bombs on Flight 182? How could a cell of single-minded terrorists trust their mission to the blind chance of collective breakdowns of Vancouver, Toronto and Montreal Security. The bag should never have been interlined, the X-ray machine should not have broken down, the PD-4 Sniffer should have detected the bomb and the bag should never have been loaded without a matching passenger coupon.

A "second bomb" theory finds support from a reliable witness. A baggage loader in Toronto who witnessed the "beeping" of the Sniffer caused by the burgundy bag remembers its being stowed in the *rear* bulk cargo hold under the last rows of seats. The full report, as carried on a Canadian Press[*] wire, reads as follows:

> "There was one bag that was big and heavy and burgundy in colour," remembers an Air Canada loader who was watching Burns International Security Services guards check luggage, including interlined bags, for Air India.
>
> The X-ray machine normally used had broken down and a male guard was using a hand-held PD-4 sniffer to check the bags.
>
> "He was scanning this bag and the alarm went off near the handle," the loader told police. "He did this a couple of times and the alarm went off each time....He did it again and again and the alarm went off."
>
> Apparently he did not think much of this as it was only a slight beep and passed the bag through.
>
> The loader told police the bag did not go in a container,

*Reprinted with permission from *The Canadian Press*

the aluminum boxes loaded with baggage and cargo and put in the belly of jumbo jets. Much of Flight 182's cargo compartment was filled with parts from a non-functioning fifth engine being returned to India for repair.

Instead, the burgundy bag was loaded in the small, sloping, bulk cargo hold under the last few rows of seats at the back of the jetliner.

Pathological evidence taken from the bodies, and engineering reports from the wreckage indicate intense vertical loading (upward, explosive force) under the final rows of seats. Wing Commander Dr Ian R. Hill, the British expert on aviation accident pathology, testified to the Kirpal Commission that the largest percentage of most severely injured victims had been seated in Zone E (at the back of the plane). Dr Hill also indicated to the Kirpal Commission that the pattern of injuries had led him to conclude that if a bomb had downed the aircraft, that bomb was more likely to have exploded in the *rear* than in the front cargo compartment.

What, then, do we make of the detailed forensic evidence, considered conclusive, of an "initiating event," a bomb, in the *forward* baggage hold?

One explanation is that there might have been two bombs, one planted on the ground in Toronto while the plane was being loaded with the spare engine parts, and the other one in the burgundy bag, a decoy *intended* for detection. Indeed, if the handler is correct in his recollection, if investigators are correct in their conclusions, there *had* to have been two bombs. One in the rear, and one in the forward baggage compartment.

As always in this case, it is possible to overendow the cell with subtlety. They made mistakes of such magnitude that one immediately suspects outside manipulation, not sheer incompetence. There is always the journalistic temptation (and historic justification) to inflate the story with counter-theories, spies and *agents-provocateurs* until a straightforward tale of amateurish bungling becomes a tangled tale of epic complexity.

We can extend the speculation a further notch. Most

apologists for Khalistan assume that the CP Air and Air India explosions were conscientiously timed for on-ground, relatively "safe" detonation. Passengers should have been off the planes. But is that really supportable? Doesn't that suggest that the cell had more scruples, less sheer hate, than their planning indicates? The Narita blast occurred thirty-three minutes after CP 003 landed (fourteen minutes early). Air India 182 went down off the coast of Ireland with the plane still an hour from London. It had left Montreal an hour and thirty-eight minutes late; it "should" have been in London, but not by a comfortable margin.

The choice of a civilian target eliminates the excuse of bad timing, bad luck or unforeseen delays. Absolute guilt is implicit in the decision. It may be assumed that a commitment was made to inflict maximum pain and grief, and to provoke an Indian government response that would cause popular uprisings in Punjab.

In any event, it is known that the perpetrators had "spotters" on the ground in Toronto. When the plane left Toronto late, they had an opportunity to notify the tower in Montreal that a bomb was aboard, and to force the plane's safe return. They could have gained a propaganda victory by demonstrating their ability to blow up a plane and taking the apparently compassionate decision not to go through with it.

Instead, it is known that the principals in the case were celebrating with pizza in the Sikh temple in Malton early in the morning of June 23rd.

As critics from within the Sikh community have put it, it seems the terrorists were incapable of rational thought, or of weighing right against wrong, or of distinguishing comparative advantage from absolute carnage. They live in a world where violence is confused with righteousness and where past crimes of "Hindus" (meaning Mrs Gandhi's Indian government) are used to justify any kind of retribution. Living twelve thousand miles from the scene has only deepened their resolve.

Only the mastermind knows everything, and nothing ties him, physically, to the scene. Even if he takes the stand, he may argue, as Birk's lawyer, William Kunstler, did in New York, that he may well have harboured murderous thoughts, that if handed a gun he might well have assassinated Rajiv Gandhi or his mother or Giani Zail Singh — but that those were only mad passions of the moment. You can't go to jail for what you're thinking, or if you do, you have a strong case for appeal.

Where, then, is the case? Legally, it is a long way from resolution.

CHAPTER 4

In March 1986, nine months after the crash of the *Emperor Kanishka*, five months after Inderjit Singh Reyat's conviction and fine for unauthorized possession and detonation of explosive material, the RCMP in Vancouver received their next major break. An "informer" — or, more likely, a deeply involved figure who decided to lighten his conscience, perhaps under pressure — came forward with a startling claim: he knew who had financed the sabotage of Flight 182. The name was a shocker: it was that of one of the most prominent Sikhs in the province.

The RCMP did some checking. He had close contacts with Talvinder Singh Parmar, who had been in the woods in Duncan, British Columbia, with Reyat. This man had made no secret of his pro-Khalistan passions. He was one of many in Canada who made available low-cost tapes of the fiery speeches of Jarnail Singh Bhindranwale, the Sikh priest who had died during the Golden Temple invasion. Digging deeper, they found that in 1982–83, a substantial amount was sent from a Toronto bank to the late Harchand Singh Longowal, then leader of the Akali Dal party, to fight Gandhi's Congress (I) party. The Indian government had managed to block Longowal's receipt of the funds.

Then came the connections to Parmar himself. In 1983, while Parmar was in jail in West Germany awaiting possible extradition to India to face two murder charges, he had looked after the financial needs of Parmar's family in British Columbia. He had also visited the West German consulate in Vancouver to attempt to intervene on Parmar's behalf. He seemed to be regarded by both the Sikh community and the Indian consular officials as a man powerful enough, ambitious enough, and implacable enough to lead such an operation. He became the immediate candidate for "key conspirator" status in the blowing up of Flight 182.

We'll call him "Sardar." *Sardar* is a term of respect, and this man with the soft, authoritative voice and the eyes glittery with *khalsa* zeal certainly commands respect. He was born into a Sikh family of lawyers and property owners in West Punjab (now Pakistan) in 1947, a bad year to be a Sikh in a region soon to become officially Muslim. Like so many other prominent figures on both sides in the Khalistan drama, Sardar was born in turmoil, another of India's "Midnight's Children."

His family fled their ancestral city when he was an infant. He grew up a refugee, hearing tales of a lost paradise. He was shaped by the knowledge that a man, no matter how hard working and blameless he might be, could lose his job, his house, even his nation, overnight. A man could lose everything he had worked and saved for, except his Sikh faith. Allegiance to anything but purity leads only to betrayal.

"The state of Punjab means nothing to me," he says. It is a balmy June night in Vancouver. We are sitting in a tastefully decorated, properly "Western-style" livingroom while his children watch "Star Trek" off the kitchen. "What I feel for is Sikh Raj. Sikh Raj is a territory in the brain." A year earlier, Lata Mangeshkar was preparing to sing in Toronto; the nightmare still had not quite happened.

The enforced dislocation in childhood, the schoolboy days as a transient have made him wary of people who aim for middle-class notions of stability and permanence. His family in India thinks of him as a rebel and is embarrassed by the rumours of his involvement in terrorism. They consider him undereducated because he did not finish university.

To Sardar, university education for its own sake means little. Power, strength of character and purity of purpose mean more. Instead of finishing university, he moved to England and worked for a year. Then he went back home, but India seemed to him a sadly corrupt place, where bureaucrats routinely expected and received bribes for issuing import-export licences.

Embittered, the restless young man emigrated to Canada. People remember him in his prebaptized days when he was beardless and without the turban. He admits to having been a "bad Sikh" in those years. But he was smart, and he was resourceful. And he believed in Canada.

"First time I turned on the shower in Canada, hot water came. First time I picked up the telephone, a voice was there. First contract I signed, no bribe was paid. These people can teach us their technology and their honesty," he tells us, "but I have no interest in the drinking and immorality." He asks us how a man can remain pure in such a country — how, for example, even a community newspaper, in printing a page of Punjabi prayers for *Baisakhi* holiday, can run stories of rapes on the opposite page? How even he, with all his will to surmount impurity, found himself reading such filth instead of the prayers?

(We are reminded of the outrage, delivered in trembling sincerity, of an old Sikh gentleman in the audience at the Birk trial in Brooklyn. During a recess he asked us, "Do you know what is the worst thing in all this?" We thought we did, but asked him to tell us. The gravest insult to the *khalsa*, he said, was the fact that Frank Camper's articles on the mercenary training school had appeared in *Penthouse*, where pictures of naked ladies had been placed next to photos of the Golden Temple.)

Canada delivered on all its promises. Sardar's fortune is, or perhaps was, much larger than his father's and his brother's. He married and raised a family. He became a Canadian citizen. To give us a sense of himself — his former self — he tells us how one day he'd found himself in Montreal, delayed at the airport. Rather than waste time, he'd called an associate and bought himself an apartment block, sight-unseen. Now all those visible assets are gone, and he declares himself glad to be rid of them. Glad of the near-bankruptcy that forced their liquidation.

The rumours are, he's spent his money on Khalistan. His own explanation for his financial setbacks turns on the Indian government's having cancelled the visa that allowed him to re-enter the country of his birth. His business had been heavily dependent on access to India. His attitude to India is strangely detached, an anger long turned to advantage. "They closed a door, but a window was opened instead. God provides," he tells us. "It is God's will. All it means is that some Hindu was given my business."

Sardar is the picture of Canada's "ideal" immigrant as he strides through the livingroom wearing his striped rugby jersey, his turban and his ceremonial dagger, and brings us the soft drinks that one of his children has poured into glasses in the hi-tech kitchen. Tonight he is a very correct host. In spite of all the rumours of his terrorist involvement, he is also the loving father babysitting his children. His wife is away on business. He's proud of her independence. For a Sikh male, he reminds us, he is very liberated.

It is a scene of the starkest, most profound irony. The terrorist as family man. We have spent a winter in Toronto interviewing other family men, now widowed and childless, sitting in their vast, empty houses.

"Sometimes I think the end is very near," Sardar says. He looks at us out of implacable eyes. He exudes a ferocity and intensity that intimidate. Sardar works for his God. "God is my provider, I owe nothing to the government of India, nothing even to my father."

There was a time when all the wheeling and dealing required for success excited him. He worked ten hours a day. Now he puts in six-hour days at the office, and spends the rest of the workday planning Khalsa Sikh community projects. He is involved with others in setting up welfare schemes — hospitals, schools, banks — to look after the *khalsa* community. The school will be modelled on Christian fundamentalist schools in the United States.

"Why?" we ask. Because, he explains, every great people — Jews, Mormons, Parsees — have provided for their own, in life and death, sickness and health.

"I go like a computer," he says. "I'm a heartless person. I'm a brain. I am a machine for converting Sikhs. I can be soft-spoken if necessary, and I can be very harsh. I use whatever is necessary. In any society, the *khalsa* must be the controlling group."

We feel he is telling us more than he thinks. The words and gestures together, punctuated by a constantly ringing telephone, add up to the portrait of a man fully in touch with two worlds.

This, then, is a story about a crusader's hatred of infidels. Sardar is a lonely crusader, looking for purity. He feels distanced from a fallen Punjab, and distances himself deliberately from mainstream Canada. Canada is a good place to do business — "to sell products at a profit" — but the society seems to him dope-crazed and sex-distracted. He even distances himself from the showy leaders of the main Vancouver pro-Khalistan groups, none of whom are smart enough, or dedicated enough for him.

"My social life is zero," Sardar says. We are standing in the front hall. It has been nearly three hours since we arrived. He has kept us here, though he senses we are enemies, because we can engage him in ideas. The scene, for all that it is extraordinary in Canada in 1986, is virtually Russian in its intensity, its overtones of zealous commitment to courses of action rooted in piety. If there is a word to describe Sardar, it is Dostoyevskian.

Now the children are anxious to be tucked into bed. "I feel so isolated," he tells us.

It is the isolation of the self-anointed prophet.

CHAPTER 5

We are called at the home of a friend with whom we are staying in Vancouver. Yes, one of the major players in the Sikh drama of the past five years wants to meet with us. But he needs time to think about where. He calls us again. There is a book he wants us to read before we meet, a book he has written on the Khalistan cause. And, mysteriously, within hours, a paperback, more pamphlet than book, appears in our friend's mailbox.

We read the material, and note with interest that the name of the publisher has been whited out. We scratch away the white-out, and the name "Babar Khalsa" re-emerges.

He calls us again. There is an Indian restaurant on Main Street where he expects to be that morning. There is something theatrical, or perhaps melodramatic, in the arrangements. We take a cab to the restaurant.

The restaurant can seat at least fifty diners, but that morning it is empty except for a handsome Sikh in a special black dress-up *damallah* turban and a full, greying beard, sitting at a table in the back, and a short, heavy man behind the cash register. The man in the black turban welcomes us. His English is fluent, his accent very slight. He had spent ten years in Britain, working as a machinist, before immigrating to Vancouver in 1969.

"No tape recorders, please," he says as we settle across from him at the table in the empty restaurant. He takes a large red datebook out of a manila envelope and places it between us. He doesn't open up the datebook; he merely moves it around on the tabletop. It becomes obvious to us that the datebook cannot be opened up, that its pages cannot be flipped through, that it is a tape recorder clumsily disguised to look like an appointment book.

He describes himself as a farmer who grows vegetables just outside Vancouver. He has to be the most elegant Sikh farmer in the province.

The farmer acknowledges that he has worked long and hard to establish a Sikh homeland. This interest in a Sikh homeland led him to support Dr Jagjit Singh Chauhan in early 1981, and to his association with Ganga Singh Dhillon, the man who headed the U.S. chapter of the World Sikh Organization (WSO) in those days, with Talvinder Singh Parmar of British Columbia and with Tara Singh Hayer, the editor of a pro-Khalistani Punjabi-language paper, the *Indo-Canadian Times*.

Parmar, Hayer and this man, we had learned from other sources, had been so close that this man worked out of Hayer's offices and used Hayer's phone to recruit adherents to the Khalistan movement. Hayer had published the pamphlet he had lent us, he said.

The farmer says that in 1981 Hayer picked the name "*Babar Khalsa*" for a small-circulation Punjabi-language paper that lasted through two or three issues before going out of business. Then, suddenly, the name Babar Khalsa came to be associated with a group in India. He denies any connection between the newspaper's name and the Khalistani terrorist organization.

When Dhillon came to Vancouver and organized a pilgrimage trip to Pakistan, the farmer signed up. Along with some other men, he went on the ostensible pilgrimage with Dhillon and Jasbir Singh, the bright and religious young nephew of the slain Khalistani leader, Jarnail Singh Bhindranwale. In Lahore, he says with a smile, the "pilgrims" were entertained by high-level Pakistani police and Defence Ministry officials. The pro-Khalistan "pilgrims" were treated as VIPs.

On this trip, the farmer had been impressed by young Jasbir — he guessed Jasbir to have been twenty-eight in 1985 — who proved his capacity for leadership and his *khalsa* nature. Jasbir was a simple man who believed truly in the Khalistan cause. He and his brother Lakhbir Singh, had been working as labourers in Dubai when Chauhan's group brought them to Britain. The brothers lived in *gurdwaras*, and kept the cause alive.

Dhillon, the tour organizer, the millionaire Washington-based man of the world, had shocked the farmer by his non-*khalsa* conduct. Dhillon is, by now, discredited in the Khalistan cause, though he had initially been one of its top leaders. The farmer believes a good Sikh must never cut his hair, eat *halal* meat, cast lustful glances at another man's wife or touch cocaine, tobacco or liquor. The farmer had liked Jasbir, who, like him, had restricted himself to a vegetarian diet.

In Britain in 1985, Jasbir worked out a plan that would put all expatriate pro-Khalistan leaders on one platform. But the poor young Khalistani had been betrayed. He was arrested and extradited to India, and stuck in a horrible jail cell where he still was.

About Dr Chauhan himself, the putative father of Khalistan, he feels unsure. It disturbs him that Dr Chauhan, after leaving India, had made anti-Indian broadcasts on Pakistan Radio in 1972. That had been a tactical error. But he supports the Khalistan movement that Dr Chauhan started.

We ask the farmer why Dhillon's pilgrims were entertained by high military and police personnel. The farmer smiles a cagey smile. Like other Khalistani leaders we've talked to in Vancouver, Toronto and New York, he hints that until mid-1985 Chauhan's Khalistan movement enjoyed the tolerance and support of the U.S. government, as well as Pakistan's.

The farmer continues his tale of disillusionment and factionalism. He fell out with Hayer over money in 1983, as had Parmar. He doesn't want to talk about that enraging episode. Hayer printed derogatory statements about Parmar and many others in his paper. Parmar, and others, are suing Hayer.

Through August 1985, two months after the Air India crash, the farmer remained close to Parmar. Then the CSIS and the RCMP investigating the bombing started to ask worrisome questions. Alliances shifted. The farmer is no longer an ally of the Babar Khalsa. There are too many factions in Vancouver. Parmar and his Babar Khalsa moved close to the International

Sikh Youth Federation (ISYF), whose spokesman is the burly restaurateur, Manmohan Singh. It is the ISYF, the farmer says, who shot the visiting Punjab cabinet minister Malkiat Singh Sidhu, on a lonely logging road in rural B.C. during the week of our meeting. The Babar Khalsa and the toughs from the ISYF are beating up members of the Khalistan Youth Organization (KYO). His sympathies seem to be closer to the KYO and the WSO. He has stayed close to the KYO.

"Sikhs never lose in battle," he says. "They only lose at the table." He looks and sounds bitter, harassed.

We press him about his relationship with Parmar. He says he had hired two German lawyers for Parmar when Parmar was detained for a year in the West German jail. He asked the lawyers to send him a copy of the conditions under which Parmar was eventually released to Canada, but the lawyers ignored his request. Parmar had been given a one-day permit to travel from Düsseldorf to Frankfurt, and back to Canada. The court decision on Parmar's case was never made public.

Parmar's year in the German jail and the failure of India to obtain his extradition is one of the deeply puzzling mysteries to everyone who has studied the case. Who paid for it, what evidence was presented, what conditions were attached to his release, if any, by India, Canada and Germany? We know that Canadian surveillance of Parmar began upon his return. We know that his militant organizing never abated.

We press the farmer for more details. Had he, for instance, driven the car that took Parmar and the straggly-bearded young man to the ferry on the morning of June 4, 1985, on their way to the meeting with Inderjit Singh Reyat?

The farmer panics.

"My wife told me not to talk to you," he says. He slips his red datebook back into the manila envelope. "I shouldn't have agreed to see you." Then he says, avoiding our gaze, "My lawyer has told me not to say anything more."

We rise to go.

"In Canada, today, we're leaderless," the man says. He looks sorrowful.

We pick up a sweetmeat at the counter. The short, silent cashier rings up fifty cents.

"I got a tip for you," the farmer whispers, his voice low and conspiratorial. "It's a tip that comes straight from Jasbir."

We stop. "Bhindranwale didn't die in the Golden Temple. He got out. He's hiding out somewhere in the area of the Persian Gulf."

"Did you see him?"

The farmer looks embarrassed. "No. That is what Jasbir Singh told me. It is up to you whether to believe or not."

We move towards the exit.

"You didn't ask to see the Khalistan passport!" he shouts, accusingly. "Everybody wants to see passports and currency and maps!"

We leave him holding the manila envelope in one hand, and a passport and colourful bills in the other. The passport and currency are impressive, professional-looking documents. The "Khalistan One" passport is made out to Jarnail Bhindranwale, and his picture is a lurid icon executed in the Indian devotional manner.

We walk outdoors. It is a warm, golden June day, the second anniversary of the Golden Temple invasion, nearly the first anniversary of the Air India crash. The sidewalks are jammed with busy shoppers, nearly all of them Sikh, old folks in full white, mothers in Western clothes, pushing baby strollers.

It is a sight not without its history, even its comedy.

It is a vision out of the "brown tide/yellow hordes" nightmare that the entire North American west coast shared at the turn of the century, and that white British Columbians had fought against with every political and religious and propagandistic device available to them. For fifty years they had prevailed.

In the summer of 1914, white Vancouverites had turned out by the thousands to cheer as the Canadian navy surrounded an old Japanese chartered tub named the *Komagata Maru*, and escorted it out to sea and back to Asia, preventing the landing of 376 would-be immigrants from India's Punjab.

It is a tangled story we'd touched on in today's Vancouver. A peaceful and prosperous Sikh community, one of Canada's oldest ethnic communities, being torn apart by events in a country many of them had never seen.

PART FIVE

When the Air India case finally comes to trial, it will be fraught with legalisms. Names and references will appear exotic, motivations and evidence displayed to Canadian judges will seem downright incomprehensible. Before the case is over we shall, very likely, find that the bombing of the Emperor Kanishka *and the massive loss of Canadian lives is entwined with Canada's immigration policies of the late sixties and early seventies. We shall find that the Air India tragedy was predictable and characteristically "Canadian," given the country's faith in the cultural mosaic and its scorn for an integrated national identity.*

The initial reaction of too many Canadians, especially of government officials, was that the Air India disaster was an Indian post-colonial tragedy in which newly independent peoples try to redraw provincial boundaries. It was a tragedy affecting only Hindus and Sikhs. The victims belonged to a group of Canadian citizenry that Pierre Elliott Trudeau's Liberals had dismissed in the seventies as "the visible minority," a second-class group whom the country had perhaps been foolish to let in. A foreign carrier had crashed off foreign seas. Canada, as a nation, though hugely sympathetic to human distress, seemed to distance itself from guilt by viewing this incident as "their" rather than "our" tragedy.

But the Air India disaster is a Canadian tragedy. The terrorist plot to bomb was conceived and carried out on Canadian soil. The majority of victims were either naturalized citizens or born in this country. Though some bereaved relatives console themselves by locating their individual loss within the design of a Hindu super-fate (whereby a soul discards its human form when its mission in that life is accomplished), our intention is to bear witness to the forces let loose by the policy of multicultural diversity.

CHAPTER 1

Portrait of a Canadian Terrorist

All the organizations in the Khalistani movement slant their appeals to two main groups: the unemployed immigrants and the romantically inclined native-born Canadians. The latter group, who bear a family likeness to the Irish Republicans, Jewish Defenders and Armenian Avengers, contribute very little at present (beyond their parents' money) to the cause. They attend Sikh youth camps in the summer (sponsored by local temples), take rifle-training and listen to fiery sermons from itinerant Khalistani preachers. This is not to say that these idealistic young men and women might not become a force in the future, especially if the movement becomes associated with heroic sacrifice and glamorous martyrdom. Until then, the Khalistan cause in North America is intimately related to the first-generation, unassimilated, Punjabi immigrant experience.

For a period of approximately four years, between 1969 and 1973, Canada experimented with near-open immigration. Foreigners arriving ostensibly as visitors were allowed to file for immigration *after* arriving in Canada. Perhaps the policy was intended to be a humane correction of sixty years of discriminatory practices or, as others have suggested, it may have been a cynical response to the call for cheap labour in the late sixties. Whatever the cause, the result was staggering, as thousands of uneducated, ill-equipped and technologically unemployable young men arrived in Canadian ports as tourists and promptly applied for immigration. Many others never bothered to apply, but simply went underground into their linguistic or ethnic ghettos. Later, they were allowed to bring over family members. Among these immigrants were Sikhs from the villages of Punjab.

Depending on whom one talks to, they were industrious and hard working, simple and pious, looking only for a chance to prove themselves — or illiterate, feudalistic and violence-prone. There is agreement, however, on one very important fact: at the time of their arrival, there was no outstanding political division in Punjab. They may well have arrived with certain predispositions, but their politics were developed entirely in Canada.

What divisions they did know were typical of rivalries from any culture in the world. Rival villages, rival gangs, rival class and religious loyalties. These petty jealousies and enmities were carried to Canada and would later serve to influence their selection of temple, or their membership in various factions of the Khalistan movement. World Sikh Organization, Khalistan Youth, International Sikh Youth Federation, Babar Khalsa, All-India Sikh Students Federation, Dal Khalsa — they shared the goal of independence for the "Sikh Nation," but were originally organized under different leaders, with different styles.

The World Sikh Organization is considered to be slightly more professional than the other Khalistani groups, more open to the educated and aspiring middle class. Khalistan Youth were more moderate, and in fact disbanded in the spring of 1986 out of a refusal to endorse further acts of violence in the name of Khalistan. The ISYF and Babar Khalsa are very close in purpose and in the means by which they achieve their ends; the ISYF is perhaps more secularly political and Babar Khalsa more religiously fundamental, but both are committed to violence.

Competition between these last two groups for influence, recognition and money led to beatings of Sikh moderates and to the assassination attempt against the visiting Punjab Cabinet minister, both by the ISYF, and aborted bomb conspiracies against Air India and the Indian Houses of Parliament by the Babar Khalsa.

No one doubts the sincerity of the young men in leaving Punjab and seeking a better life for themselves in Canada.

They left dreaming of material success. The dream was fed by travel agents who pocketed huge commissions and rehearsed their clients in the litany of customs forms and immigration questions they would be expected to deal with on arrival. Many of those young men found the better life they were looking for. Those with some training and some education have prospered.

Many others, however, have remained untouched by their Canadian experience. They work in Sikh-run shops, they live in near-dormitory conditions and they do not have a hope of gaining meaningful, rewarding employment. Lacking English or skills, they have no contact with mainstream Canadian society. If they have married, their wives are working as maids or cleaning women — an unthinkable occupation for a Jat woman (a woman of the prosperous landowners' caste in the heart of Punjab). If they have children, their children's lives in Canada are beyond their influence. Daughters refuse to marry the groom of their father's choice. They have pressure from home to send for brothers and cousins, to send money to marry off sisters, to provide for aging parents. There is no real Punjab for them to return to. To return as poor as they'd left is intolerable for any immigrant, especially for a proud Jat Sikh male.

They are time-bombs, ripe for conversion.

If persuasive orators in the community successfully appeal to the code of *izzat* and convince the undereducated and underemployed Sikh youth that their honour, their dignity, their manhood, their women's virtue are all in their hands, and that second thoughts are a sign of weakness, that any opponent is the agent of the devil and that death given or death received in the defence of the *khalsa* is noble service and, finally, that lies and denial are justified in the higher service of the faith, then the leaders have created the nucleus of an armed cult.

The situation of the unemployed Sikh in Vancouver or Toronto was hopeless until Khalistan came along. There are no community centres for him, so the only place he can go and feel himself vaguely important is the *gurdwara*. He sees that the "old Sikhs" — those who arrived forty or fifty years ago or who were born here, the ones with shaved beards and short hair and no turbans — are not good Sikhs, as he understands it.

By now, he has fallen under the spell of Bhindranwale, an uneducated villager much like himself, whose sole criterion for judging between good and evil seems to have been the presence or lack of hair.

He sees that when he speaks in the temple, people listen. His earthiness, his uneducated village Punjabi is not an object of derision. He sees that his group is in the majority and could lead if it learned how to organize. He may not have money or influence or cozy connections with the Canadian establishment, but he can at least have some influence in temple politics. He sees that *his* leader, Talvinder Parmar, enters the temple as though he owns it, and takes the front row for himself and his family. Parmar behaves in foreign, frightening Vancouver as though he is in his village. No one has the courage to oppose him.

The old Canadian Sikhs are toothless, he realizes. Push them a little and they back off. The Canadians were never too concerned about ritual, about covering the head, taking off the shoes. They were too busy making it in Canada, proud of their contacts with mainstream businessmen and politicians. They don't think, obsessively, about being good Sikhs. They don't want to look or sound too strange and prejudice their children's chances. Their children are in universities, doing well, marrying outside the *khalsa*.

He sees, for the first time in his life, that he is a better Sikh than most of the Canadians. He has kept his hair, his purity. He sees that the same people who cut their hair and don't wear turbans also laugh at Bhindranwale and at the idea of Khalistan. To him, Khalistan sounds like a great idea, especially if the rich and impure are against it. Khalistan appeals to the dreams of revenge of any embittered, alienated ethnicity. In a pure Sikh state, he would be somebody. Hindus are trying to kill us. Indian agents are sitting among us. Anyone who speaks against Khalistan is an Indian agent, no better than a killer of Sikhs.

He sees how uneasy the old-timers in the temple get when anyone starts talking about Khalistan. Whenever the talk turns to Khalistan he finds that he has something funny or moving to say, it's his only area of expertise. His group applauds him. He sees that his relative power in the temple depends on maintenance of tension. It's in his interest to keep the kettle boiling.

For the first time since he's been in Canada, Khalistan makes him feel he belongs somewhere. Portrait of a terrorist, Canada, in the 1980s.

CHAPTER 2

Punjab

We are looking at a generational phenomenon. A few young Jat Sikh males who emigrated to Canada in the early seventies, and a great many more who stayed behind in the villages of Punjab have been subjected to the same intense pressures, and given voice to much the same nationalist protest, no matter where they live.

But when did this hatred begin? Sikhism and Hinduism are as close as religions can get — not that doctrinal propinquity ever guaranteed political harmony. Punjabi Sikhs and Punjabi Hindus are the same people, separated by an arbitrary line of tonsorial convenience. All ten Sikh gurus were born Hindus. Sikhs and Hindus have fought together bravely and repeatedly against Muslim (mainly Punjabi Muslim) Pakistan.

Most Sikhs agree that the hostility between the Hindu and Sikh communities in the Punjab began seriously in 1951, at the time of the first Government of India Census. The internal map of India was being drawn along linguistic lines. Sikhs speak Punjabi, and write the language in Gurumukhi script. Hindus in the Punjab, who were far more numerous than Sikhs in the Punjab immediately after the Partition, also speak Punjabi, but in order to prevent Punjabi from becoming the official language of the state (which already had Sikh political leadership under the Akali Dal party), they declared their mother tongue to be Hindi. Sikhs saw this as the first blow against their culture, a sign of Hindu perfidy and distrust. For some, a tiny minority, the idea was planted that Sikhs would never truly own the Punjab as long as Hindus, with their 350 million Hindi-speaking brethren at their backs, shared the state.

The dream of a separate Sikh state would not go away. Always in Sikhism is the fear of annihilation, the perception that the *khalsa*'s enemies are bent on nothing less than extermination. In the fifties and up through the elections of 1964, the call for independence was kept alive by Tara Singh, but with diminishing effect. Nevertheless, the "Tara Singh" wing of the ruling Akali Dal party did not perish with the master's death in 1968, as we shall see.

After the war with Pakistan in 1965, in which the Sikhs acquitted themselves with their usual valour (rejecting in the process assurances of an independent Sikh state under Pakistani protection), the official state of Punjab was created, with Punjabi as its language and Chandigarh as its joint-capital (with the neighbouring, Hindu-dominated Haryana). At last, Sikhs were dominant (by 56 percent originally) in their own Punjabi-speaking state. The Akali Dal, the main Sikh party, which had as many factions as the Congress party, was theoretically in a position to dominate state elections. The fact that they have very often failed, even playing on a tilted field (Hindu-majority areas of the old Punjab were whittled away into the separate states of Haryana and Himachal Pradesh), indicates that difficulties lay ahead.

In 1971, while India was waging a successful war against Pakistan over the secession of East Pakistan (now Bangladesh), a little-noticed event was taking place at Nankana Sahib, the birthplace of Sikhism's founder, Guru Nanak, in Pakistani Punjab. A former Cabinet minister in the Punjab legislature, Dr Jagjit Singh Chauhan, announced the birth of the latest incarnation of Sikh independence, this to be called Khalistan. He even made broadcasts for Pakistan in the midst of the war.

He took the dream with him to England, where he has settled, somewhat like Lenin in Zurich, in his "Embassy of Khalistan," to wait out the millennium. From Reading, he has appointed his other ambassadors and shadow Cabinet. His pro-Pakistani, pro-American, anti-Indian and anti-Soviet rhetoric falls on sympathetic ears in Washington. When he visited the United States, his visa request was supported by Senator Jesse Helms. The maps of Khalistan distributed in Vancouver by his "Ambassador to Canada," Surjan Singh Gill, even list the ten appointed leaders. All of this media manipulation was comic opera until events conspired, in the early eighties, to turn Khalistan from one man's dream into a national tragedy.

Inscriptions on the Khalistan map, dated June 8, 1984, read, in part:

> It is the duty of the members of the Government in EXILE to carry on the liberation struggle up to the last ounce of strength in their body. The Hindu imperialists and their henchmen are hell bent on disreputing and destroying the Ministry in EXILE.

> But we have high hopes and our resolve is further strengthened by their antics. We have created a defence committee to intensify the LIBERATION STRUGGLE still further.

The document (a handsomely produced map, generous in its reapportioning of Indian territory to Khalistan) is marked "Approved and released by Govt. of Khalistan, 8 Burgess Court, Fleming Road, Southall, Middlesex."

Khalistanis and moderate Sikhs agree in their assessment of the next major phase of Punjabi history. It should have been a glorious chapter. Instead, it has created chaos.

Nothing prepared the Punjab for the peaceful revolution launched in 1963 by the Nobel Prize winner, Norman Borlaug. His weapon was dwarf wheat, bolstered by fertilizer. By 1967, with full co-operation of the central government's Food Minister, the "green revolution," had caught on in the grain-growing state of Punjab. Production tripled in one generation. And in that same generation, new wealth created new problems, at least for some.

Many educated younger Sikhs trace the rise of religious fundamentalism, which has always been connected with Punjabi nationalism, as a reaction to Punjab's new-found prosperity. Modernization, communications, travel, education — especially education — entrepreneurship, intermarriage, urbanization, secularism: all of these "dangerous" influences have flooded Punjab in the past twenty years.

Statistics begin to tell the tale: the number of secondary schools and colleges in Punjab more than doubled between 1967 and 1981. Statistics also tell another story: in 1971, Sikhs constituted 61 percent of the Punjabi population. A decade later, the figure had dropped to 52 percent and was falling. The "best and the brightest" were fleeing Punjab for education abroad or business opportunities in other parts of India.

The agricultural fieldwork that had been the pride and the calling of Jat Sikhs for centuries has become mechanized or has been relegated to Hindu migrant-workers from neighbouring states. Migrants now do 40 percent of Punjab's agricultural labour. These migrants, most of them necessarily landless, low-caste, Hindi-speaking Hindus, illiterate and desperate for work and resigned to living in abominable conditions, see conversion to Sikhism as an immediate way of improving their prospects. Sikhism, with its doctrines of non-caste openness, never had to confront such a "sinister" Hindu challenge before.

Conversion *to* Sikhism is a hidden threat to the traditional community, perhaps more frightening than attrition from it. Loss, after all, purifies the flock; conversion only adulterates it. The more liberal elements among Sikhs feel that Sikhism could easily be the dominant religion of northern India: it is a simple man's faith with some inspiring visions behind it. Untouchable Hindus, especially, undergo an immediate transformation on accepting baptism. And that, of course, is the problem. Sikhs, despite their doctrines, are no less caste- and colour-conscious than any other Indian religious group (including Indian Christians, Jews and Muslims).

Many thinkers, then, would see the source of Sikh fundamentalism in the internal struggles of traditionalists (that is,
Punjabi-speaking Jat landowners) as they strive to maintain
control of a world they no longer understand. And they recruit
their supporters among the lost, embittered and alienated
young men who have failed to take advantage of Punjab's rapid
development. Moderates see the invasion of the Golden Temple
as an irrelevance — as, at best, a convenient Khalistani
recruitment tool that was made available by Mrs Gandhi's
stupid blunder at the very moment when Khalistani agitation
was dying from its own violent excesses. For them, the Golden
Temple invasion was the Reichstag Fire of the Khalistani
movement. They *needed* it, desperately. If it had not happened,
it would have been invented. Sikhs had been turning away from
fanatics; they had had no interest in returning to a purified
seventeenth century run by illiterates, and dooming themselves, at the time of Punjab's greatest ascendancy, to becoming the Palestinians of India. The Invasion reversed all that.
The tiny minority's view that Hindus were bent on their
extermination was borne out. The *khalsa* turned violent.

An analogy can be made with Iran, where modernization
and prosperity were unequally distributed, and where those
left behind in the rush to Westernization took their revenge in
the name of traditional Islam. The Punjabi Jat claim to speak
for all of Sikhism was threatened on two fronts: modernization
from an impure world and conversion from what was perceived
as an inferior one. In many Punjabi villages, there are now two
gurdwaras and two separate rings of settlement, one for Jats
and the other, contrary to traditional teachings, for *Mazhbis*,
the low-caste converts.

To the world, say the moderates and educated political
analysts, the current crisis may appear to be an Indian civil war
between Punjab and the rest of the country or between Sikhs
and Hindus. To Sikhs it is primarily a *Punjabi* civil war, fought
among classes and generations of Sikhs, to determine the
shape of their future.

Here is where Khalistanis raise strong objections. They
see the invasion of the Golden Temple as the major cause (and

justification) of Sikh militantism. For Khalistanis, the Golden Temple invasion is proof of Hindu intentions to destroy Sikhism. It prejustifies any action against Hindus as an act of collective revenge.

Collective revenge inverts the pyramid of guilt by insisting that the perpetrators are really the victims, and the victims are really to blame. The invasion and the Delhi riots free the young militants from any scruples. The passengers of Flight 182 are not seen as innocent civilians, but as soldiers.

In many Kalistani homes in North America, we have encountered poster-sized, full-colour blow-ups of the Delhi riots: of the still-smouldering bodies of old Sikh men thrown off trains, of street dogs pulling on the arms of children, dead under the rubble of their houses. It is upsetting game-room decor, and it is strange to encounter the posters again in the foyers of Sikh *gurdwaras*. Yet there it is, the call to *shaheedi* (martyrdom) among the expatriate or the suburban North American youth, the need for continual rededication.

The Khalistan movement was already in place, however feebly, by the late 1970s. People of little consequence in their various communities had been appointed "ambassadors" and had tried to drum up support, but had failed for nearly ten years. Chauhan, a tireless traveller, made several organizing trips to Canada and at least one to the United States; reports are that he was laughed from most temples in the late seventies and early eighties, even in cities like Vancouver.

But then things slowly changed. In the early eighties, particularly in 1982-83, the movement was resurrected by money. Khalistani newspapers came into existence. Suddenly, in the ethnic press of Toronto and Vancouver, the normal high rate of violent crime in Punjab was redefined as "commando raids" and "Khalistani agitation." Free-swinging editorials that would have resulted in instant libel suits in the mainstream press were written against members of the community known for their anti-Khalistan views. Khalistani organizations, all of them apparently well funded, proliferated.

These events all predated the Golden Temple invasion, but paralleled the rise of the charismatic Sikh priest, Jarnail Singh Bhindranwale, in Punjab. He was the catalyst, the soldier-priest in the mould of the ancient gurus (as understood by uneducated peasant boys). The phenomenon of Bhindranwale is one of those electrifying events in a region's history that are hardly unique to Punjab or to India but which remain inexplicable in ensuing years. His theology seems devoid of any complication, his politics are muddled (but applicable to all factions) and his strategy seems, on balance, anarchic. He recruited violent young men, set them upon his enemies, encouraged acts of outrageous violence and then retired to the Golden Temple, where he felt his religious status and the temple's sheer majesty would protect him from any secular retribution.

His supporters, wanted for uncountable murders and other crimes, had stockpiled an arsenal inside the Golden Temple, in violation of all outstanding agreements with political and religious authorities in India. Why Mrs Gandhi was so late in acting is an area of intense speculation in India, but when she acted with Operation Blue Star on June 4-7, 1984, there can be no doubt that she intended her act to be an extirpation. The first chapter in the struggle of Khalistan was over, and a new, unforeseen future of violence stretched before the country and the *khalsa* wherever it found itself. That violence would claim the lives of Gandhi and Bhindranwale, the two central players, and thousands more in India. And in Canada, 329 who had thought themselves entirely removed from the politics of their homeland.

Hanging over the tragic history of Bhindranwale and Mrs Gandhi is a narrative worthy of Shakespeare himself. Bhindranwale was originally Mrs Gandhi's creation. She, who could not tolerate any kind of opposition, waged political warfare against even moderate elements in the Akali Dal. Following the advice of her Punjab expert, the Congress party Sikh (and now President of India) Giani Zail Singh, she had unleashed the obscure priest as a means of embarrassing the secular, anti-Congress elements of the Akali Dal.

Theoretically, the strategy makes perfectly good sense. Since the Akali Dal was opposed to the Congress party, any enemy of Akali Dal was a potential friend of Mrs Gandhi's. This form of political tinkering — the "my enemy's enemy is my friend" philosophy — infected Congress (I) party thinking under Mrs Gandhi nearly from the outset.

Back in 1977, "Year One" in the violent phase of the most recent history of the Punjab, Dr Chauhan returned briefly from England and helped organize a hand-picked wing of his own Khalistan movement, to be called Dal Khalsa. In the same year, the thirty-year-old Jarnail Singh was named the fifteenth *sant* (leader) of the religious order of the Damdama Taksal (the honorific "Bhindranwale," indicating the village in which the order is based, was added after the election). He was to succeed Kartar Singh, who died as the result of a motor accident. (The fourteenth *sant* died in hospital rather than allowing his hair to be cut for an operation). Kartar Singh's son, Amrik Singh, became the leader of the All-India Sikh Students Federation (AISSF), the major terrorist organization in Punjab.

Dal Khalsa began contesting for seats against the Akali Dal in Punjabi elections. They lost, but enjoyed the financial support of the Congress (I) party, who did not run candidates against them. Chauhan returned the favour by raising the Khalistan flag from a temple in the city of Anandpur, in March 1980. By June of the same year, the government of Khalistan was proclaimed both in Amritsar (the city of the Golden Temple) and in England, to which Chauhan had beaten his retreat.

By 1981, Akali Dal weakness, Congress (I) meddling, Dal Khalsa and AISSF violence, and Bhindranwale's itinerant preaching had sown the crop of dragon's teeth. The plan to rid Punjab of non-Sikhs had taken the form of street assassination. Punjabi police looked the other way or, in some cases, provided the firearms. The leader of a rival Sikh sect was assassinated and Bhindranwale was named the lead conspirator but was never arrested. The power to do so rested in the hands of Zail Singh, who was then Mrs Gandhi's Home Minister.

For three years, the situation in Punjab was allowed to deteriorate. Bhindranwale and his forces took up residence in the Golden Temple, which became the focus of political as well as criminal activity in the state. The Akali Dal, as Mrs Gandhi had planned, was exposed as ineffective. The next step would have been the removal of the elected state government, on the amply demonstrated grounds of its inability to govern, and the imposition of direct rule from New Delhi.

She never got the chance. Events were moving too quickly. The announced plan of the Akali Dal — by now a tail being wagged by the AISSF dog — to halt all grain shipments from Punjab and to call for a suspension of all taxes paid by Sikhs to the central government goaded Mrs Gandhi into her final action.

On the night of June 4, 1984, she ordered the invasion of the Golden Temple complex. The battle raged until the morning of June 7th, when troops entered the basement of the *Akal Takht*, the administrative headquarters of the Sikh religion, which was part of the complex. Among the bodies discovered were those of Amrik Singh, the chief terrorist; Major-General Shahbeg Singh, the military strategist; and Jarnail Singh Bhindranwale, the would-be messiah, or ayatollah, of Khalistan.

CHAPTER 3

The Foreign Hand

In January 1985, when Birk and Lal Singh met with Frank Camper in the Hilton Hotel in New York City to discuss mercenary training and arms sales, Birk boasted that the Khalistan cause was receiving help from Pakistan and China. This should come as no surprise. Destabilization scenarios make perfect sense: Pakistan and China are India's traditional enemies.

Of China, little evidence exists, apart from some captured weaponry — whatever that means, in the contemporary world of international arms dealing. Pakistan is a different matter.

Pakistan had been in the business of encouraging breakaway factions in Punjab and Kashmir for many years before the announced "birth" of Khalistan in 1972. Both regions are volatile, non-Hindu, adjacent to Pakistan, and may be considered, arguably, as much in the Pakistani sphere of influence as in New Delhi's. Pakistan has offered a haven for several Khalistani leaders from overseas, among them the Canadian ISYF head, Satindrapal Gill. Evidence from trial transcripts in Canada, and Birk's taped transcripts all name Pakistan as the jumping-off point for surreptitious penetration of India. Confessions gained by Indian border police from apprehended Khalistani infiltrators have pinpointed the Pakistani border towns of Gujranwala, Hajipur, Mianwali and Abbottabad as containing Khalistani training camps.

Overseas Indian magazines, such as the London-based *Sandesh*, have reported that Pakistan military assistance to the Khalistani cause was channelled through the Dal Khalsa.

Indian journalist Ahmed Malik has reported that financial assistance was paid through the Zurich branch of the Pakistani Habib Bank, through Pakistani businessmen resident in Britain. All of this makes perfectly good sense — that is, it conforms to one's expectations, or prejudices. Actual figures are not mentioned in these reports, nor are names. In much the same spirit, we have read, or have been told, that "millions of dollars" have been raised in *gurdwaras* in Canada and the United States, allegedly for the relief of Sikh widows and orphans in India. It is assumed that at least some, perhaps even most, of this money goes towards the purchase of arms.

It would be reassuring to be able to trust the unassailable integrity of the overseas Indian press (and a great deal of its domestic press as well), but we cannot. We would like to believe all that we read, within reason, and most of what we're told, in confidence. We cannot. It is in the interests of the Indian government, and of its overseas supporters, to blame outside agitators (the so-called "foreign hand," in Mrs Gandhi's frequently used terms), overseas communities, and lax supervision of spurious "refugees" in Canada, the United States and the United Kingdom, rather than to undertake politically risky negotiations with Sikh leaders in Punjab. But the hard evidence of active Pakistani involvement, apart from so-called "blind-eye" tolerance, is impossible to find. When proof appears, or when it seems to, it may very likely turn out to be a classic piece of disinformation.

Indeed, the BBC's longtime reporter in India, Mark Tully, in his (and Satish Jacob's) study of the Golden Temple invasion, *Amritsar: Mrs Gandhi's Last Battle*, specifically exonerates Pakistan from any but a minor, smuggling role in fomenting the Punjab crisis. According to Tully and Jacob, Pakistan President Zia-ul-Haq "did not openly support the Sikhs and we have found no evidence he gave them covert help." They suggest that he was kept in line by his fear that a distracted and frustrated Indira Gandhi might be tempted to launch a strike against Pakistan as an artificial unifier of domestic opinion.

It is attractive to think that the truth may lie somewhere in between, but politics is not simple accountancy. Help has come from Pakistan, we feel, but that help has been carefully shorn of government involvement.

The question is, who besides Pakistan is possibly involved? The answer, of course, is the United States and the Soviet Union.

The wild card in the region is Afghanistan, where superpower conflicts intersect with local rivalries. The late-1979 Soviet invasion of Afghanistan is considered by nearly all Western observers to be the opening shot in a long-range Soviet strategy aimed at delivering, through steady pressure on Pakistan or Iran, a warm-water port on the Indian Ocean adjoining the Soviet landmass.

That is the nightmare haunting American policymakers. If the Soviets consolidate their power in Afghanistan, and if they maintain or even strengthen their long-standing friendship with India, Pakistan is effectively isolated. All of Pakistan's natural ethnic fissures — far deeper than India's, on balance — can be exploited. Should the Soviets gain access to the Indian Ocean, American experts foresee an inevitable blackmailing of Saudi Arabia and the oil-producing Gulf States, an all-out assault on Israel, a militarization of the Indian Ocean, and the breech of America's southern strategy to protect the West's oil, and political interests.

"Losing" Pakistan, moreover, a loyal military client since 1954, on top of its strategic implications, would be a psychological and political blow unacceptable to any American president. Accordingly, insurance against such a loss carries a steep price. In late 1984, the New York *Times* projected the fiscal 1985 cost of *covert* military aid to Afghanistan supplied by the CIA through Pakistan at $280 million, which represented more than double the 1984 outlay. Overt military aid to Pakistan in the decade of the eighties has been budgeted at over $7 billion.

In other words, the preservation of an intact and militarily strong Pakistan is a primary American policy. Actions taken by others in the region inimical to that policy are viewed as hostile. So when the General Assembly of the UN met to consider a condemnation of the Soviet invasion of Afghanistan, and India abstained, its action was considered to demonstrate hostility towards the United States.

As we have noted, the Khalistan cause, translated into

Western (especially North American) terms, is extremely right wing. With "socialist" and "secularist" India as the enemy, the Khalistan cause becomes "capitalist" and "fundamentalist" almost by default.

Conversely, those Sikhs in the West who oppose the Khalistanis have been, at least in our experience, predictably liberal-to-leftist in their politics, secular (i.e., shaved, non-turbaned), well educated, articulate and instinctively suspicious of American motives. Their attitude to Pakistan would be patronizing, based as much on its theocratic nature as its American dominance. They would assume that initiatives seeming to come from Pakistan are being directed by a foreign hand out of Washington.

One leader of the WSO, a suburban professional man in the New York area, boasted to us: "Six days a week I work for Reagan. Seventh day, for Khalistan." His game-room walls were hung with full-colour blowups of scenes from the Delhi Riots. Dr Satindrapal Sekhon, head of the ISYF in the United States, wants to put the Khalistan question to the UN for a vote — providing the Soviet Union and all socialist states are denied the franchise. Senator Jesse Helms himself has intervened on the behalf of Khalistan's "founder," Jagjit Singh Chauhan, by arranging for his visit to the United States, despite a State Department refusal of his visa request.

There is a reason, then, apart from amateurism, that the Khalistani cells in North America have been so easily infiltrated by the FBI and the RCMP, and why they have turned to commercial mercenary schools and to gritty *Soldier of Fortune* types for help. Organized terrorists with broad international support, such as the various Middle Eastern factions of the PLO, do not flash their VISA cards and answer ads in the backs of magazines, as did Frank Camper's three Khalistani students. Camper's school, an FBI flypaper operation to lure and monitor would-be mercenaries, vigilantes, white supremists and survivalists, became a trap for the Khalistani commandos partly because of their naïveté, and partly because of the self-image they shared.

Birk, the would-be weekend terrorist with the six-figure

salary, was trapped by Camper and "Nichols." The Montreal cell of Babar Khalsa activists, two of whom were convicted and sentenced to life terms for conspiring to blow up an Air India flight (out of New York in 1986), were set up by Frank Miele, an apparently unsavoury "underworld" plant from the New York FBI office. The Hamilton (Ontario) Babar Khalsa cell arrested for conspiring to blow up the Indian Houses of Parliament and kidnapping an Indian politician's child to help gain entry, were successful property owners and small businessmen, trapped in part by their innocent trust of the telephone system.

Inevitably, the dispute over Khalistan takes on an east-west, left-right, USSR-US configuration. In the view of those on the right, Khalistanis are freedom fighters defending their faith and their homeland. They are the Israelis of the subcontinent. To those on the left, they are revanchist chauvinists, Nazis, racists, ignorant storm troopers led by bigoted *mullahs*.

One of these leftist gentlemen offered us a helpful document. It was a copy of a speech ascribed to (then) UN Ambassador Jeane Kirkpatrick. The copy seemed to have been taken from a book, *Agony of Punjab*, but no further citations could be discovered. The speech was titled, "Operation Balkanisation of India" and it was reprinted from the leftist *Link* magazine. The speech had apparently been delivered before 1300 delegates at the Mayflower Hotel in Washington, on February 27, 1982, before the convention of the Conservative Political Action Conference. A bit of research revealed that that was the conference in which James Watt was named Reagan's best cabinet appointment, and Alexander Haig was heckled for his Kissinger connections.

The speech reads like classic Kirkpatrick: hard, slashing, and, as regards the "Third World," utterly unsentimental. Harming Soviet interests (such as by harming India) and Soviet prestige (by highlighting India's breakaway ethnic movements) becomes a helpful adjunct of American foreign policy. The India section of the speech closes with the lines, "The United States could watch the erosion of the Nehru-Gandhi tradition, almost irrespective of the form it takes, with some complacency."

Through newspaper files we dutifully tracked Mrs Kirkpatrick to the Mayflower Hotel and to attendance at the Conference on the given date. But the national and local papers merely reported two conference speeches, one by the Attorney-General, the other by Haig. Surely her speech, so full of innuendo, so contemptuous of the Third World's aspiration to human rights, so generous to South Africa, deserved some commentary?

It was not until late September 1983, that the story broke: Kirkpatrick's "speech," along with a number of other "documents" (one relating to a planned assassination of Nigerian officials, another to "proof" that the Korean Airliner that was shot down by Soviet air defences on September 1, 1983, had been on an American spy mission) had been concocted in Moscow, "leaked" to an Indian Communist paper, then legitimized by being "reported" by TASS and then disseminated to friendly, leftist papers, like *Link*, around the world. Moscow Radio even beamed the news back, in English, on its International Service.

Moscow Radio's "analysis" of its own manufactured document played like this, transcript courtesy of the BBC: "In my view, Boris Vasiliyevich, Washington is particularly attracted by the idea of the Balkanisation of India. Jeane Kirkpatrick the US representative at the UN, even holds forth publicly about it. The lady is making a great song and dance about the idea. But the essence of Balkanisation amounts to splitting India into tiny, mutually hostile states, so that the imperialists, having turned them into submissive puppets, would be able to take them in hand." In other words, by repetition and seemingly offhand citation, the lie takes on substance and enjoys an underground, "Protocols of the Elders of Zion" type existence long after the objections and retractions have made their dutiful appearance.

Presumably, the release of the disinformation was timed to coincide with Indira Gandhi's taking over the leadership of the World Non-Aligned Movement from Fidel Castro. The Soviets were worried that in her power to set the Movement's agenda for the next three years, she might move to censure the Soviets for the war in Afghanistan. The "Kirkpatrick Speech" was intended to drive her from any American embrace, at a time when she had been making her first overtures to the United States.

The stakes in the region are obviously very high. Nothing, and nobody, is quite what it appears. Touch the region at nearly any point, such as the crash of Air India 182, and, slowly, enormous shapes begin to appear from behind banks of impenetrable fog.

In the course of our inquiry, we spoke to a well-connected Indian national living in the United States — let's call him "Babu" — who was in a position to clarify some of the Big Power machinations. On condition that he remain anonymous, he told a fascinating story.

Of course there is American involvement with the Khalistanis, he said. America is pouring hundreds of millions of dollars into Pakistan for the alleged defence against Soviet incursions. You know how these arms dealers operate — their mark-up is fantastic! These middle-men are growing fabulously wealthy; they're a government unto themselves. This Afghan war is the biggest thing that's ever happened, the chance of a lifetime. They don't answer to anyone. If Sikhs want some arms, or anyone else, including rebels in other parts of Pakistan, they'll sell them.

Babu is actually quite sympathetic, in an ironical way, to Pakistan. All they wanted was a few billion dollars more for the ruling Twenty Families and some extra hardware to flash at India. Now they've invited a Trojan Horse into their midst: three million lawless, dope-dealing Pathan tribesmen squatting on their border in refugee camps. So the Soviets will get their way in the end, because Pakistan will collapse under Pathan pressure and other ethnic rivalries without the Russians even firing a shot. There have already been serious riots over dope and arms seizures between Pathans and earlier refugees in the slums of Karachi. The Pathans are a greater threat to Pakistan than the Khalistanis are to India.

By the way, he asks us, did we know that the Soviets offered India a destabilization plan for Pakistan, and India turned it down? India doesn't want the Russians next door any more than Pakistan does. India wants to preserve Pakistan as a buffer state. The ultimate irony in all this, from an Indian perspective, is that Pakistan has become India's client, as well as America's.

According to our informant, and to widespread opinion among both Sikh and Indian government sources, the Indian government of Mrs Gandhi's time, true to its own obsessions, had gathered convincing evidence of "the foreign hand," or CIA involvement, in Khalistani agitation. In India and in much of the Third World, the very word "CIA" carries nuances in the popular mind that Americans might find flattering, if not amusing. When Mrs Gandhi was assassinated, the first reaction of a segment of young businessmen in Bombay was that it represented "the triumph of the CIA over the KGB." The CIA is given credit for having initiated just about any event from which the United States might profit.

Indian officials have never been shy in playing the CIA card. Mrs Gandhi nearly discredited its effectiveness by overuse. Why now, we asked, when CIA involvement in the Khalistan agitation seems a logical extension of American foreign policy, a way of influencing Indian behaviour, and of punishing India for its apparent acceptance of the Soviet invasion of Afghanistan, are Indian officials so silent, so reluctant to voice their views?

The reason, says Babu secretly, and the reason, announces William Kunstler flamboyantly in the Birk trial, is that a deal was struck on June 12, 1985, between Rajiv Gandhi and President Reagan. The new prime minister was in the United States ostensibly to open the Festival of India, but the real reason was to discuss India's grievance with American destabilization policies in the region. Fortunately, America also wanted to change its policies, in light of Rajiv's openness to American free-market economics. For the first time in Indian history, the United States felt it had someone in power in New Delhi with whom it could do business.

The United States agreed to suspend help, aid and comfort to the Khalistanis. It would take steps to purge the so-called "Punjabi Pipeline" of its illegal aliens and funding, it would stop the fraudulent marriages that were bringing militants into the country and it would start scrutinizing the legitimacy of requests for amnesty from Sikhs looking for refugee status. It would investigate with particular thoroughness the petitions for visa extensions by certain high-level spokesmen for Khalistan, like Major-General Jaswant Singh Bhullar.

And one more thing of special interest to Rajiv Gandhi. At that meeting, the FBI was able to present the evidence it had gathered on the Birk–Lal Singh cell of extremists that had been plotting his assassination. Birk and four others, including his close associate Sukhvinder Singh, who had also attended Camper's mercenary school, had been picked up on May 14th in New Orleans. According to FBI charges, the cell, minus Lal and Ammand Singh, had gone to New Orleans to assassinate Bhajan Lal, the Chief Minister of the state of Haryana, considered one of the Sikhs' major enemies in India. Had they not made that impulsive trip down from New York, the planned FBI sweep of the New York cell would have netted Birk, the other four, and the two still-fugitive Singhs.

"We saved your life, Mr Prime Minister." The price to India? Silence. And the continued deregulation of its economy.

This, at least, is a leftist view. As we have pointed out, it is not without its own agenda. The Punjab crisis plays to many constituencies, and contains room for ample villainy from all sides. If, in the early years, there was a "logical" role for American and Pakistani support of Khalistan, there is today justification for a certain Soviet interest. If India has indeed rebuffed Soviet intentions, and if the new economic and military order in New Delhi favours American free enterprise and American weaponry, and if the Khalistan leadership is starved for arms and training (and especially if it feels humiliated by the Western "tilt" to India), the movement could easily be taken over by a well-trained cadre of the Left. After all, it has no articulated economic or social policy; it lacks a coherent constitution; it is a movement rooted in vengeance.

The right-wing position, as articulated by Birk at his trial and in subsequent letters to us from prison, is that the Khalistan cause has been abandoned by its supposed friends. He sees himself in the tradition of citizen-soldier and freedom fighter, taking arms against tyrannous Hindu colonialists. How dare the country that bombs Libya, that funds wars against communism in Nicaragua, Angola and Afghanistan convict him for "violation of American neutrality"? The Sikh *khalsa* is America's most sincere friend in the world; Birk's pain is the pain of betrayal. Khalistanis around the world assume that the lure of Indian trade, mere profits, has sold out the Khalistan cause in the West.

Birk's lawyer, William Kunstler, accused the judge who sentenced Birk of panicking before the word "terrorism," and of bending to the new political line that saw Rajiv Gandhi as a sudden friend, and the Sikhs as a major embarrassment.

Shortly after that Reagan-Rajiv meeting, India rotated one of its major Punjab policy makers, Gouri Shankar, into its Washington embassy. Many observers have speculated that Shankar's presence dovetailed with significant policy changes in Washington, among them the newfound zealousness of the Immigration and Naturalization Service in processing, and rejecting, Sikh refugee claims. Since these changes all occurred prior to the bombing of Flight 182, one is forced to assume that it was Rajiv's opening to the West that initiated the policy review.

Canada, on the other hand, ended its moratorium on the deportation of Sikhs who had unsuccessfully claimed refugee status after the invasion of the Golden Temple. By December 1985, Secretary of State for External Affairs Joe Clark had gone to India to discuss a treaty with India to permit the extradition of Sikh separatists. It is doubtful that these significant policy changes would have occurred without the overwhelming political impetus generated by the loss of Flight 182.

CHAPTER 4

Canada

Why Canada?

Canada has always defined itself by its orderly settlement, domestic tranquillity and good government. Its mission was the preservation of civility on a barbarous, republican continent. For Canada there was no Revolution, no Civil War, no Manifest Destiny. In Toronto in the late eighties Sunday closing laws are challenged; films are censored; a ballplayer is arrested for killing a seagull with a thrown baseball.

What explains the gap between a country's self-image as a tolerant society, comfortably stuffy and exempt from madness, and the reality of having hosted the worst terrorist act of modern times? The victims and perpetrators were Canadian. The terrorists met and trained in Canada, they developed their politics in Canada. The Canadian government had been warned repeatedly of terrorist cells and terrorist camps operating within its borders and had done nothing to stop them. Why?

Two explanations, we feel: complacency, and multiculturalism not as an ideal, but as an expedient. Multiculturalism is a Canadian invention, a convenient contrast to the American "melting pot." It is also a way of dealing with — or excluding — the non-French, non-English "ethnics" and "visible minorities" by rewarding their resistant diversity, not their ability to assimilate.

An example of the process at work in the Indian community: the federal Ministry of Multiculturalism funds specifically "Punjabi" dances at a generically "Indian" function. No one objects to that, except when "Punjabi" becomes "Sikh" and

"Sikh" becomes "Khalistani." The nuance seems subtle to outsiders, but not to Indians, and not to the videotapers who use the footage, complete with Khalistani flags and slogans, as evidence of Canadian approval for Khalistan. Ironically, Canada itself suffered the same outrage twenty years ago, when President de Gaulle of France used a "Canadian" stage to serve the purposes of Quebec (and France) in booming out, "*Vive le Québec libre!*" at the opening of Expo '67.

Canada is no stranger to secessionist movements. The greatest political challenge to Canada in this century, the election of René Lévesque's legally constituted separatist government in Quebec in 1976, was met peaceably, allowed to go to referendum and to sputter out. One can hardly imagine a more civilized response, given the threat that was posed.

Just six years earlier, however, the same Liberal government of Pierre Trudeau that was in power when Lévesque was elected had placed the entire country under martial law in the wake of a single political kidnapping by a cell of the banned, separatist Front de Libération du Québec (FLQ). At the time, the country overwhelmingly supported Trudeau's extraordinary measures; in retrospect, it has come to be seen as one of the most excessive and illiberal acts in Canadian history. The lesson seems to be that anarchy, however anæmic, will be crushed with a sledgehammer; orderly secession, however threatening, will be calmly debated. The real lesson is that Canada is unprepared to deal with terrorism without dismantling its own liberal democracy, and thus prefers to turn a blind eye as long as it can.

Canada's peacefulness, good government and domestic tranquillity have been purchased at a high cost.

The attempt to prosecute Khalistani terrorism in Canadian courts, particularly in Inderjit Singh Reyat's trial in Duncan, British Columbia, has already raised an issue at least as serious as Trudeau's invocation of the War Measures Act sixteen years earlier. Most Canadians do not realize that they are living in a potential police state, whose potential has already been actualized. During the Reyat trial, a spectator was able to stand from the gallery and address the court. After identifying himself as an officer of the CSIS, the super-elite "security intelligence" service, he was effectively able to suspend the trial, denying the defence its right of cross-examination, and declaring the judge "functus," or impotent, in his own courtroom. (The actions were undertaken to block the identification of witnesses to Reyat's and Parmar's detonation of the bomb in the woods. One can speculate — indeed, it is the only speculation that in any way justifies the action — that it was not CSIS agents who were being protected, but members of the Sikh community who would have been endangered by exposure.) Such actions are entirely consonant with police-state behaviour.

Canada's uneasy balance between authoritarianism and liberal democracy is upset only when threats to its stability are perceived as challenges to mainstream society. This is consistent with British political traditions, in which Parliament, not the individual, is sovereign. (Other examples of reversion to authoritarianism are the uprooting of west coast Japanese Canadians in World War II; the mustering of a small flotilla of naval gunboats in the "*Komagata Maru*" incident to oust a boatload of would-be East Indian settlers in Vancouver in 1914; and, of course, the military actions against Louis Riel's short-lived *Métis* (French–Indian) "nation" in western Canada in the 1880s.) Race has been a prominent issue, a challenge to white supremacy, in most of these major overreactions. However, if mainstream society is not directly affected, incidents like the Air India disaster or the communal tensions leading up to it can be treated as something "ethnic," a disturbance in the multicultural mosaic. Many of the grieving Air India families and many anti-Khalistani Sikhs wonder why their requests for government review of slanderous broadcasts and libellous editorials in Canada's Punjabi-language media, of death-threats and even assaults were not followed up. Some feel that strong government action in 1983 and 1984 would have indicated to the Khalistanis operating in Canada that they were under close surveillance, and not exempt from accountability.

Police sensitivity to the new area of "intracommunal" crime still needs refinement. Just as rape victims and battered wives have been made to feel guilty by police or the courts and racially assaulted Canadians in the seventies had to overcome police skepticism before racism was accepted as a proper motive ("You say he spat on you and pushed you, but how do I know he doesn't do that to everybody?"), so do the victims of "ethnic" attacks by members of their own community feel, at times, patronized ("You guys settle it among yourselves, or I'll have to run you in") by police who have no background in the particular dispute. People simply don't want threats to their safety or their dignity minimized because of their foreignness, or treated less seriously than threats to English speakers in Quebec, French in Manitoba or Jews in Alberta.

Beyond a certain insensitivity to minority feelings, which is hardly a Canadian monopoly, police work in Canada — this is an important consideration — is as heavily bureaucratized as any other branch of government. The various levels of law enforcement have different mandates and different lines of Cabinet authority. The RCMP are charged with the investigation of crimes *after* they are committed; the CSIS with the developing of cases leading to apprehension before the actual crime. The RCMP generally work closely with municipal police; the CSIS, with Interpol and international intelligence. Both are likely to conflict with the work of the Ministry of Multiculturalism, which may, in fact, be paying the legal appeals of certain individuals under police scrutiny or funding some of the projects of a "cultural" nature that police take to be dangerously political.

Perhaps the most telling example of counterproductive rivalry was the slack follow-up on the surveillance of Reyat and Parmar in Duncan, British Columbia. Security forces knew that Sikh fundamentalists were desperately assembling a bomb-making capacity, but when the Air India flight went down, the attitude at RCMP headquarters, according to an undercover agent present at the time, was, "We blew it." They had assumed that the bomb was intended for export to India. They had not anticipated the viciousness of the terrorist mind.

National character contributes to certain kinds of tragedy. Seymour Hersh suggests in *The Target Is Destroyed*, his study of the Soviet downing of KAL 007 off Sakhalin Island on

September 1, 1983, in which 269 civilians were killed, that the paranoia of Soviet air defences and the rigid hierarchy of the Korean airline's command structure overrode the elaborate fail-safe devices supposedly built into the defence and navigation systems.

In this context, the Air India disaster was a Canadian tragedy from the beginning, growing in part from a national character flaw: the comfortable myth of instinctive goodness. The bedrock certainty of "it can't happen here," which translates into complacent airport security, yields only slightly to a partial revision: "Sad as it is, it's not really our problem." That attitude lay behind the misplaced condolences in Prime Minister Mulroney's call to Rajiv Gandhi on learning of the crash: it's theirs, not ours, and it's a terrible pity. It *still* hasn't happened here.

At a Toronto-area memorial service one year after the tragedy, the prime minister's office was still referring to the disaster as a tragedy for the "Indo-Canadian community," and it was left to an Opposition member of Parliament, Roland de Corneille, to state openly, "Not enough Canadians are deeply touched. Not too many realize it was Canadians who were killed. There still remains racism, a separatism that the loss affected them, and not us." The failure to acknowledge the victims of the crash as Canadians remains for most of the families the enduring political grief of Air India 182.

For that reason, it was important that Canadian Secretary of State for External Affairs Joe Clark heard the petitions of bitter relatives in Ireland a week after the Toronto ceremonies. It was significant that he noted in his speech at the Cork memorial service that Canada, and not just an obscure appendage called "Canadians of Indian Origin," had suffered a terrorist loss. It's important to see that Canada, for all its high-mindedness and self-exemption from blame, had brought much of the tragedy on itself.

At the very least, the Air India disaster strikes at Canada's smugness. A country that so piously guards its seagulls and its civic virtue will almost certainly confuse propriety with real protection. But in a political and historical sense, Canada was not just smug, indifferent and unlucky. Canada contributed more to the tragedy than it has ever acknowledged.

The miscalculation that admitted thousands of unskilled immigrants into Canada in the early seventies was only one contribution to the disaster. Far more important are the thousands more, over the course of eighty years, who were barred on account of race or national origin. It was not until the mid-sixties that restrictive laws were rewritten and a point system that favoured education and aptitude was instituted. Almost immediately, the East Indian community, which had been predominantly Sikh, working-class, and west coast-focused, became Hindu, professional, and Ontario-centred.

This group quickly established itself in medicine and the professions, as bureaucrats, teachers and entrepreneurs. Arriving with certain advantages, they became Canada's most successful immigrant group, an oft-cited "model community," if one looks only to income and comparative lack of transitional strains.

What is more difficult to grasp is the problem they have faced in *acceptance* by white Canadians. The seventies were a difficult time of overt discrimination, but even with obvious improvement in the area of casual public harassment, the latest polls and sociological inquiries place the "East Indians" nearly at the bottom of the ladder of social esteem in Canada, ahead only of "Pakistanis" (the difference is minimal, since both are known, in bad times, as "Pakis"), and trailing blacks.

A great many of the husbands and fathers of Flight 182 are part of that carefully selected late-sixties trickle of Indian immigration. The contribution of the Air India families to Canada's scientific life has been enormous: Dr Radhakrishna's thermal property analyser (patented by Ontario Hydro and in use around the world); Vishnu Pada's mining engineering, which had seen him serve as a consultant to several foreign governments; Dr Bal Gupta's laser spectroscopy; Dr Balvir Singh's much-cited papers on government spending and private income; Dr Yogesh Paliwal's development of barley seeds resistant to yellow dwarfism — just these few, taken at random, have generated millions of dollars in savings, or in income, for

Canada. The children might have accomplished even more. All of their children, and dozens more, are dead.

Their life contrasts with the peculiar nature of Sikh-Canadian life (which began in British Columbia at the turn of the century), with its long history of alternating abuse and tolerance, its heavy representation in the lumber and trucking industries, its low-profile marginality — the result of generations of racial quotas and noncitizenship (the right to vote was not granted until 1949) — which led to its *gurdwara*-based culture and comparative indifference to the professions and higher education. The pervasive west coast fear of a "brown tide" or "yellow hordes" was used to keep Asian immigration at a minimum and to discourage normal family life (immigration of women for purposes of marriage was not permitted). Partly as a result, the community never grew in the explosive, variegated fashion that characterized the later, southern European arrivals, and later still, the Indians, Chinese and West Indians of the present day.

Air India 182 was not just a jumbo jet on its way to India when tragedy struck; it was also a symbol of Canadian immigration policies, failed and successful. The two communities of Indian immigrants met that morning off the coast of Ireland; the financially successful and professionally assimilated Canadian suburbanites in the plane, and the unilingual, desperate Canadians on the ground. Those families died for their continued attachment to India; these terrorists killed for the same reason. They are the two sides of the immigration drama, one unintelligible without the other.

We cannot leave this topic without casting out a few final words of hope. There will be bitterness between the communities of Indian-born Canadians, particularly between Sikhs and Hindus, for a long time. Moderate Sikhs want the Hindus to speak out on their behalf; Hindus who have lost everything say that, deep down, there are no moderates. As with victims of the Holocaust or their children confronting a German or his children, it may take a generation or more before the two communities can speak again.

Mukul Paliwal was fifteen, a boy gifted with engineering genius, as well as a bright gift for life. His father's house is still

full of his working inventions, headphones and tape recorders
discarded by the school, a complicated multitracked electronic
train, a calculator. His first words were "it moves," in Hindi,
referring to the spinning head of a tape recorder. Inscribed on
each of his inventions is the mark of the artist: Mukul
Productions. On his walls are hockey posters and an International Development Agency map of active aid projects. His
record library includes rock and Hindi. His soccer clothes are
laid out on the bed.

He was a boy in perfect balance, like so many of the young
men and women who perished. They embodied an immigration
ideal that comes round only once in a community, in the brief
window between nostalgia and assimilation.

We were struck by a simple letter, and poem, sent to Mukul's
father by his next-door neighbour, sixteen-year-old Indrapal
Jaswal, a Sikh. Hindu and Sikh, but also Canadian. In the
letter, Indrapal writes:

> Almost every day that I knew him I talked with him. In the
> mornings we would walk to school. I, usually downtrodden
> for one reason or another, and he happy and content as ever.
> We would walk to school and observe others, talk about the
> weather; anything that came into our minds. During school,
> we would invariably meet in the halls and greet each other.
> We would walk home together and talk about school, full of
> new learnings, and our stomachs rumbling in hunger. Then
> we would each enter our own house and not less than half an
> hour later call each other on the phone and then come back
> out and play something. Whether it was hockey or soccer or
> football, we didn't care, it was fun.
>
> Nowadays I am alone. I walk to school alone. I meet
> people in the halls at school, but I don't meet him. Walking
> home once again I am immersed in my own thoughts. When
> I get back home I slowly trudge into my room and wait, wait
> for his call.

And in the poem, "Mukul," written two days after the crash:

> As I am writing this, I can still hear him saying,
> "See you in September."
> Goodbye, Mukul, I will never forget.
> And may the flame of happiness
> That you illuminated in everyone you knew,
> Continue to burn, brighter than ever.

CHAPTER 5

The Sikhs

In Montreal, we spoke with an old friend, a Sikh, about his religion. Typical of friendships between Hindus and Sikhs back in the sixties and seventies, the "issue" of religion had never arisen. In those years a Hindu would use the words "Sikh" and "Punjabi" interchangeably.

Outwardly, he is an observant Sikh, bearded and turbaned. The religion suits him, he's comfortable within it. As with Hinduism, there is little besides the habits of devotion to mark Sikhism's "theology." One reads the Holy Book (the *Granth*), recites the prayers and meditates on their meaning. For him, the beard and the turban are secondary signs of the faith, not inessential but certainly not supreme. He rejects the Bhindranwale-inspired devotion to outer appearance and the linkage to a "pure" Sikh state.

He realizes there are others in the same Montreal *gurdwara*, from the Babar Khalsa, with very different agendas. He knows the men recently convicted for conspiring to blow up an Air India plane out of New York. He describes for us the change they have undergone since their "baptism" into the new, pure faith. He does not use the word, but we have; what he describes is conversion to cult behaviour, cult thinking, cult exclusiveness.

"Sikhism is a new religion, so it combines the best of all thoughts," he explained for us. "It is a simple man's religion; its whole theology is summarized in a single phrase: *Sat Sri Akal* — 'it is true,' or 'God is Truth.' And it's a very practical, peasant religion: only once in every 8.4 million *avatars* (births) are we permitted to be human beings, so we must not waste it, and must not deprive another being of his life."

For him, what is happening in Punjab is not Sikhism, nor can it be undertaken in the name of Sikhism.

We spoke to another gentleman who's been involved in Toronto community life for over thirty years, not as a Sikh, but as an Indian. Through his liaison position with the Toronto School Board, he was instrumental in eliminating the exclusive use of the Lord's Prayer and replacing it with readings from every religion practised in the city. In the mid-seventies he worked with the police for more foot-patrols in troubled areas where Indians had suffered attacks at the hands of white youths. In the late seventies he led the protests against police brutality in the "Albert Johnson Case," where a deranged Jamaican immigrant had been pursued by the police from the street into his house, and killed.

These would be acts of traditional Sikhism. Self-defence, social conscience. Sikhs, even well-disposed ones, often tweak Hindus for their lack of a social vision. Hindu social policy, say the Sikhs, runs like this: "Don't just do something, stand there!" Sikhs, by contrast, are seen as full of valour, though they may not have the slightest idea of what they're fighting for.

This gentleman is agonized by the current violence. The world that he's fought for as a labour organizer and teacher in India, as a community volunteer in Canada is falling to pieces. The community is tearing itself apart. He longs for exculpatory evidence, proof, in the matter of Air India 182, that the Indian government was involved. Mainstream Sikh opinion has rejected the possibility of a Sikh-planted bomb. "It is not our way," he insists.

"I can see a desperate act of desperate people directed specifically against the Congress party officials in New Delhi, and only against those officials who organized the riots after Mrs Gandhi's death. I can understand the killing of Mrs Gandhi after the Golden Temple. All that I can see happening. But this — these women and children — a Sikh cannot do. A Sikh is commanded to help the weak. He will fight, but he is forbidden to harm innocent people."

But what about *these* desperate people? What about underground cells composed of uneducated and underemployed young
men, Punjabi-speaking, hearing only the fiery rhetoric in their
local *gurdwara*, hearing only talk of vengeance against the
Indian government who killed the saviour of Sikhism, Bhindranwale, and the hundreds in the Golden Temple, and who organized the systematic slaughter of innocent Sikhs in Delhi in the
days after her assassination?

What about the psychology of all breakaway underground
movements, their fear of infiltration, their need to satisfy their
financial, religious and political backers? In such a group, anyone who preaches moderation is viewed as a traitor, a possible
Indian government agent. Each new baseline of contemplated
activity becomes ever more violent.

"Then they are not Sikhs," said the old gentleman.

(Certainly he is right; it is a cult offshoot of Sikhism, just as
the Moonies are "Christian" or the Rajneeshis were "Hindu." A
great deal of confusion in the minds of the general public, not
to mention hurt and humiliation to mainstream Sikhs could be
redirected if the media would stop referring to the terrorists
simply as "Sikhs.")

It's in Vancouver, the traditional centre of Sikh immigration in
North America, that the divisions are felt most sharply. Vancouver is the home of Talvinder Parmar; of the men we've called
"the farmer" and "Sardar"; and Manmohan Singh, the spokesman
for the ISYF; and Hardial Singh Johal, the man whose phone
number was given to CP Air as a contact number back in the
days before the plane was bombed. It's where the two bombs
began their journey on June 22, 1985. Three hours away, on
Vancouver Island, a bomb was tested, and a few hours' drive
north of Duncan is where the convoy of the Punjab Cabinet
minister was ambushed by would-be assassins.

It's also the home of Ujjal Dosanjh, the most outspoken anti-
Khalistani Sikh in the country, the man loosely categorized as
"the spokesman for moderate Sikhs." It is a role he has accepted
by default, and one that has cost him a severe beating and several
death threats. He is a forty-year-old lawyer, twice an NDP

candidate for the provincial legislature. As a "Sikh lawyer," he has written many contracts, closed many property agreements, probated many wills, for people with whom he is in profound disagreement.

In February 1985, he was beaten in the parking lot of his office by a much larger Sikh wielding a three-foot metal sawmill screw with bolt. Eighty stitches, in a double layer, were taken to close the wounds on his head. He identified his attacker, naming him, but police investigation could not turn up a serious enough "motive" for the attack. (The victims of such assaults are often made to feel somehow responsible: if they'd only piped down, kept a low profile and not gotten those hotheads all excited.) Dosanjh's alleged attacker was let go. Some small satisfaction attaches to the fact that he was arrested again fifteen months later, and faces life imprisonment, for the attempted assassination of the Punjab Cabinet minister.

To his detractors, Dosanjh is just another ambitious politician. To committed Khalistanis, he is something worse, of course — a traitor, an Indian government spy. (Most Khalistanis cannot conceive of a world in which holding Canadian political ambitions would be antithetical to serving the government of India as an informer.) To others, Dosanjh is a statesman. He defines his own role as that of a bridge: between the immigrants and the mainstream, between old Sikhs and new. If he has a cause, it is Canadian, not Indian or Punjabi; he wants integration of the community into the Canadian mainstream, an end to its terrible isolation and to the forces that prey on its alienation.

To him, it's the illiterate, skill-less recent arrivals who support terrorism. "They're worse than the militants in the Punjab, because they are waging a long-distance battle without commitment and without suffering any physical consequences. They enjoy the adrenalin but suffer no pain. They have no commitment here, and no commitment there. But all the same they feel fulfilled. They have the best of both worlds."

So far as resolving Sikh-Hindu problems in India, he feels that the Indian government has to come clean about the Delhi riots and deal justly with the issue of police activity during the riots. Then it must implement the long-standing agreements reached years ago between the Akali Dal and the central government. Both leaders (Longowal and Mrs Gandhi) have since been assassinated, but the accords still stand. The terms were simple enough when they were negotiated in the late seventies. They had to do with the return of Chandigarh to Punjab for its exclusive use as the capital, the inclusion in Punjab of some Punjabi-speaking villages currently in Haryana, greater control of river waters that originate outside the state. But they were repeatedly "sabotaged" by the Congress (I) party leadership. By now, politics have been replaced by religion and language and the notion of a "Sikh nation," and a negotiated settlement is temporarily out of the question.

As for problems between Sikhs and Hindus in Canada, or between Sikh factions in Canada, he feels it's basically a matter of the need for tight law enforcement. If police had dealt adequately with the complaints of assaults on moderate spokesmen and with the provocations in the ethnic press and on ethnic radio, the problem would not have escalated to its current level. By ignoring the problem or dealing with it leniently (or, worse, "politically," by knuckling under to the vehemently Khalistani factions within the Sikh community), a message was sent to the criminal elements that they could get away with any outrage.

It is very dangerous for moderate Sikhs to speak out against Khalistan. One young man who did in Toronto was attacked by five young Khalistanis with field-hockey sticks in the below-ground parking lot of his apartment complex. Now he carries metal plates in his arm, a permanently misaligned finger and scars on his face and scalp. He was accused by the investigating officer of secretly knowing his attackers, but being afraid to name them.

This young machinist sees unemployment and lack of education as contributing to the increasing violence of the cells. "There are some young men sitting at the bottom who cannot think logically. They are ready to do anything. Violent men at the bottom force the top leadership to do something, produce some results, to look active. The leadership might try in the beginning to do small things like beating a person like me who is nobody. 'See? We have beaten up a traitor' — that kind of satisfaction. But that only works once — what will they do the next time? There has to be a bigger show. Each group is competing with other groups. They have to be able to show they are strongest or the least afraid, like gangs in a city. After they beat me up and no one was caught, they can say, 'See, we are stronger than the police. They are afraid of us.' And these boys believe it, because they have no experience and no way of evaluating what they are told. They cannot think about right and wrong. For people who deeply believe in violence, in taking sword-in-hand as they say, the Air India crash will have no chastising effect."

Dosanjh remembers a similar incident, which happened just before his beating. When Sikhs are ready to martyr themselves for a cause, they cite the early martyrs who told the guru, "we have our heads on our palms." Dosanjh was visited by a similar group, for purposes of a threat. Their heads were on their palms, to which Dosanjh answered, "You've had them on your palms so long you don't have any on your shoulders."

Dosanjh still places his faith in politics and the law, provided they are fairly applied, and open to all.

The police have their own view of communal violence, which runs counter to that of the young machinist. They believe the pressure comes from the top, from the money-men who fund the cells but prefer not to be associated with their everyday running. "A man gives five thousand dollars, he expects something for it," says Inspector Ron Prior, lately with Minority Group Relations for the Metropolitan Toronto Police. He feels the militants are more concerned with pleasing their backers, and thus commanding more funds and influence within the community, than with impressing their own membership.

Manmohan Singh might qualify as a sworn enemy of Ujjal Dosanjh. One night after closing his "Punjab" restaurant, he described for us a "typical Indian agent," and the words would fit Dosanjh or any shaved, Westernized Sikh perfectly. "He might be born in a Sikh family, but he does not wear the signs of a true Sikh. He goes to the media and speaks against Khalistan."

Singh is a tall, powerfully built man in his early fifties, formerly an Indian Air Force pilot. As befits a restaurateur, he wears his beard carefully gathered under a fine, dark mesh. The restaurant sells liquor, which places him in an awkward position with many fundamentalists. Clearly, he is not a purist; he's been divorced. He acknowledges uneasiness with the Babar Khalsa ("...more fundamental, less educated. If they get a Khalistan, they won't let us in either"). Even so, he declares them to be doing their part, good or bad.

We pointed out to Manmohan Singh that "the part" contributed by the Babar Khalsa, with all its violence and murky membership, is at odds with his goal of making Khalistan somewhat respectable. But in June 1986, he could not go so far as to condemn them. "If I speak out against them, I'll be perceived as betraying the cause. It is a religious matter. We are too far from Khalistan for it to be a political matter. Sikh people don't want violence, but they don't want decency taken as weakness. We don't believe in not defending. When fighting is in the name of God, you don't worry over this life, you worry over the next life."

The wide divergence between militant Sikhs like Manmohan Singh and the government of India draws as much on the deeper Punjabi codes of *izzat* as it does on simple politics. We asked Singh what India would have to do to satisfy the more extremist Sikhs of the ISYF. The answer was not couched in the political accords at all. His answer was a psychological profile of Khalistan.

"If Rajiv has any common sense," he said, "he does not want to repeat the history of the *Mahabharata* (in which a battle was fought between two brothers, Kaurava and Pandava, simply because one brother did not want to give rights to the second brother. They destroyed the whole fabric of Indian culture in that war). Injustice and oppression — that is the whole history of Hinduism. We are brothers, we are part of India, part of Hindus. But the amount of injustice they give us will destroy them.

"I never thought of Khalistan before the Golden Temple was attacked. And I still want to live as if India was one and to feel the whole of India as part of my life. I still want it. But I don't want to live where my turban is hooted at or I have been manhandled or my children are beaten up. I can't tolerate that. So they have to take some strong measures, socially, politically, legally to restore honour to the Sikhs.

"First thing if you want to make any compromise you go and say I am guilty, I am at fault, it is my mistake and I am sorry for it. The healing starts with the accepting of guilt. They must declare whatever they have done to the Sikh nation was totally wrong, non-democratic, cruel, and they will compensate every Sikh the best they can.

"It must pass ordinances that anyone humiliating Sikhs must be sent to jail. They must punish those who were responsible for the massacre (100 persons should go to the gallows for that), so we'll feel we're getting some justice. Then they should remove the military in Punjab and leave just the Sikh military there, even if they are under command of the Indian government. Get out of the temples, leave the temples open to the priests, never ever try to influence people in the Sikh community directly or indirectly. And assist the community to build itself back up as they were.

"Then some basic needs: electricity, water, grain problems can be done with a fair mind. Punjab should be compensated. And they must restore respect to the Sikhs in the general public by putting a strong law that any Sikh who's proved he was humiliated or insulted by anyone, he must be punished heavily.

"If they do that, I think Khalistan will melt away by itself. There is still time; they can stop Khalistan."

We do not believe for a moment there will ever be a Khalistan. Not for lack of will on the part of committed Khalistanis, but merely for strategic reasons. India is Punjab and Kashmir and Tamil Nadu and Assam and Sikkim — all those regions around the Hindi-speaking Hindu heartland that force India to be democratic and secular, and not just another, larger Burma.

Indian journalists and politicians are predicting severe unrest in Punjab for the rest of this century. If the elected moderate wing of the Akali Dal cannot cope with the violence, or if Punjab again threatens to withhold its financial and agricultural contributions to the nation, the mechanism exists in the Indian Constitution to suspend the state's elected government and to install "President's Rule" directly from New Delhi. The appointed governor of Punjab, S. S. Ray (a Bengali from the same distinguished family that gave the world the filmmaker, Satyajit Ray) is a Gandhi-family loyalist with vast experience in "cleaning up" terrorists and breaking an insurrection's back, as he did during the "Naxalite" crisis in West Bengal in the 1960s. Terrorists and the central government are playing a waiting game today, with the ultimate threat and response — total anarchy or police rule — not quite ready to assert itself.

The Indian government played politics when it should have conceded some power; it relinquished power when it should have exercised it firmly. Khalistan is the price of Mrs Gandhi's pursuit of power, without discernible purpose.

Ultimately, however, the madness in Punjab must end not by external threat, but by the voices of reason once again asserting themselves. Sikhism, like many religions, is based on moving visions of love and harmony. In its time and place, it was superior to the visions and practices around it. But like all religions, Islam and Christianity particularly, it has an intolerant streak that corrupts its vision and lends itself to the opposite interpretation of its original intentions.

We all know by now, because we have nearly lived through the twentieth century, the inevitable destination of religious movements that turn political. We know from Western history the fate in store for any mass movement that prides itself on purity alone and has no core of beliefs but vengeance, no code of behaviour except an unbending obedience to ritual observance.

———————————

On a rise of rocky shore above Dunmanus Bay some sixty miles southwest of Cork, a monument has been erected by the three governments to the Air India dead. Conceived and sculpted by a Cork artist, the memorial is in the form of a marble compass pointing out to sea in the direction of the crash, with the time, date, and co-ordinates carved on the surface. Around the edge the inscription reads: *Time Flies. Suns Rise and Shadows Fall. Let It Pass By. Love Reigns Forever Over All.* In a low stone wall behind it is a brass plate with an inscription in English, French and Hindi, listing the names of the 329. Cork County donated the land and the upkeep; India and Canada each contributed $65,000 to building it. Some parents have already seen memorials erected by their children's schools in Detroit and Toronto vandalized within days, and they are grateful that this place, the closest they have to a grave, is safe and in a better place.

Speaking on behalf of the families that morning, Dr Yogesh Paliwal of Ottawa, the father of fifteen-year-old Mukul, says:

It is exactly one year today that we woke up on a Sunday morning to hear the dreadful news which was to change our lives permanently. A large number of us did not even receive the bodies of our loved ones and have not been able to lay them to eternal rest with our own hands within our sight and with proper religious rites. The subconscious mind still keeps wondering as to where have the loved ones gone. So vividly do we remember the going into the departure gates at the airports, laughing and waving. Illusions that they will come back keep flashing.

Our grief and despair continues and will persist all our lives as we helplessly miss the loved ones who were so much a part of our daily lives, our flesh and blood, our link with the past and our hopes for the future.

The 329 innocent people who were brutally murdered by the sabotage of Flight 182 were an extraordinary collection of people that included many world-renowned scientists, doctors and professors from both Canada and India. The 84 young Canadians on the flight need a special mention. Most of them were brilliant, first-class-honours students, and there were many highly accomplished performing artists among them. Young people are a nation's wealth, as they are the ones who will shape the future of the country. Canada lost some of its most promising national wealth in the tragedy. So many of the children had said to their friends, "See you in September." September has come and gone. They never came back....

...I would like to close with a message of Lord Krishna from the *Bhagwat Gita*, which reads, about the human soul: "No weapons can cleave him, nor the fire burn him, no waters can make him wet, nor the wind dry him up. The soul is immortal; only the body is mortal."

Thank you and God bless.

"I will come back over here when it's quieter," says Dr Radhakrishna, a frail, almost boyish-looking engineer at Ontario Hydro. "This will be a good place to meditate."

He's lost everyone — his wife, his son and daughter. Outwardly, he seems at peace, perhaps the most peaceful man in the entire gathering. He'd mentioned on our first meeting back in the winter, "I'd gotten up very early that morning for prayers, at my usual time. I heard the report on the radio and something came over me — I accepted it immediately. I knew people would start coming over as soon as they heard, and I worried how I was going to look after them." Now he's come over to the rows of folding chairs behind the dais to comfort a middle-aged white man hunched in tears.

Then, looking over the gathering, at the flags and the dignitaries and all the Irish sailors and soldiers who contributed to the rescue, at the staff of the Cork Regional Hospital who'd come down for the services, at the world's journalists and cameramen packing up their gear, and at the lone mourners staggering up from the water's edge where they'd tossed blessed fruits and flowers to the sea, he adds, "This is the first time I'm seeing everyone together.... I did not realize the magnitude. Last year, I came, I identified their bodies and I left for India before the others came."

Down by the water, Kamal Saha of Calcutta folds up the legs of his white cotton pyjamas so they will not get wet. From Calcutta he has brought sweetmeats and blessed flowers and now he arranges them lovingly on a tray. And he adds something else, a can of Coca-Cola. His brother, Bimal, was crazy about Coca-Cola. Then he wades into the still, seductive waters and lets the flowers, the sweets, the Coke float away. Friends have to pull and half-carry the sobbing Kamal Saha back up the slope to where the dignitaries are drinking tea under a blue tent. For the moment he is a big, bearded weeping man in a holy-orange kurta, whom sorrow has robbed of self-restraint. In a week he will return to his responsibilities in Calcutta where he is a division manager with a multinational shoe-manufacturing firm and the head of a household, which, through air crash and road accident, has already lost too many men.

We walk down to the water's edge, visitors with no mission here, only a job. Mr Swaminathan of Detroit and Dr Radha-krishna pass by us on the stone stairs leading to the shingled beach. "Sam" is a man of iron self-discipline, unyielding to grief. He, too, has lost everyone: the accomplished son on his fifteenth birthday, his wife, two daughters. To Radhakrishna he is saying, "I thought f/8 at a sixtieth, because I'm using Ektachrome."

Mr Raju Sarangi, a man who lived for his fourteen-year-old daughter, Lita, and her dancing, who has built his Toronto house around a basement stage for her recitals, is standing at the water's edge, his body strapped with the latest video equipment, bags bursting with videocassettes ready for insertion. He is taping everything, and everyone, every last precious second of Irish air and water, as though they are embodiments of Lita. Tears are washing down his cheeks. One wants to reach out, to hold him, his pain is so poignant. He had made himself a professional stage manager for his daughter's sake, the quiet, bald man with the extraordinary daughter, radiant behind the curtains, con-trolling the sound and light.

That morning in his Cork hotel, even then arranging his cameras and cassettes and lighting-bar for the day ahead, he had come over to us and pulled us aside. "Mr Clark and Mrs Mukherjee," he'd said, "tell the world how 329 innocent lives were lost and how the rest of us are slowly dying."